NUECES REPRISE

THE TUMBLEWEED SAGAS

MARK GREATHOUSE

DEFIANCE PRESS
& PUBLISHING

Nueces Reprise

First Edition: February 2020

Printed in the United States of America

10 9 8 7 6 5 4 3 2 1

ISBN-13: 978-1-948035-56-9 (Paperback)
ISBN-13: 978-1-948035-38-5 (eBook)

Edited by Janet Musick
Interior Design by Debbi Stocco

Published by Defiance Press and Publishing, LLC

Bulk orders of this book may be obtained by contacting Defiance Press and Publishing, LLC. www.defiancepress.com.

Public Relations Dept. – Defiance Press & Publishing, LLC
281-581-9300
pr@defiancepress.com

Defiance Press & Publishing, LLC
281-581-9300
info@defiancepress.com

DEDICATION

Dedicated with love to my wife, Carolyn,
and to our two sons, Mike and Matt.

ACKNOWLEDGEMENTS

Book writing simply doesn't happen in a vacuum. The author provides the creative talent and crafts the stories, but there's so much more that demands acknowledgement. I've been blessed with many friends and family who have supported my writing of The Tumbleweed Sagas. My wife Carolyn's reviews and encouragement were a huge help, along with very important tech support from our sons Mike and Matt. Other supporters have included Cara Miller, Jim May, Ernie Angell, and cousins Jim & Cindy Holmgreen and Johnny Dunn. Many more friends have contributed support at some level to the creation and publication of Nueces Reprise, be it encouragement or advice.

Naturally, I am major grateful to the great folks at Defiance Press & Publishing. The team they bring to publishing is first rate from promotion to editing, cover design, narration, arranging media interviews, and the myriad tasks that lead to successful book sales.

While most of my authoring occurred in my office, decorated so as to channel my inner Texan, my creative juices were often inspired in cafés and coffee houses. My favorites were Hester's Café & Coffee Bar in Corpus Christi, TX; Nueces Café in Robstown, TX; Java Ranch Espresso Bar & Café in Fredericksburg, TX; Ragged Edge Coffee House in Gettysburg, PA; and Frederick Coffee Company & Cafe in Frederick, MD. These décors, combined with savory cups of coffee and easy-listening music, tended to set me in the right frame of mind.

Thanks to all of you.

THEME

Reprise:

A recurrence, renewal, or resumption of an action.

THE CAST

Lucas "Long Luke" Dunn – Soon to become one of the greatest Texas Ranger captains ever, Luke escapes the Great Famine in Ireland to seek his fortune on Texas' Nueces Strip. He gains repute as Indian fighter and respected lawman. Later conflicted between being lawman and rancher. Comanche calls him Ghost-Who-Rides.

Elisa Corrigan Dunn – Marries Luke Dunn after losing her family to frontier rigors, including fighting off Comanche. She and Luke build the Heaven's Gate Ranch and a life on the frontier.

George Whelan – A dutiful and well-intended sheriff of Nueces County. His weakness for the ladies lands him in trouble.

Scarlett Rose – Red-headed prostitute from Laredo whose conflicted interests and bad choices of men could prove deadly.

Doc Andrews – The alcoholic Nuecestown doctor is the rheumy conscience of the town.

Three Toes – Comanche chief, son of famous Penateka Comanche War Chief Santa Anna and favored by Buffalo Hump. He develops a friendship with Luke that contradicts tribal ways.

Carlos Perez – Cattle thief and killer embarrassed by Luke. Perez stalks his nemesis, seeking revenge. He blames Luke for the loss of his eye and Scarlett Rose for the loss of his manhood.

Bernice & Agatha – Nuecestown town gossips with hearts of gold who run the boarding house.

Colonel Horace Rucker – U.S. Army veteran of Mexican-American War who fights a dilemma of self-respect and the need to support his family, versus helping in the schemes of his commanding general.

General Booker Truax – U.S. Army general caught up in using his Washington, D.C. connections to defraud the Indian agencies.

Lieutenant Gordon Belknap – Fresh West Point graduate assigned to fighting Indians in Texas. Faces several encounters with Three Toes before receiving a special assignment.

Thaddeus Brown – Indian agent who colludes with General Truax.

Horatio Thorpe – One of the wealthiest men in Texas, descended from a

Carolina plantation family, comes to build his own plantation on the Texas Gulf plains. Uses power of money to greedily influence Texas politics.

Roy Biggs – Feared throughout the southwestern U.S. as one of the most cold-hearted, vile villains ever to roam the region. As a gun for hire, he's loyal to whomever pays the most. His hideout in the far northern reaches of the Nueces Strip is an impregnable hacienda.

Berne "The Fixer" Culthwaite – Hired hand of Horatio Thorpe who specializes in political fixes.

HISTORICAL CHARACTERS

Colonel Henry Lawrence Kinney – Entrepreneur, rancher, and trader. Founder of Corpus Christi, originally as a trading post, who was a leader in the settlement and economic development of the eastern part of the Nueces Strip.

John Salmon "Rip" Ford – Soldier, elected official, newspaper editor, and Texas Ranger, Ford was critically important to taming the Texas frontier. He was a renowned Indian fighter and led a campaign against Mexican rebel Juan Cortinas. He would later be intimately involved with secession, fighting in the War Between the States, and post-war redevelopment.

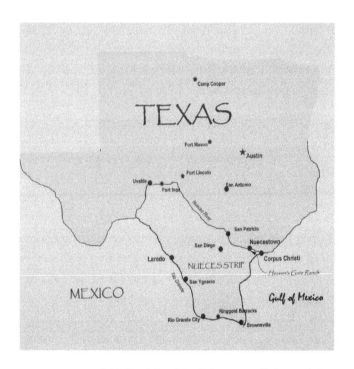

Nuecestown, established in 1852 by English and German settlers, was developed by Corpus Christi founder Colonel Kinney as a ferry crossing. It frequently serves as a setting for Tumbleweed Sagas. Thanks to being bypassed by the railroad, it's now a "ghost town" marked only by historical markers. All that remains is a preserved schoolhouse and the Nuecestown Cemetery.

CONTENTS

PROLOGUE

Warm breezes eased across the vast prairies that comprised much of the Nueces Strip of 1857. It was mostly tall grasses and loamy sands that stretched as far as the eye could see and then some. It encompassed the territory south from the Nueces River all the way to the Rio Grande, its eastern boundary being the Gulf of Mexico. Mottes of live oak or mesquite popped up here and there and offered the prospect of shade for both man and beast. Weather? Hang around long enough on any given day, you just might find weather that suits you.

Flushed with rain, the once-dry creek beds and arroyos eventually emptied into Nueces Bay and, farther to the east, Corpus Christi Bay. Settlers and travelers were at the mercy of flash floods during especially heavy rains. Summers tended to be hot and made even hotter by the humidity. Gulf breezes didn't reach far enough inland to offer much relief from the oppressive damp heat.

Animal and plant life were in abundance. Coyote, deer, javelina, fox, jackrabbits, armadillos, coons, and even mountain lions were fairly common with occasional spotted ocelots and even wolves. Ferocious-looking horned lizards or horny toads were bountiful. Red-tailed hawks and bald eagles kept watch from their high vantage points in the skies over the Nueces Strip and contributed to keeping the varmint population under control.

The Diamondback Rattlesnake is part and parcel to the culture of the region and is included in many so-called Texas-isms, like, "he's as touchy as a teased rattlesnake." Or "more nervous than a rattlesnake's tail." Bite was nasty for sure. Travelers were wise to listen for the tell-tale warning rattle.

Wildflowers swept across the landscape like a rainbow, with scarlet sage, hibiscus, daisies, poppies, lilies, and the ubiquitous bluebonnets. Groves of cypress, juniper, and palmetto could be found farther south. There was also the omnipresent cactus, along with yucca and agave.

The plentiful and accessible longhorn cattle could be called the "low-hanging-fruit" of the Texas economy. Brought from the Iberian Peninsula by early Spanish priests, the longhorns eventually escaped the failing missions, roamed free, and proliferated. Eventually, millions of the beasts covered Texas and especially the grazing lands of the Nueces Strip. But, as sheer numbers of prairie wildlife went, none surpassed the wild horse, not even the buffalo. In fact, the Nueces Strip was often referred to as the Wild Horse Desert.

It's natural to ask, who was attracted to this often harsh and unforgiving land? Many sought fame and fortune, and permanent homes weren't part of their destiny. The early migrants to Texas were seekers and entrepreneurs, often profiting outside the law before moving on to the next opportunity. It was the settlers, beginning with Moses Austin and his son Stephen, who would set the stage for the civilizing of the Texas frontier. Communities, laws, and commerce followed.

There weren't many settlements on the Nueces Strip in 1857. Dwellings such as they were might be built from dried mud bricks to wood transported in from afar. Roofs tended to be of thatched grass or animal skins. There weren't any large trees to be chopped down, so log cabins were few and far between. Finished lumber was still a luxury. In the triangle between Corpus Christi, Laredo, and Brownsville, there were a few way stations for stage and mail service. The military had established forts along the periphery of the Strip. Other than a few towns like Corpus Christi, San Diego, Laredo, Brownsville, and Nuecestown, the landscape was mostly wide-open space. Corpus Christi founder Colonel Henry Kinney had seen to the construction of a road of sorts from Corpus through San Diego and on to Laredo. A few folks felt the Strip reached as far north as Uvalde, but that was indeed a stretch.

If the demographic composition of Texas were to be visualized in the simplest geographic terms, the Indians held full possession of the western plains, Mexicans held the southwest as defined by the Rio Grande, and the Anglos possessed the remainder.

Ranches and farms were popping up throughout the eastern portions of the Nueces Strip. The economy was mostly about cotton, horses, and longhorns. The range was as wide open as it was beautiful. While the frontier expanded inexorably westward, there was worry about Comanche, Kiowa, and Lipan Apache, as well as the rogue marauding bandits from south of the Rio Grande. In fact, the last thing you'd wish on anyone was to be captured by Comanche, as they weren't equipped to sustain or house prisoners. This all served to keep early Texans ever vigilant. It was easy to make the case for calling companies of what were unofficially called Rangers, as they took it upon themselves to go where the military found it politically unattractive. Unfortunately, there was insufficient money in the government coffers to fund companies of Rangers on a daily basis. Texas Rangers, as they would become known, initially appeared as a result of a governing council resolution in 1835 to provide security between the Brazos and Trinity Rivers. The Rangers alternately increased and decreased in number over the decade of the Republic, mostly as a consequence of the militaristic perspective of whomever was president.

The aforementioned Nueces Strip of that time with its threats by Indians demanded the unbridled devotion of a special breed of men like famous Texas Rangers Ben McColluch and Jack Coffee Hays. Fortunately, the threat from Mexico was mitigated by their rebellious internal squabbles south of the Rio Grande.

By September 1855, settlers of the Nueces Strip were being increasingly terrorized by thieving bands of Lipan Apache. The U.S. Army was no help at all in civilian matters. A Texas Ranger company was formed under the notorious James Hughes Callahan to chase Lipan Apache out of Texas. With the debatable benefit of an erstwhile adventurer named W.R. Henry, Callahan and his company of little better than one hundred men chased the Lipan Apache across the Rio Grande into Mexico. They were counter-attacked by the Apache and a force of Mexican troops. This initiated an incident on the Rio Escondito in which a small number of men were killed and wounded on both sides, the town of Piedras Negros was looted and burned, and Callahan re-crossed the Rio Grande into Texas.

Nueces Justice protagonist Luke Dunn, a youthful Irish immigrant, joined Callahan's force after serving as deputy sheriff in Corpus Christi for a few months. Dunn was credited with being in the thick of the battle and reveled in his first taste of Texas Ranger action in kicking out the Apache and bringing justice to the Nueces Strip. Dunn was frustrated to learn upon returning with Callahan that, while public support for another expedition was favorable, the politicians were not inclined to risk another international incident. Notably, Callahan died the following year in a fight with a fella named Woodson Blassingame.

It's said that the Nueces Strip never gave up its secrets. One thing for sure, justice was swift and certain. When Nueces justice was rendered, there was no question that lawbreakers were dealt full punishment for their misdeeds. While it might seem to offer hiding for lawbreakers, the vast perilous and unpredictable vistas of grassy prairie offered little or no place to hide. Once the law was involved, Nueces justice was indeed the invariable outcome.

From here, our story picks up with Luke Dunn having begun to establish himself as a force to be reckoned with in bringing justice to the Nueces Strip as a Texas Ranger under special authorization from the nominal head of the Rangers, John C. "Rip" Ford. While companies of Rangers were funded at various times when threats arose and money came available, Luke was left to almost single-handedly exercise law across vast reaches of prairie. When not on his Texas Ranger assignments, he worked with his wife at building their Heaven's Gate ranch near Nuecestown just west of Corpus Christi.

With Luke's success in eliminating the likes of Bad Bart Strong and Dirk Cavendish, and weakening Carlos Perez, came a high level of notoriety. Luke continued to find himself conflicted between the roles of Texas Ranger bringing justice to the Nueces Strip and rancher and family man contributing to the settlement of the region. But with the notoriety of killing lawbreakers came threats of those looking to make a name for themselves. Rip Ford's assignments were woven into the context of Luke dealing with the very real menaces that he must face on the vast reaches of the Strip. Carlos Perez was hardly the least of the perils Luke faced, as he also had to hunt the powerful, obsessive mastermind of an intricate defrauding of the military and Indians in Texas.

ONE

Heaven's Gate

The rain the night before had turned the normally dry creek beds around the ranch to mud interspersed with pools of water. A longhorn bull had been drinking from one of these pools when he found himself beginning to sink into the mud. As he instinctively tried to push off, he just mired himself deeper. Soon enough, his hind legs were sunk just about their entire length.

Luke Dunn, erstwhile notable Texas Ranger captain and rancher, had set out early to see what damages the rains might have wrought. He knew there'd been a bit of flash flooding, but he was more concerned with how his modest herd of cattle had weathered the storm. He knew he could even be dealing with drownings. On a small ranch with less than twenty head of cattle, every life was sacred. The economic loss of just one longhorn was significant.

Luke was tall as men went, pushing six-foot-three or thereabouts. He'd thus earned the moniker "Long Luke." He wore a broad-brimmed tan hat with a simple leather band. His ruggedly handsome Irish face framed a well-tended fiery-red mustache that gave him an appearance of maturity beyond his years. He wore a buckskin vest over a blue shirt with gray trousers stuffed into well-worn cowboy boots. His gun belt accommodated his Walker Colt plus plenty of ammunition. When on duty as lawman, he pinned the Texas Ranger badge to his shirt, where it stood out so as to be impossible to miss.

Before long, Luke came upon the hapless longhorn. He was one very tired bull. His big brown eyes pleaded for relief from his predicament. Luke surveyed the situation. Normally, this sort of work might take at least three men with horses, extra horses at that. All he had was himself, a couple of ropes, and the handsome big gray stallion he rode. As he thought on how to rescue his bull, he dismounted and hung his gun belt on the saddle horn.

A solution finally came to him. Luke fashioned a halter with one of his rope lines. The bull had sunk deep enough that there was no way a rope was going to be threaded under his belly. His left foreleg was just free of the mud enough to offer the beast a little leverage. Luke spotted a nearby live oak. Using a tool that doubled as hammer and axe that he'd had the presence of mind to carry with him that morning, he chopped three reasonably long pieces that he then lashed together into a tripod of sorts. The idea was to produce enough upward lift to help the longhorn climb out.

Hitching one end of the halter rope to the longhorn and the other to his saddle horn, Luke backed the big gray until the line was taut. The bull likely weighed in at around fifteen hundred pounds, and Luke needed to get the frightened and exhausted beast out of the muck just enough to get a rope under him. He backed up his horse a bit more, glaring at the bull. "Come on, you big piece of meat. Fight! Climb!" He cajoled the longhorn into making the effort to climb out. The suction from the mud did not want to let him free. At last, however, there was a loud sucking sound, and the longhorn lurched forward just enough to create a small space under his belly. Luke had the big gray hold steady, dismounted, dodged the longhorn's five-foot horn spread, and threaded a rope under its belly. He ran it over the tripod and back to his horse.

Again, Luke backed his horse. Slowly but surely, the longhorn worked free of the muddy morass. Luke dismounted and pushed the beast onto dry land. The longhorn was breathing heavily from the exertion, as was Luke. The beast showed his discomfort with a lot of snorting, and Luke stroked his head in an effort to calm him down. The longhorn gave Luke no trouble in detaching the rope from around his belly, and Luke was able to easily lead the bull over to the shade of the motte with its remaining live oak trunk. It didn't take much persuading to get the bull to lie down.

Luke only had a canteen, but he did his best to get the longhorn to drink. He made a few trips to the pool of water, and repeatedly emptied the canteen onto the longhorn to cool him off. Now he could only hope the bull had learned his lesson. Likely as not he hadn't, but Luke could hope.

Only after caring for the longhorn did Luke finally take a moment to look down at himself. He was covered in drying cakes of mud. Elisa wasn't going to be happy about his wallowing around in a mud hole with a longhorn. He chuckled to himself as he mounted up. They hadn't been married long. She'd just turned seventeen, and Luke was an old man of twenty-three. Elisa had grown up on farming, so she had no trouble getting used to her man coming home now and then covered with dried Texas mud. In any case, she had plenty to do as a frontier wife from sewing to cooking to keeping their humble cabin habitable.

Having immigrated from Ireland only a few years before, Luke missed the wars that ultimately resulted in Texas statehood and U.S. possession of the Nueces Strip. He'd already become an exceptional tracker of men, and his exploits at capturing or killing lawbreakers would become legendary.

Tired from the morning's extraordinary effort, he decided to head home. He took one last look at the longhorn, smiled, and turned the big gray stallion toward the ranch.

Luke had pretty much hung up his Texas Ranger spurs, at least for the present. Now that he was married and had a modest spread to maintain, he didn't feature himself on month-long adventures, risking life and limb tracking lawbreakers. When he was Rangering, he typically furnished his own horse, bedroll, and armament. His weapons of choice included a pair of Walker Colts, a Colt rifle with revolving cylinder, and a Bowie knife. The weapons he carried on his ranching chores were pretty much the same, just one fewer Colt.

In effect, Long Luke Dunn was at present little more than a bounty hunter, a very good one, with a Texas Ranger badge. He'd already proven himself at taking down Indians and bandits. It didn't take long to establish a reputation and to earn the ire of powerful folk that sought to grow powerful by any means possible.

Luke rode past the arching gate he and Elisa had erected on the trail leading to their cabin. He'd carved the ranch name, Heaven's Gate, into the wood slats across the top. They saw the ranch as their heavenly gateway to a new life.

As he approached, he saw an unfamiliar horse tied to the hitching post, but the man talking with Elisa was a familiar face. Luke immediately wondered why Rip Ford was visiting.

"Rip!" He spurred his horse to a trot and was quickly dismounting and extending his hand to his old friend.

"Luke, what on earth happened to you?" Rip immediately noticed the now-dried cakes of dirt on his clothes.

"Just wrestling with a longhorn that got himself stuck in the mud." He caught himself and turned to Elisa. "Sorry, Darlin." He kissed and hugged her. "Lisa, this is my old friend Rip Ford."

Elisa dusted herself off as best she could. "Well, we have met, Lucas, and been chatting bit."

"Rip, what brings you to Nuecestown. You keeping them politicians straight in Austin? How's the newspaper business? They going to reauthorize the Rangers?" Luke hit Rip with a veritable staccato of questions.

"Lucas, I just fixed some coffee. Let's enjoy Mr. Ford's visit."

Ford tipped his hat. "Now that's the best offer I've had all day."

Luke had just completed the construction of a gallery across the front of the cabin. Back east, they called them porches. Gallery had a certain ring to it, as it implied a place to gather. Elisa went inside but quickly emerged with three cups of coffee.

"Dang, this is right good coffee, Mrs. Dunn." Ford, a handsome man with a steely tough visage that belied his compassionate side, took a couple of long sips of Elisa's brew. His nickname of Rip was derived from his writing letters home to loved ones lost in the Mexican-American War. He'd served in an adjutant role to General Taylor, and Rip stood for "rest in peace."

Elisa had some vague notion of Ford's exploits as an officer in the Texas War for Independence and the Mexican-American War and knew that Luke held him in high regard. "What brings you to Nuecestown, Mr. Ford?" she asked.

Luke was all ears awaiting Ford's answer.

Ford's eyes went from Elisa to Luke. He considered what a lovely family they'd be making, and it pained him to have to ask for Luke's help. "Luke, you've impressed folks in Austin, bringing Strong, Cavendish, and Perez to justice. That would be a handful for an entire company of Texas Rangers." He leveled his eyes on Luke's. "I've been authorized to offer you the opportunity to be a special agent, and I can't think of a more capable man."

Luke cocked his head inquisitively. "Special agent? What's that, Rip?"

Elisa was immediately concerned. Was her new husband going to be heading off chasing lawbreakers and leaving her to care for their growing ranch by herself?

"From time to time, we have special situations. We wouldn't want to send, much less pay, for an entire company of Rangers when a single Ranger could get the job done more effectively." Ford glanced at Elisa almost apologetically. "It's not full time, Luke, so I think you'd still be spending most of your time right here with your lovely wife at

Heaven's Gate." Ford stood and added. "Think on it, Luke. I've got to head into Corpus Christi for a couple of days. I'll stop by on my way back." He took a couple of steps toward his horse. "If it makes any difference, it pays five dollars a month just to be available plus you can collect any rewards." He mounted up. Once in the saddle, he tipped his hat to Elisa. "Thanks for the coffee, Mrs. Dunn."

Luke returned Ford's tip of the hat as he rode off to take care of his business in Corpus Christi.

"What do you think, Lisa?"

What does an expression of resignation look like? Apparently, this was to be something she was simply going to have to accommodate. The very principles she admired in her man drove him to right injustices.

Three Toes, a chief among the Penateka Comanche, and his band of six warriors had easily managed to leave the reservation near Camp Cooper up on the Brazos River and head southwest toward the Llano Basin. Upon his arrival at the camp a couple of weeks earlier, Three Toes noticed that the U.S. government was not living up to its end of the latest treaty. To his knowledge, there had been dozens of treaties, and the white man never lived up to them. Almost laughably, and certainly naively, the federals would make a treaty with one band of Comanche and expect the other bands to follow its terms. They had no idea that each Comanche band was a separate entity.

Three Toes quickly recognized the Indian office at Camp Cooper as corrupt caretakers prone to cheating the Comanche of gifts or annuities or gift allotments. This corruption often led to bloodshed. He noticed a man named Thaddeus Brown who traveled from fort to fort, supposedly inventorying the supplies provided for the Indians at the various camps and forts. Three Toes wondered at what was in the agent's wagons, which were kept covered and well-guarded. They looked as though they carried heavy loads.

As Three Toes departed Camp Cooper, the U.S. government was moving toward an end to a policy of what amounted to utter passivity toward the Indians. Soldiers had been directed never to fight Indians unless they attacked or had committed some criminal act. In his journey from the Nueces Strip to join his people, the chief noted that the long string of U.S. Army forts were understaffed and soldiers inexperienced. It was blatantly obvious. The young lieutenant he'd encountered on his journey to Camp Cooper weeks ago was further evidence of the soldiers' naiveté. They were ignorant of the basics of Indian culture, much less warfare, so they were neither equipped nor trained to fight Comanche. Many a bluecoat scalp wound up as a trophy hanging from a Comanche lance.

Three Toes wasn't interested in being trained to become a farmer like other Comanche on the reservation. He was a highly-respected hunter and warrior. Farming was women's work to a Comanche warrior.

While he mostly rode in silence, Three Toes was able to talk with his warriors on their travels southward. The Penateka Comanche did not have an extensive language. It was comprised of roughly eighteen characters combined in often guttural sounds with various vowel lengths. Hand signs also played into their communications. Interestingly, they called themselves "Nermurnuh," which translated to "true humans."

Eagle Eyes rode alongside Three Toes for a while. "Great Chief, how will we know when we have found a new home?" he questioned.

It was a simple but profound question. The Comanche had never thought of any confined space as a home, but rather considered the vastness of the land to be their home. The Great Spirit owned the land and, at his will, they rode upon it, hunted, proliferated, and made war. He considered the question carefully. "The Great Spirit will tell us when we have found it." He feared that day might never come. The white man was encroaching farther day by day.

Eagle Eyes pondered Three Toes' answer. Like the other warriors, he had left his family behind. He feared his people might starve over the winter or catch a white man's disease and die. He was anxious to find them a new home.

The band rode to the top of an escarpment from which they had an expansive view of the countryside. Off in the distance, Three Toes pointed to a long line of perhaps a dozen mounted soldiers heading westward with several freight wagons. It was tempting prey but for the fact that his band was significantly outnumbered. It would be a triumph to delay the construction of another fort on the Comancheria. Tempting indeed.

The white man had labeled this region the Comancheria, that vast land west of the 98th Meridian. It was filled with danger. Aside from marauding Comanche, there were the Kiowa, Apache, and the ubiquitous Mexican bandits. The U.S. Army had been singularly unsuccessful in cleaning up the region, sending under-manned, under-equipped patrols as essentially token defense.

Eagle Eyes caught Three Toes' attention and motioned to the west where the soldiers would soon be riding through what appeared to be a narrow ravine. The confines of the ravine could negate the soldiers' numerical advantage.

Soon Three Toes' band found themselves peering into the ravine and watching the approaching soldiers and their wagons. Should their battle not go well, they had an easy escape route, as the soldiers would be hard-pressed to get out of the deep ravine and stage a pursuit. Best case, the warriors could inflict serious damage.

Once the first six soldiers had passed their position, the Comanche began shooting their arrows. They were fine marksmen. Nearly half the soldiers were wounded or killed before the rest could fire their first rifle shots in self-defense. One mounted soldier waved his sword and tried in vain to get the wagons to turn around in the cramped ravine. Three Toes put an arrow through his chest.

The soldiers dismounted and sought defensive positions behind anything that might protect them from arrows. The battle lasted not three minutes. One of the wagons turned over in its attempt to turn within the narrow confines of the ravine. Its contents effectively blocked the ravine and trapped those remaining. Two wagons accompanied by five of the mounted soldiers successfully turned around and headed back at breakneck speed from whence they'd come.

Three Toes counted perhaps four dead bluecoats. His warriors would be too vulnerable to go into the ravine to take scalps. The chief wouldn't have them suffer the same fate as the soldiers in the event the retreating bluecoats regrouped and staged a counterattack. He waved to his warriors to mount their ponies and leave the scene. They'd at least temporarily delayed the building of another military "hacienda."

Three masked men came barging through the door to the Laredo sheriff's office. It fell from its hinges easily. Carlos Perez sprawled on a cot in one of the two cells.

Sheriff Stills had been sleeping soundly in the other cell. Startled awake, he realized it was too late to react as the masked invaders locked his cell. Besides, he could barely see, as it was dark save for the flame from a lone candle on the desk.

"Damn tarnation, what the hell do you think you're doing?" He couldn't be positive as to identities due to the masks and dim light, but was sure one of them was a man he'd seen in Nuevo Laredo. However, with a rifle aimed at his gut at close range, there wasn't much point in him making a fuss.

Using the straw-filled mattress as a makeshift stretcher, the invaders hoisted Perez and carried him out the front door. They never said a word, though Perez groaned some. His wounds still hadn't healed, and he had considerable discomfort from the combination of the castration he'd received thanks to the marksmanship of the whore in San Patricio and the damage from the extraction of the Comanche arrow when Luke Dunn had captured him with Three Toes' help. He was just aware enough of his surroundings that his hopes of exacting revenge on those who'd caused him such pain were vaguely renewed.

His grimace turned to a weak smile.

The men placed him as gently as possible in the back of a wagon. The rig rattled, lurched, and swayed along the road and was soon crossing the Rio Grande into Nuevo Laredo and the relative safety of Mexico. Perez took a final look at Laredo through his remaining good eye, then passed out.

He had no idea what lay ahead. In any case, he was at the mercy of these men who'd sprung him from the Laredo jail. He suspected that they weren't interested in being hiders. His days of skinning rustled cattle to sell their hides were now in the past.

"I've never missed it before, Lucas." She was torn between joy and concern.

"You're certain?"

"I can count, you know," she said. "It's been twenty-eight days."

Luke had learned long ago to always expect the unexpected. Still, fatherhood had not been in his immediate frame of reference.

It should have made the choice as to whether to accept Rip Ford's offer much easier. He gazed down at his beautiful wife. She was young, but a full-grown woman by any measure. This woman who'd fired a pistol that killed attacking Comanche would soon be holding a vulnerable little baby in her arms. Luke marveled at the paradox of frontier life.

"Are you going to be able to look after Mike when I get called away?" Mike was Elisa's young brother and had been essentially bed-ridden as the result of a rattlesnake bite. He was being kept under the watchful care of Doc, Nuecestown's answer to frontier medicine... when he was sober. Luke and Elisa still had hopes that Mike might one day return to the ranch, but the rattler's venom made that doubtful. The boy was lucky to be alive, if it could be called luck.

"Doc says he's struggling. He's trying to keep him comfortable and hoping his young body will heal." Sadness colored Elisa's words.

"Do you want to bring him out here?" Luke asked. "He loves this place."

"Let's think about that, Lucas. We can talk with Doc when we visit Mike tomorrow."

Luke held her close. The possibility of her being pregnant was pleasantly overwhelming, yet the real world beyond Heaven's Gate was making incursions into their wedded bliss.

General Truax was livid. His glare was so fierce, so intense it seemed to fully penetrate the man standing before him. Colonel Horace Rucker was sweating profusely. It was as much nerves as ambient temperature. He stood at attention before his commandant.

"You simply left?" Truax's question was almost rhetorical. "She's still there?"

"Yes, sir, no excuse, sir."

Truax knew that Rucker had taken three bullets in pursuit of the Laredo whore, Scarlett Rose. "Exactly, Colonel. There are no excuses." He lit a cigar and took a long pull. "So, this Captain Dunn faced you down."

"Yes, General, yes, he did."

"Did he threaten you?"

"Not directly. He's a very capable Texas Ranger, sir; he seemed a step ahead of me." He might have added that Luke's presence was also intimidating. He towered over Rucker.

"What about this Sheriff Whelan?" Truax asked. "He's the one who spirited her away from your ranch."

This was the toughest part for Rucker. "I didn't see him in Corpus Christi. I saw Colonel Kinney and then went to the bank. Turns out she was being held in the bank vault, but Captain Dunn was there to intercept me." He looked down, then back up at Truax. "He's not just any Ranger, General. He's big, smart, and has already built an impressive reputation bringing justice to the Nueces Strip."

"I can't go to Washington, Colonel, with this business hanging fire. Did you learn what they intend to do with her?" Truax tapped his fingers impatiently on his desk.

"I understand they'll charge her with accessory to a bank robbery and to murder. But it's complicated."

"Complicated?"

"She's with child, sir."

Truax exhaled as though punched in the stomach. "Who's the father?" he demanded. Given that she was a whore, he could only hope the possibilities had been narrowed to only a couple of men. He wasn't to be disappointed.

"As I understand, sir, it's either her dead outlaw lover Dirk Cavendish or Sheriff Whelan himself, who raped her in her jail cell."

Truax quickly concluded that they'd likely reduce the crimes they were charging her with due to her condition. "Learn what you can, Colonel." He looked past Rucker and saw a wagon pulling into the yard. "I've got business to tend to, Colonel. See me before you head out." He distractedly arose from the desk. "Oh, and Colonel, I hope your wounds heal well." He had a bit of a heart after all.

Thaddeus Brown drove the lead rig around behind the general's headquarters building. These were not the sorts of business dealings one conducted in plain view, and it was risky to even be inside the fort. He peered around furtively, climbed down from the wagon, strode over, and knocked on the back door to Truax's office.

"Come in." Truax could barely bring himself to look at the man. He hadn't earned the rank of general to be dealing with sleazy characters, but such was the nature of the illicit merchandising of government property that he'd become involved with.

Thaddeus Brown was as slimy a crook as could be found west of the Sabine. And he was very good at his craft. It was said that the man was so good at selling that he could sell cowboy boots to sailors and they'd pay extra for spurs. He dropped five heavy bags on the general's desk. "'Bout five thousand in gold, General."

Brown had sold most of what he'd "bartered for" from the camps and forts that served as Indian agencies in the eastern part of the Comancheria, that region of Texas west of the 98th Meridian running north to south through Austin. Anything intended for the Indians was fair game to steal, which made acquiring the supplies for the forts a little more challenging. Much of his loot had necessarily been converted to gold coin. It was more convenient than having a caravan of several wagons.

These bags contained a king's ransom in Texas frontier terms. Truax tried to maintain self-control. He owned Brown, but feared him as well. The man could be unpredictable. "Anything else?" he asked.

"Got some right nice weapons, General. Latest from Colt Firearms. Also found some clothes the ladies might like." He was saving what he saw as the best part for last. One of his men entered with a large crate, which he placed on the general's desk. "Lastly, I found you some fine wine, General. It's imported from France. It's a Bordux." He announced the wine with a proud grin, even though he'd murdered the pronunciation of *Bordeaux*. He felt that it lifted his less-than-savory stature to identify fine wine.

The presentation of the wine brought a smile to Truax's lips. "Have you taken your share, Mr. Brown?" He'd established at the beginning of their relationship that Brown did not like receiving any pay-off. It made him feel like a prostitute, as if that should have mattered. Of course, what he felt like and what he was were pretty much one and the same. He'd taken his cut of the bounty.

"Yes, sir. Where would you like me to unload, General?" It was a rhetorical question. Brown knew full well where Truax kept his loot. The nondescript barn was one of those places that aroused no suspicions. It was chock full of the general's collection of material that had been intended for the Indian agencies.

"See you in a couple of months, Mr. Brown."

TWO

Decision

"Lisa, sweetheart, it won't be long. I'll be back long before the baby comes." Luke had been wrestling with the decision on the matter that Rip Ford had proposed. With winter on the horizon, he'd take half the longhorns to market and buy a few head more before heading out on his special assignment. As a Texas Ranger special agent, he'd be taking assignments that didn't entail a typical 130-man company of Texas Rangers.

Elisa uncharacteristically pouted a little, but it was difficult to stay upset with her man. "Promise, Lucas?"

Luke placed his hand over Elisa's belly. She didn't even have a bump yet, but he'd swear there was one. "Shouldn't take long, Lisa."

She liked the intimate nickname he had for her. Lisa and Lucas were the names they reserved for each other.

"I've arranged for Dan to come out and check the cattle now and then. He'll help you with any more difficult chores, too." Dan was the boy in Nuecestown that took care of the livery stable. He'd also proven himself during the skirmishing a couple of months back with Dirk Cavendish and Carlos Perez's *Caballeros Negros* gang. Luke and Elisa trusted him implicitly. "Doc promised to ride out and bring Bernice and Agatha along for a visit."

"What about Comanche?"

"Three Toes' promise of my protection from the Comanche is strong. I trust his word, Lisa."

The decision had been made. Luke had received his first assignment from Ford. He'd be headed down to Corpus Christi to investigate some hiders. They'd been killing local cattle, skinning them, and smuggling the hides out of Texas.

Three Toes knew the end of the Comanche way wasn't far off. The camps and forts that served as reservations and the ever-more-numerous treaties were clues that couldn't be missed.

He motioned for Eagle Eyes to join him at the front of their party. Their attack on the U.S. Army supply wagons was still fresh in their minds. "More come. They build their camps to where the sun sets. We know no end of them."

Eagle Eyes nodded agreement. "What shall we do, my Chief?"

Three Toes had been mulling the answer to that question ever since they'd left Camp Cooper up on the Brazos River. It was a major dilemma, to be sure. To maraud through the Llano Basin would likely not end well. If he had a hundred warriors, it would not be enough. He had only six.

He remained silent to Eagle Eyes' question for a few moments until they arrived at a small grove of trees. He dismounted from his prized pinto pony and motioned the others to join him. They circled around him. A light breeze picked up, catching the feathers in his headdress and war lance. To the casual passerby, he would appear as a rather majestic being, a man of powers, a man filled with the Great Spirit. He was.

"My Comanche brothers, you need follow me no longer. I free you to return to Long Feathers and our people at Camp Cooper."

Eagle Eyes was perplexed. He'd been observing Three Toes for several days, but this caught him by surprise. "What if we wish to go with you?"

Three Toes measured this brave warrior's response. "I ride to a meeting with the Great Spirit," he said. Clearly, he was no longer searching for a new home for the Penateka Comanche. He recognized that this adventure might not end well.

The warriors looked at each other. Three had families and many years ahead of them. They were nearly done fighting, and Three Toes had represented perhaps their final resistance to the white man's incursions. They had no incentive to die. They'd lost their Comanche fighting spirit.

Three Toes nodded. "Go, brothers. You served me well."

Eagle Eyes and the other two remaining warriors began to make camp, and their three brother Comanche rode off toward the north to rejoin their families. Three Toes had a sense that what lay ahead just might be the final journey for him and his small band.

At dawn, they broke camp, mounted their ponies, and headed due south. They'd ridden perhaps half a day when they came upon the tell-tale smoke of a cooking fire. Whoever it was made no attempt at hiding their location.

Three Toes and his band rode cautiously toward the smoke. They weren't close enough to identify who was camping. Soon enough, they heard noises from cooking utensils and voices. There was definitely no attempt at camouflaging. He wondered if it might be a trap. He deduced that, with so much racket, they must be U.S. Army soldiers, as they were often so naïve as to not hide their activities from possible threats. These soldiers may have believed there were no Comanche remaining in the region.

The soldiers soon came into view. There appeared to be eight soldiers. Three Toes had his warriors spread out. He nocked an arrow on his bowstring. At about thirty yards, a soldier spotted one of Three Toes' warriors.

"Indians!" He screamed and ran for his rifle. He never made it, as he took two arrows in his back. Either would have killed him. A second soldier was felled. The manpower odds were evening out. An officer was yelling to rally his men in a defensive position. The soldiers had yet to fire a shot. A third fell victim to an arrow from Three Toes himself.

Three Toes let out a blood-curdling war whoop and charged his pony headlong into the soldiers. He was determined to count coup; it was the bravest act a warrior could perform against an enemy. He sought to touch his war lance to a soldier without killing him. He rode low and hard, tapped a soldier on the shoulders as he rode through the defensive line and went on a short way before twisting on his horse and shooting an arrow into the very soldier he'd just touched. The remaining soldiers seemed frozen, totally aghast at what was happening. Their number had been halved in seconds.

The first shot fired was by a soldier and aimed into his own head, as he dared not be taken captive.

Three Toes waved the attack to a halt. Three bluecoats stood helplessly, as though in surrender. In mere seconds, he'd defeated a numerically superior force.

Slowly, Three Toes advanced toward the soldiers. It was at this moment that he recognized two of the remaining three. It was the lieutenant that had confronted him on his trip north to Camp Cooper weeks ago and his sergeant who'd convinced the lieutenant to allow Three Toes to pass. Three Toes nocked an arrow and held it aimed at the lieutenant. The officer dropped his pistol and raised his hands. The chief allowed his warriors to scalp the dead soldiers, and then they waited while he took the scalp of the soldier upon whom he'd counted coup. One of the soldiers standing helplessly before the Comanche nervously wet his trousers.

The lieutenant and Three Toes locked eyes. The chief nodded, raised his hand as a sign of no further aggression, and then turned and rode away with his warriors. Once the Comanche had turned their backs, the lieutenant bent to grab his rifle, but the sergeant stopped him by bumping him. "Sorry, sir," he apologized. "I lost my balance." He knew he was saving his lieutenant from certain death. As it was, he'd have a lot of explaining to do.

For his part, Three Toes had the sinking feeling that such attacks would be far less frequent in his future.

Colonel Rucker sat in the window, looking out on his ranch. He was pondering his future. He needed to make choices that were difficult by any measure. He had gotten caught up in General Truax's little game with the red-haired whore from Laredo, but had become increasingly aware of the general's other illicit activities. He'd already put his family at risk and was in danger of getting caught in the web of deceit that was being woven. He needed to change course or risk being unable to free himself from the spider's web.

He decided to reach out to an old friend from his Mexican-American War days. He expected Rip Ford would be returning soon from his business in Corpus Christi. Ford was experienced in these sorts of things.

"Sir, are you going to go back after that woman?" Stephen asked the question of his father innocently enough but had the temerity to have interrupted the colonel's thoughts uninvited. From Rucker's expression, Stephen recognized that he was treading on thin ice.

Rucker's initial thought was to put the young man in his place, but then it struck him that Stephen was exactly that, a young man. He and his brother Rex weren't children any more. He'd even taken the risk of taking them along in pursuit of Sheriff Whelan and the whore. That had worried their mother to no end. He softened. "Come here, Stephen. Sit, please." He motioned to the chair next to him.

Stephen sat, uncertain as to what to say.

"I'm sending Rex to New York in a couple of weeks. He'll be entering West Point. You'll be going next year."

"Yes, sir."

"I have some business to tend to that may be dangerous. While I'm gone, you're charged with being the man of the house."

"Yes…"

"Stephen, for just once you can call me father." He uncharacteristically smiled.

"Yes…Father. I'll take care of the ranch."

"Thank you, Stephen, thank you." He paused. "And I was proud of you and Rex when we fought the engagement with that sheriff." He shook head resignedly at not having succeeded in capturing Scarlett Rose, the Laredo whore, as he'd been directed. He felt in his bones that someone powerful was obsessed with her and was using Truax and him as mere pawns.

Luke had never felt this way before. He'd always headed out on the trail fully engaged with his mission. Now, his mind churned with thoughts of a wife and soon-to-be child. It was a good feeling, but it added a new dimension that he had to get used to. He longed to be with Elisa. As he rode, his mind conjured images of her so real it was as though she were with him. He found himself fantasizing over the sweet touch of her full lips and her angelically soft skin as she lay with him. He figured it was likely a good thing, so long as he could focus on his mission when it mattered.

He decided to give Corpus Christi a wide berth as he headed south. He'd skirt the eastern bounds of the King Ranch. From his previous experience as deputy sheriff, he had a rough idea of where the hiders might be working their lawless trade.

Roughly a day into his ride, he came upon his first sign. Longhorn carcasses, perhaps a dozen, lay about rotting in the hot prairie sun. He judged them to have been skinned no more than two or three days before.

He expected there'd be three or four hiders, likely Mexican, but that wasn't a given. Given his experiences on the Nueces Strip, he'd learned to never assume anything. The challenge would be to capture one to find out who was organizing their endeavors. It wasn't likely they were acting alone, as someone was taking a cut of the proceeds to coordinate the sale of the hides. His job was to find out who that agent might be.

The hiders had left a trail. It was old, but he'd learned enough from his few days with Three Toes to be able to pretty much read sign. He'd look for hoof prints in the sandy soil, broken shoots of grass, occasional broken cacti, and perhaps places where they'd stopped to rest or answer nature's call. Luke found that his strategy of traveling through the night generally resulted in quickly closing the gap between hunter and prey. Once he found them, he'd have to take in the terrain and judge the best approach. If at all possible, he'd prefer avoiding any shooting.

Dan had visited Heaven's Gate a half-dozen times already per Luke's request. He appreciated the opportunity to get away from Nuecestown, if only for a few hours at a time.

There were no young girls resident in the town, though a couple of the nearby homesteaders had daughters nearly of age for him. He was only a couple of years younger than Elisa and sought her relative experience and expertise toward eventually sparking one of the young ladies. He'd noticed that Elisa's belly was starting to grow, and that intrigued him. Fortunately, that was about as far as his curiosity about pregnancy went.

One day after working especially hard, Dan prepared to head back to Nuecestown. "I'm 'bout done for today, Mrs. Dunn. That fence should hold up just fine." He stood with his weight shifting from one foot to the other, as though he wanted to say more.

"Dan, thanks again for coming out here. I truly am thankful for your help."

"You're welcome, Mrs. Dunn. I'm pleased to help while the captain is away." Before climbing aboard the sorrel nag he'd borrowed, he decided it was time to open a subject with Elisa. "Mrs. Dunn, may I ask you a couple of questions?"

"Why, sure, Dan. What do you have in mind?"

"What do girls look for in a man?"

"That's a great question." She'd sensed that he was building up to this inquiry the past couple of times he'd come out to help. "Naturally, there's a spark, Dan…an attraction. But most important is a man who respects her, a man whom she can trust, can rely upon."

He gave her a curious look. "What about love?"

"Well, that's important, but true love happens over time. It's not a sudden thing that blows away at the first sign of trouble." Elisa appreciated that he wanted to know. Not many young boys seemed interested in what women wanted. "You also need to be able to provide for her, Dan. A woman wants to feel secure."

That last piece of advice about security resonated. It made him realize he had to find something as a career besides caretaking a livery stable. "Thank you, Mrs. Dunn. I'll be back in a few days."

Carlos Perez was well on the path to recovering from his wounds, though the psychological damage was borderline devastating. The friends who had spirited him away from the Laredo jail were incentivized to helping him. Their blood brothers had ridden with the *Caballeros Negros*, and it had cost all of them their lives. They shared Perez's passion for revenge.

"*Dónde estamos?*" Perez had been in and out of delirium for nearly two weeks. He had no idea where he was. He knew every move pained him.

"*Estamos en Nuevo Laredo, patron.*"

"*Por qué?*" Of course he wanted to know why. It was almost surreal that these strangers should be concerned about him.

"*Queremos venganza.*" It seemed they shared Perez's lust for vengeance.

Perez looked them over and scanned the room. He felt so tired. His eyelids grew heavy, and he fell asleep.

The four young men seemed mere children as contrasted with Perez. But they were patient. They crossed the Rio Grande by twos and stole whatever they needed to subsist. After all, Carlos Perez had become a legend and was well worth waiting for. They would help Perez "*mata at guardabosques de Texas.*" It didn't matter that he was half a man owing to Scarlett Rose's accuracy with a gun. The scars from the Comanche arrows healed well, but the loss of his testicles had been a demoralizing outcome. Even the loss of his eye thanks to Texas Ranger Captain Dunn was more tolerable than what the red-haired Laredo whore had done. He was driven completely by vengeance.

Three Toes knew the U.S. Army wouldn't take kindly to his attack. However, he'd make it as difficult as possible for them to find him. If the Comanche were exceptional at tracking, they were equally successful at covering their tracks.

They calculated that the soldiers wouldn't expect them to head south. Logic would dictate that they'd ride back to the relative protection of Camp Cooper and the Brazos River. Heading south would buy them valuable time until the soldiers caught on to the ploy.

It helped that Lieutenant Belknap and his remaining soldiers were now on foot. A key part of Comanche battle tactics was to deprive their enemies of their horses. On foot, they were vulnerable to the rigors of the frontier, whether cold, rain, fire, or other such natural extremes. It might be days before they found horses. They'd most likely find wild mustangs before locating mounts suitable for their less-than-adequate riding prowess. The bluecoats would likely head back to their fort. Three Toes permitted himself a hint of a satisfied smile.

Eagle Eyes didn't miss his Chief's fleeting expression of triumph.

He too understood that their future was clouded. The Comanche were dwindling in numbers and impact. This small band might yet wreak havoc, but they knew intuitively that it was a losing endeavor.

THREE

Hiders

The hiders appeared to be heading southwestward as though intending to slip past Brownsville on their way to Mexico. It was mostly flat grassy countryside. They would eventually come close to but bypass what used to be called the Ringgold Barracks, which had been upgraded to a fort.

Two days into tracking the hiders, Luke noted that they'd made a sudden right turn to the west. Was it simply an evasive move, and they'd turn southwest again? They were traveling heavy, given the nature of their cargo. Luke calculated they could be heading to San Ygnacio, where they could easily cross the shallow waters of the Rio Grande.

Luke became aware of darkening skies as he focused on the hiders' tracks. Heavy storm clouds that contrasted to the slate-gray sky were gathering just to the south. The warm breezes off the dry prairie created conditions that fed whatever tempest was brewing. The changeability of the weather on the Nueces Strip was legendary.

He heard faint rumbles of thunder from far off, and thought about the oilskin duster he'd left at home. It might have afforded some protection from wind and rain.

A different sort of rumble reached Luke's ears. Instinctively, he spurred the big gray away from the sound. Too late.

A cattle stampede was one of the most unimaginable terrors that could beset anyone on the open prairie. Few beasts were wilder when panic-stricken. Everything in their path was trampled as they fully succumbed to whatever caused them to flee. Luke nearly made it to the edge of the herd. The big gray was pushed and buffeted by the terrorized longhorns. He reared up, and the unthinkable happened. Luke was caught in the leg by a passing horn and flipped from his mount. He was now on foot doing battle with the stampede. The gray had a wild look in his eyes, tried to stay near Luke, but was pushed to the side. Luke was finally knocked to the ground by the last cattle of the herd.

Bloodied and covered with Nueces Strip dirt, he staggered to his feet and took inventory. He had plenty of cuts, scrapes, and bruises. The left leg of his pants was ripped where the longhorn had hooked him, and his shirt was tattered. Incredibly, he hadn't lost his hat. Both Walker Colts were accounted for.

The big gray stallion came limping over. Luke calmed him down and looked him over. The saddle had remained in place, likely protecting him somewhat. As far as Luke could tell, there were no serious cuts, but the horse may have suffered some bruising. In any case, it wouldn't do to add to the beast's woes by mounting him. They'd be walking for a bit.

As if in some comic ironic relief, the edge of the storm passed by. Its rains offered some soothing comfort from what they'd just endured.

They'd now have a tougher time closing ground on the hiders. Luke wondered whether they had faced the same stampeding herd. He concluded they likely had not.

He walked for about a day, giving the big gray time to recover. The horse had finally stopped limping.

The hiders' tracks had been wiped out by the stampede for quite a distance, but he'd soon picked up their trail. Once he found the trail, he decided to rest up a bit. He found a sheltered spot under the only live oak to be seen for miles.

What was to be a couple of hours of rest lasted through the night. Waking to the rising sun, Luke was disappointed in himself. It was as though he had let himself down. Mentally, he couldn't let the aftermath of the stampede be an excuse. Now, he felt pressed to make up for lost time.

He needn't have hurried. After about an hour of riding, he came upon a grisly scene. Two dead horses, a nearly dead pack mule, and three trampled hiders in grotesque defensive positions were collected in an arroyo. There was a stack of perhaps thirty hides and many more strewn about. It was clear that the hiders had not avoided the longhorns after all.

Luke scanned the near horizon and spotted two saddled horses perhaps two hundred yards away. Three bodies and four horses. Someone was missing. He pulled one of his Walker Colts from its holster and began walking concentric circles around the scene to see what he might find.

He spotted the signs of a body dragging in the dirt at pretty much the same time he heard a pitiful groan. The man in the brush was in horrible shape but was trying to aim a gun at Luke as he approached.

"*Hola suelta tu arma y levanta los manos,*" Luke ordered. It would be the only warning the hider would get to drop his weapon and raise his hands. Then Luke saw the blond hair. This man didn't appear to be Mexican at all. "You speak English?"

The hider dropped the gun, but not for want of trying to lift it to shoot Luke. It was clear that one leg was badly broken and his ribs on one side looked to be crushed. He struggled to breathe. Luke wasn't sure the hider would live much longer. "What's your name?"

He grunted something barely intelligible.

"How's that?"

"C-c-cow...boy."

It came to Luke that this man wasn't one of the hiders. He'd been a drover trying to bring the stampeding herd under control. He watched helplessly as the man struggled to breathe and then passed away. The Strip had taken another soul.

As he was concentrating on the dying cowboy, he didn't hear the horse approaching.

A voice called out, delivered between pain-tautened lips. *"Hola, gringo!"*

The hider's first shot missed, giving Luke time to react. He pulled the second Walker Colt from his waist and aimed both pistols at the man. *"Levanta los manos!"*

The hider aimed his rifle to shoot again and pulled the trigger, but it misfired. Luke aimed and fired, hitting the man in the shoulder and dropping him clean out of the saddle. He fell with a sickening thud. The Walker Colt packed a wallop.

Luke repeated, *"Levanta los manos!"*

No matter. The hider had passed out. Luke let out a sigh, shrugged, and manacled the man's wrists. Luke pulled his bandana up over his nose. The man stunk to high heaven. He smelled like cattle hides, combined with the feces he'd fallen into and terrible body odor. He had no weapons other than the rifle and a skinning knife.

Luke rode out, gathered the horses, and tethered them. There was nary a tree or shrub in sight, so he did what any resourceful horseman on the prairie would do. He dug a hole with his knife, knotted the end of the tether rope, stuck it in the hole, and tamped down the ground around it. It was an old technique and just about as good as a hitching post.

He had no idea where the dead cowboy might be from, and he wasn't up to hauling a body around draped over a horse for some undetermined time. He grabbed a small shovel from his gear and dug a grave. There wasn't any wood around to serve as a grave marker, so he took the cowboy's saddle and placed it as a headstone. Might have been a waste of a good saddle but, if anyone happened on the site, it might serve as identification. What were apparently the man's initials were carved into the saddle horn.

He turned his attention back to the hider. The thief was starting to come to. He'd lost a bit of blood from Luke's shoulder shot but was otherwise in decent shape.

From Luke's point of view and despite the stampede, he was pleased that it hadn't been necessary to risk his life trying to ambush the hiders. He bound the hider's ankles together and tied the other end of the rope to the horse tether. He took a dead hider's canteen and swabbed out the man's wound as best he could. All the while, he tried not to breathe in the near-toxic fumes emanating from the man. "*Señor, estas bajo arresto.*"

The hider gave him a rather nonplussed look. "*Qué?*"

"*Hables ingles?*"

"*Si*...I mean yes, dammit!" He looked down at his bloodied shoulder. He was in obvious pain. The slug had broken the shoulder pretty badly, and the manacles prevented his finding a position that relieved the wound's torment. "Who the hell are you?" he asked through clenched teeth.

"Texas Ranger Captain Luke Dunn at your service." Luke smiled as he delivered the last couple of words.

"No, not another goddam Dunn."

"You got an issue with my family?"

The man obviously had experience with Luke's cousins. He smiled ruefully. "You could say that."

"What's your name?"

The hider thought about that a moment. "John Smith."

"Perhaps you didn't hear me." Luke jostled the man's wounded shoulder. "What's your name?"

The hider grimaced. "Cord Crawford...really, no lie."

Luke figured it wasn't worth asking him where he was from. "Who do you work for?"

"Trust me, you don't want to know."

To Luke, this meant the hiders were tied into someone important.

"We'll see if you might be up to talking when I get you back to Corpus Christi." With that, Luke lifted the hider upright and half-walked, half-carried him to one of the horses.

The hider tried to squirm loose, but his broken shoulder simply proved that resistance was futile. Luke being a lot bigger physically served as further dissuasion. Despite the struggles, Luke got him into the saddle and tied him in. He strapped the man's upper arm to his body so that riding the horse wouldn't jerk the shoulder around too badly.

"Guess we're going to get better acquainted, Crawford."

About a day into the ride to Corpus Christi, they encountered three cowboys returning from a cattle drive. Luke determined that they were possibly part of the dead cowboy's outfit. When he got close enough to talk to the men, they told him they had realized early on that their fellow drover was missing but had lost hope of finding him. Luke gave them rough directions to where they could find the grave.

They looked at Crawford's manacles. "What have you got here, Ranger Dunn?"

"I've arrested this man and am taking him to Corpus Christi."

"What'd he do?" The drovers looked inquisitively at one another.

"Suspected of being a hider." This was like waving a red cape in front of the cowboys, given that hiders seriously impacted their livelihood.

One of the three moved his hand to his pistol.

Luke was quick to respond. "Now, gents, perhaps you didn't hear me."

Perhaps it was Luke's Irish-Texas accent, his size as he sat astride the big stallion, or the .44 caliber Colts in his hands, but the cowboy decided discretion was the better part of valor. "Guess it ain't worth getting killed over, Ranger Dunn." He tipped his hat. "Did you by chance ride with Callahan?"

Luke nodded.

"You have a safe trip to Corpus Christi, sir." Obviously, the cowboy's demeanor had shifted. "Thanks for kicking them savage Apaches out of our range."

Colonel Rucker entered the courthouse in Austin. He hoped against hope that what he was about to do would matter. He knocked on the office door and was invited in.

"May I help you?" The young man was apparently some sort of clerk or secretary.

"I'm looking for Rip Ford."

"He's not expected back for a couple of days. Would you care to speak with his assistant, Pete O'Rourke?" He saw the doubt in Rucker's eyes. "Mr. O'Rourke is Mr. Ford's assistant."

Adjutant to adjutant would work. "Thanks, I'll be pleased to talk with Mr. O'Rourke."

After introductory niceties, Rucker got down to business. "I have information about some fraud involving the Indian agencies."

O'Rourke raised his eyebrows. "Does this relate to your military service, Colonel?"

"I'm afraid it does."

"Why don't you take it to General Truax?"

Rucker took a heavy breath. Could he trust O'Rourke? "I report to General Truax."

A hint of knowing something about the general's activities swept briefly across O'Rourke's face. "I understand, Colonel. How widespread is this fraud?"

"Mr. O'Rourke, it involves nearly every camp and fort in Texas that has an Indian agency assigned. It's large scale. It involves cash, livestock, food, and trade goods." Rucker made sure this was fully registering with O'Rourke. "Shoot, he even operates a prostitution ring with three brothels."

O'Rourke shook his head. "Would you like Mr. Ford to follow up with you, Colonel?"

Rucker thought a moment. It might place both himself and Ford at risk. "If you could let me know when he's in town, I'll be pleased to reach out to him."

"I hope I've been of some help, Colonel."

Rucker departed but had an uncomfortable feeling about O'Rourke. Something wasn't right about the man's reaction to his revelations.

O'Rourke watched from the second-floor window as Rucker mounted his horse and rode off. He grabbed his hat and headed out the back of the courthouse. He then walked to the nearby livery, saddled his horse, and headed toward the Army post. He tipped his hat as he rode through the gate and up to the general's office.

"All rise. Court is in session. The Honorable Thomas Wells presiding."

Scarlett dutifully stood and then sat as ordered by the court clerk. There was now no question as to her pregnancy. Despite her condition, she'd led Sheriff Whelan on quite a chase to bring her to justice. He'd finally recaptured her up in Austin and then had to deal with Colonel Rucker and his sons trying to steal her back for some as yet unknown reason. He was still conflicted, as he couldn't be certain whether the child she was carrying was by the desperado Dirk Cavendish or his by virtue of having raped her in the Nuecestown jail cell.

The clerk called the first case…the only case. "The City of Corpus Christi versus Miss Scarlett Rose to the charges of accessory to murder, accessory to bank robbery, and escape from lawful imprisonment."

The judge looked over at the prosecutor. "Mr. Williams, what do we have here?"

"The prosecution is pleased to present a very straightforward case, your Honor. The accused has waived trial by jury and trusts her fate to the judgment of this court. Miss Rose has pleaded guilty to all charges."

With Luke still out on the trail and Sheriff Whelan considered a biased witness, there were no witnesses to call for testimony.

"Miss Rose, do you have an attorney?"

"No, your Honor. I can speak for myself."

The judge shook his head. "I never advise that, but please go ahead, Miss Rose."

It occurred to Scarlett that the judge looked familiar. He looked different sitting up high on the bench as he was, but she vaguely recalled him in a horizontal position with no robes.

"Have you ever been to Laredo, your Honor?"

Judge Wells wondered at the question. "Does that have anything to do with this case, Miss Rose?"

"Could be, your Honor. I was in Laredo for a time and met the possible father of the child I'm carrying."

Wells squinted down at her. She began to look a bit more familiar. Where had he seen her before? He needed to bring the matter back to the business at hand. "You've pleaded guilty to all the charges, Miss Rose. What do you have to say in your defense?"

"Nothing really, your Honor. I got myself partnered up with a man that turned out to be a murderer and thief. I followed my heart and expect I made a poor choice."

Suddenly, Judge Wells recognized her. She certainly did make mostly bad choices in men. Lots of men. "Is that your defense?"

The prosecutor looked over at Scarlett sympathetically.

"Yes, your Honor. I'll take whatever punishment I have coming." By now, she'd seen the hint of recognition in the judge's demeanor. She decided he must have been a happy man when he left her bed.

Judge Wells sat back thoughtfully in his chair. "Does the prosecution have anything further to present?"

Scarlett noticed for the first time that Sheriff Whelan had slipped into the courtroom and taken a seat in the back of the nearly empty gallery. They exchanged knowing looks.

The judge brought the court back to attention. "I've considered the case and am prepared to pronounce sentence."

The clerk stepped forward. "The defendant will please stand."

"To the charges of accessory to murder and bank robbery, I hereby sentence the defendant to two years' probation." There was an audible sigh from the courtroom. The wife of the businessman who'd been murdered in the bank robbery hung her head tearfully. "As to the charge of escape from lawful imprisonment, I sentence the defendant to time served. There being no further business, the defendant is free to go. Court is adjourned."

Just as the clerk was about to have everyone stand to honor the judge's exit, the murdered businessman's wife stood. "Murderer! Murderer!" She tearfully aimed a pistol at Scarlett, but Whelan was faster. Before she could pull the trigger, the report of the sheriff's Walker Colt shattered the otherwise near-quiet of the courtroom. Killed instantly, the woman slumped to the floor.

Judge Wells exited quickly. Scarlett turned to Whelan. "George?" She'd never called him George before. She ran to him and wrapped her arms around him.

Whelan was rather dumbstruck. Yes, he'd saved her life from prostitution for whomever Colonel Rucker worked for, and he'd likely found a way to keep her out of jail and able to be mother to her child… the child that might be his. "You're welcome," he whispered in her ear.

Scarlett emerged onto the steps of the courthouse. Suddenly, it struck her. Where was she to go? What was her future to hold? What of that colonel? Was Carlos Perez really dead? These thoughts swirled about her. Then it struck her. What about Nuecestown? There was Doc Andrews and, of course, Bernice and Agatha at the boarding house. Maybe she could buy enough time to figure out answers.

Whelan followed her out of the courthouse front door.

"George," she asked, "can I trouble you to take me to Nuecestown? You've been good to me these past few weeks and I hate to impose further, but could you?"

Whelan smiled. "Sure, Scarlett. It'd be my pleasure." He looked her up and down and especially at her growing belly. "You think you're up to riding a horse?"

FOUR

Gathering Storm

Carlos Perez was just beginning to feel like his old self…or mostly his old self, given that parts of him were now missing. With Luke Dunn's knocking his eye out with a bullet ricochet and that Laredo whore Scarlett Rose's well-aimed shot that left him essentially a eunuch, he was fully incentivized to recover. He even prettied himself up just a tad with a brand-new eye patch. It made his appearance not quite so repulsive. The four young men who'd rescued him from sure death at the Laredo jail were anxious to become his new *Caballeros Negros*, and Perez was anxious to leverage their enthusiasm to achieve his vengeance.

Perez, for his part, shared with them how he had required his original *Caballeros Negros* to wear black vests, thus earning the name he'd given his band of hider cutthroats. The Caballeros were a distinctive lot, like warriors. In addition to the black vests, they fancied braid-trimmed trousers, broad-brimmed black sombreros, and rode on embossed and inlaid saddles. They tended to be devastatingly skilled with the knife, though over all they were inferior fighters to the Comanche. They preferred parlay over fighting and were known for

making and then breaking promises

Today was a big day. Perez was going to sit a horse for the first time in many weeks. He was physically healed, but still bore psychological wounds. "*Caballeros, traer el caballo alrededor.*" The thought of his tender crotch astride a saddle held no attractiveness in the least.

The young men positioned the horse. They were unsure as to whether it would insult Perez to help him mount. They wisely decided to stand back ready to catch him if he fell.

He slowly raised his left leg and inserted his foot into the stirrup. He paused as if gathering his strength. He pushed off and swung his right leg up and over. His right foot found the stirrup such that he was standing in the saddle. Slowly, he eased himself down onto the saddle.

There was a collective sigh of relief. "*Bueno, jefe.*"

Perez smiled at his accomplishment and gently chucked the reins and gave a gentle touch of his spurs to get the horse moving. He rode real easy-like around the corral a few times. "*Abre la puerta, amigos.*"

They opened the gate, and he walked the horse up the road. He was a long way from hard trail riding yet, but he was feeling his confidence coming back. Knowing he could ride helped prepare him mentally for the mission ahead. Soon enough, he'd cross back into Texas and transit the Nueces Strip in search of his prey.

Whelan and Scarlett gathered her belongings and headed up to Nuecestown. Soon enough, they were hitching their horses in front of Bernice and Agatha's boarding house.

Bernice was so excited, she ran out the front door to greet Whelan. "Sheriff, welcome. And who is this?" Agatha sidled up next to Bernice.

At least, Whelan wouldn't have to tell the story twice. "Ladies, you might recall Miss Scarlett Rose?" He gently nudged Scarlett forward. "Miss Scarlett is looking to enjoy the peace and quiet of Nuecestown."

Bernice's eyes riveted on Scarlett's belly, and she nodded

knowingly. "I expect so, Sheriff." Given some of the religious zealotry in the region, an unwed pregnant woman was scorned if not outright rejected.

Doc heard the commotion and ambled over from his place. "Good to see you back, Sheriff." He gave Scarlett a once-over. "And you, too, Miss Scarlett."

With Scarlett starting to feel uncomfortable, Bernice broke the ice. "So, you're looking for a place to stay, dear?"

"Yes, ma'am. I won't be no trouble." There was no way she was going to mention the men who might be hunting for her.

"That surely does appear to be the case, dear." Bernice figured that Scarlett's whoring days were on hold, at least temporarily. "I expect we can put you up here. You do have the means, don't you?"

"I'll pay for the room, Miss Bernice." The sheriff was torn between genuine altruism and obligation owing to the possibility of the child being his.

Scarlett was surprised by Whelan's offer. "Why, thank you kindly, George."

Three Toes and his braves slowly made their way south along the eastern edge of the Comancheria. They sought what the military might call targets of opportunity. They had already accommodated their likely fate as a small vulnerable band.

They made camp. Three Toes had shot a deer earlier, so they'd be enjoying a fine repast of venison. Soon, the venison was cooking on a spit over a small cooking fire alongside a broad stream that the settlers called the Frio River. They had given San Antonio a wide berth but were closer to Fort Mason than they'd have preferred. They'd have to be wary of mounted Army patrols on scouting missions. While the patrols rarely were comprised of more than a half-dozen soldiers, Three Toes could ill-afford being surprised. He much preferred being the hunter rather than the hunted.

A watch was set, and the warriors settled in for the night with bellies full and spirits high. Eagle Eyes took first duty as lookout. The four of them took turns through the night.

At first light, Three Toes heard what sounded like wagons off in the distance. He'd taken the final watch and was constantly alert. As the sounds drew closer, he became certain that it was the creaking of wagons. He awakened his warriors one by one. "Listen."

They judged the sound to be coming from the east and upwind of their position. Three Toes and his band cleaned up their camp, making it appear as though no one had camped there at all. They mounted their ponies and slowly moved in the tall grass toward the sound. They were still in hilly country, so given arroyos and occasional live oak mottes, the lines of sight could be challenging for tracking purposes.

A hill was ahead of them, so the band rode to its crest to get a better view. Once at the top, they spotted three covered wagons. They appeared to be homesteaders. From what they could see, there were three men, three women, and four or five children. There were several horses and, at another time, those would have been of great interest to Three Toes' band.

The warriors knew what to do. By eliminating the men, the rest of the prey would be left vulnerable. They decided to lay an ambush. They'd painted their faces with broad black horizontal stripes typical of the Comanche, creating a fearsome sight to any person being attacked. Bows and arrows were at the ready as they positioned themselves on both sides of the trail the wagons were inching their way along. They'd be catching the unwary homesteaders in a deadly crossfire.

The homesteaders had relied on assurances that the Comanche and other tribes had been driven from the region. They planned to make it to Fort Mason before sunset.

Three Toes launched the first arrow, and the lead man fell mortally wounded. The other two men were dropped from their horses in rapid succession. Women and children dove for the cover of the wagons, screaming in horror at what had just befallen them.

The Comanche ignored the women at first, choosing to take scalps from the men. Once their initial blood lust was satisfied, they turned their attention to the women and children. Three Toes' band was not returning to Camp Cooper or any other tribal village. There was not to be any taking of prisoners. The children were disposed of in short order with lances and war clubs, leaving the three women cowering under the limited protection of the wagons.

Three Toes was unable to control his warriors. He watched as years of Comanche mistreatment by Anglos and Mexicans, unexplainable diseases like cholera, and the taking of their heritage fueled their rage. The massacre was only ended after full satisfaction of the Comanche lust for revenge. None of the homesteaders survived. Anyone happening upon the aftermath and seeing the mutilations still could not begin to fathom the horrors that were endured. The men were blessed to have been killed and spared being witness to the warriors' savagery.

Three Toes had mixed feelings as he led his band away on its southern track to seek their next quarry. He'd journeyed far from the vision quest the Great Spirit had sent him on and, try as he might to ignore it, it was beginning to haunt him. His world had turned upside down, but he was as yet unable to see it. Life was not as it should have been.

Luke arrived in Corpus Christi with Cord Crawford in tow and pulled up in front of the sheriff's office. Fortunately, Sheriff Whelan had just returned from depositing Scarlett with Bernice and Agatha in Nuecestown.

"George, how you doing? Been a long time."

"You have something for me, Captain?" Whelan couldn't miss the wounded captive tied aboard the horse trailing Luke's big gray.

"Hider, George." Luke handed the lead to the sheriff. "Hold that while I get this man dismounted. He tells me his name's Cord

Crawford, but hasn't said who he's working for." He dragged the man down from the saddle and sat him on the steps to the office. "Caught up with him about a week west of here after a cattle stampede. The cattle wound up killing three of this man's hider gang plus a drover trying to gain control of those raging longhorns. Hell, George, they even knocked me from my horse and nearly ran me down."

"I can likely get him to talk, Luke."

Luke could only imagine what techniques Whelan might have in mind. "Apparently, it's someone important." He smiled. "You figure to use one of those Comanche tortures?"

Crawford's eyes grew wide. "That…that wouldn't be legal," he stammered. A look of panic set on his face. "Would it?"

Whelan looked at the hider, then at Luke. "Luke, why don't you take a little walk while I deal with this boy."

"Captain Dunn…Captain Dunn…please don't leave."

Luke looked down at Crawford, shrugged, and turned as if to walk away.

"Brown…Thaddeus Brown. He's the one we sell our hides to. He's connected with some higher-ups in Austin."

Luke and Whelan exchanged knowing looks. Unsaid was that this technique worked nearly every time. "Luke, let's dump this piece of cow pie in a cell and grab some grub. I've got some news."

Over some tasty fried catfish, Whelan filled Luke in on Scarlett's situation and the goings-on in Nuecestown.

"Have you seen Elisa?"

"Bernice says she's doing great. Dan's gone out there every few days to take care of the heavy chores, and Doc's visited a time or two."

"Well, I expect I ought to get my sorry butt up to Heaven's Gate. I could sure use some wifely loving." He thought on what he'd just said, then thought on Whelan's situation. "You softened any on Scarlett?"

"Not sure how I feel, Luke. The child could be mine, though I'm not proud of how that happened." After the escape incident in Nuecestown, Whelan felt he could talk more openly with Luke. A trust had been built by Luke not snitching on the means of Scarlett's escape nor Whelan's raping of the prisoner.

"That's a decision only you can make, George. She's a life-toughened woman…been through a lot of hard times." He smiled reassuringly, then got up. "But I think she's got some softness in her heart, my friend." He picked up his hat. "I think I'll clean up a bit and head home."

That had a nice sound to it for Luke. Indeed, it was a true home. "I'm pleased to leave Mr. Crawford in your hands. I'll write a short report and leave it on your desk. *Hasta la vista.*"

Elisa saw Luke approaching when he was perhaps a hundred yards from the cabin. She ran so fast that he'd barely had a chance to dismount before she was wrapping him in a huge hug. He could feel her growing belly against him.

"My, but you're so beautiful." She was radiant. The pregnancy seemed to lift her spirits even more as life grew in her womb.

"I love you, Lucas Dunn. God, I've so missed you." She couldn't let go of him. At last, she broke away and grabbed his hand. "Come see what I've done in the cabin."

She pulled him through the door. There arrayed before him on their bed was a comforter she'd made just for them and next to the bed was a crib with blankets she'd knitted. She pulled the both of them onto the bed.

"Are you sure?" She seemed so fragile.

"I'm not going to break in two, Lucas. He or she won't be ready for at least five months yet."

"I love you, too, Lisa." Luke had married a true woman of the frontier.

The big gray stallion waited patiently by the hitching post for the next couple of hours.

Lieutenant Belknap, the sergeant, and the private finally found their way to Fort Mason. Tired, embarrassed, and on foot, they reported in to the commanding officer. The lieutenant described the ambush and how inexplicably the Comanche chief had let them go free. He couldn't bring himself to admit that Three Toes had shown him a courtesy because he'd allowed the chief to pass unharmed from their initial encounter weeks earlier.

The sergeant confirmed the lieutenant's story, adding that the Comanche had ridden off to the north, possibly toward Camp Cooper.

"What would you have me do, Lieutenant Belknap?" It was rhetorical.

"We could set a trap, Major."

"What do you have in mind?"

"We could hide soldiers inside a covered wagon. From the outside, we'd look like homesteaders."

The major appreciated the lieutenant's resourcefulness. "Hmmm… not a half-bad idea. What do you think, Sergeant?"

"Just so I don't have to dress like a woman, Major."

"We'd need at least a half-dozen men, sir. Four hidden in the wagon, plus a driver and outrider."

"I'm a bit concerned, Lieutenant Belknap, at you wandering over the vast prairie in a wagon with not the faintest idea where those savages might be. You say they headed north, but that could have been a trick. Also, you'd be cut off from resupply." The major shook his head. "Good idea, Lieutenant. It's just not feasible. We need a lot more information as to their location."

The lieutenant considered the major's words of wisdom. "Sir, may I have permission to take a detail to scout for the savages?"

The major sighed resignedly. "Lieutenant, I'll give you two weeks. If you find some actionable pattern by the Comanche, we'll reconsider your idea." He arose from his desk. "Do you have any idea whom you are chasing, Lieutenant?"

"If I may, sir?" The sergeant stepped forward. "Rumor has it that the Penateka Chief Three Toes was disappointed with life at Camp Cooper and left to find better hunting grounds. The leader of this band was definitely a chief of some influence, sir. Likely, it was Three Toes."

"Three Toes? If it's him, you have a serious challenge ahead." The major shook his head with concern. "I'll be praying you return from your scouting in one piece."

"There's only four of them, sir."

"And he whupped your asses when you had him outnumbered the last time you met." He paused. "Sorry, I just hope you come out of this alive and learn something about how to fight Indians, Lieutenant Belknap."

FIVE

Setting a Trap

"You asked to see me, sir?"

"At ease, Colonel."

General Truax rarely commanded Rucker to report in. There was something in Truax's tone and manner that was deeply concerning to the colonel.

Truax came around from behind his desk and stood nose to nose with Rucker. "Who the hell do you think you are, Colonel? You seem to have suddenly developed a conscience." He was right in Rucker's face. "Nobody turns on me," he snarled. "Nobody."

A trickle of sweat ran down Rucker's sideburns. He felt Truax's hot breath full on his face. The general was nearly spitting as he spoke. "Yes, sir." Rucker realized that O'Rourke had probably tipped off the general.

"A source tells me you're talking with the Texas Rangers about some things I may be doing. Is this true?"

It was time to lie. "Totally untrue, sir. I've taken bullets for you, sir. I could never betray you." Damn that O'Rourke.

Truax looked at him suspiciously. "We'll see where your loyalties lie, Colonel Rucker." An almost diabolical smile appeared. "Word has it that Scarlett Rose is in Nuecestown. You're to bring her to me. Do whatever it takes, Colonel."

Rucker had been convinced that this was a settled matter, at least for the present. His expression of surprise belied his inner offense at Truax's order.

"I'll give you a month to get her here, Colonel." Truax smiled again. "Dead or alive." At least, he recognized Rucker would spend nearly two weeks traveling to Nuecestown and back. His condescending expression told the colonel that he held low confidence in mission success.

"Yes, sir," Rucker half-blabbered. He turned to go.

"You forgetting something, Colonel?"

Rucker turned, came to attention, and saluted. He left with his tail between his legs like a whipped puppy. He'd been given an assignment with no upside. To fail would mean losing all he'd worked so many years to achieve. The Washington, D.C. assignment would not happen, his ranch would be lost, and his sons would not follow the family tradition at West Point. The stakes had become extremely high.

Three Toes and his warriors continued moving south at a slow but steady pace. They sought targets of opportunity, such as the homesteaders. They were still moving along the Frio River. It was an easy ride with access to water and game. They stayed highly vigilant for bluecoats.

The band found a suitable place to camp for the night. As was his custom, Three Toes walked off to commune in solitude with the Great Spirit. Something inside still did not feel right. His conscience gnawed at him. Had he chosen the right path? Was this the path to which his vision quest had led him?

Eagle Eyes stood near the campfire watching his chief. He admired Three Toes and was possibly the most loyal of his warriors. He barely cocked his head as he heard the faint click of flint on metal. Too late; the musket ball tore its way through his heart. As he dropped to his knees, he looked down at the blood pouring from the gaping hole in his chest. A helpless, pleading expression passed over his face. One moment, he was standing as a proud Comanche, the next he was a dead man.

Upon hearing the shot, Three Toes ran toward Eagle Eyes. The chief arrived to find him having already taken his final breath.

Three Toes and his warriors scanned the trees along the river banks from whence the shot had come. Nothing. Whoever had shot Eagle Eyes was very good. The three warriors ran to the river bank to look for sign. It didn't take long to find the tamped-down grassy spot from which the shot had been fired. They were perhaps a hundred and fifty yards from where Eagle Eyes had stood. The marksman had been impressive. The sign led up river from where they had come. The killer had apparently been tracking them for some time and was experienced, as they found that the sign led in both directions so as to confuse anyone tracking him. The odor of burned gunpowder still hung in the air.

They cautiously headed back to the campsite on the lookout for the assailant. Upon reaching the campsite, they were horrified to see that Eagle Eyes had been scalped. Who was this killer?

Lieutenant Belknap assembled his patrol. He led six mounted soldiers plus two pack mules. He judged himself about as ready as he was going to be to take the first steps toward eventually setting his trap. He knew he'd face a difficult task in persuading his commandant to go along with his plan.

Belknap had thought for some time on the major's theory that Three Toes had actually headed south. The more he ruminated on the idea, the more it made sense.

The major smiled as he watched Belknap leave the fort and turn southward. Perhaps this wet-behind-the-ears lieutenant would yet turn into an effective leader.

Soon enough, Belknap's patrol had wended its way to Fort Martin Scott and then on to Fort Mason. After five days of riding, they'd seen no sign of Comanche, though they had the feeling they were being watched.

At Fort Mason, they decided to take a break from the trail for a day. It was a chance to clean up and resupply as needed.

At the commanding officer's invitation, Belknap was invited to dinner. "Welcome to our humble abode, Lieutenant Belknap." The commanding officer's wife was a petite and quite friendly lady who greeted Belknap with the sort of extra-welcoming smile practiced by the wives of many army officers on station. Women were scarce at the forts, so the wives learned to be especially congenial to visiting men. "The colonel and I are pleased that you could join us."

"Thank you, ma'am."

The dinner was not so special other than being home-cooked. After dinner, the colonel invited Belknap to join him on the porch to smoke cigars. "So, you have quite a quest ahead of you, Lieutenant." He lit his cigar and then lit Belknap's from his.

"Yes, sir, but I've seen no sign of Comanche as yet."

The colonel chewed on that a moment. "So I gather, Lieutenant. Hopefully, you'll see them before they see you. I assume you're traveling on a track that takes you from fort to fort?"

"Yes, sir. Why do you ask?"

"Do you think the Comanche would travel from fort to fort?"

Belknap's eyes grew just a bit wider as he grasped the sense of what the colonel was saying. "I think I understand what you're suggesting, sir."

They continued smoking and sharing soldiering stories until the wee hours of the morning, when the colonel ultimately sent Belknap off to the officer barracks.

Next morning, Belknap headed out once again in a southeasterly direction. In consideration of the string of forts the Army constructed, his route would take him well to the west of the next fort. He wasn't more than four hours into his travels when he came upon the aftermath of Three Toes' massacre of the homesteaders. The buzzards and coyotes had already feasted on the victims, but Belknap's patrol did their respectful duty and buried what remained.

The lieutenant was horrified at the obvious torture inflicted on the women. The Comanche had apparently released the horses, leaving the wagons to eventually fall into a state of total disrepair and disintegration. He couldn't help but note the homesteaders' personal belongings. Lives filled with hope for a bountiful future had been brought to a sudden and tragic end. Husbands, wives, and children would never again share lives in this world.

The sight of the homesteaders reinforced Belknap's determination to set his trap for Three Toes. His sergeant figured that the homesteader attack had likely occurred four or five days previous. They were on Three Toes' trail to the extent that they'd confirmed his southward movements. Belknap needed to find an officer with the willingness to think outside the normal strategies of Indian fighting, one that would let him carry out his plan and set his trap. He set his sights on Fort Inge near the town of Uvalde on the Frio River.

Luke had been thoroughly enjoying his time at Heaven's Gate with Elisa. He found himself ever more the rancher and ever less the lawman. There was a growing appeal to spending days on horseback tending to their growing herd of cattle and coming home to a great meal. Occasionally, they'd go to Nuecestown for supplies and to visit Doc and the ladies.

Elisa's little brother Mike was not getting any better. The rattlesnake's poison had done its dastardly work, gradually breaking down the boy's body functions. Elisa gave further serious thought to bringing him out to the ranch.

Their idyll wasn't to last long. Apparently, O'Rourke was playing both sides of the game, as he told Rip Ford that Colonel Rucker was headed to Nuecestown with orders to kidnap Scarlett. Ford sent a courier with a message asking Luke to prevent that from happening.

Luke happened to be standing on the gallery as Ford's courier arrived at a full gallop. He nearly didn't stop in time to avoid crashing into the gallery. "Captain Dunn? I've got a message from Mr. Ford." He handed Luke an official-looking envelope

"What's that, Lucas?" Elisa called from inside.

"Message from Rip Ford, sweetheart. He's got something he's asked me to handle." Luke's expression revealed inner conflict of some sort. He absentmindedly started to wave off the courier, then thought better of it. "Get yourself some water and rest your horse. Then head back and tell Mr. Ford I'll handle this."

"What's wrong?" Elisa came out onto the gallery.

"Apparently that Colonel Rucker fella that George Whelan dealt with is headed this way under orders to kidnap Scarlett Rose."

"I thought…"

"That he was satisfied, and that her pregnancy had caused him to break off the assignment." Luke shook his head and sighed. "Guess whoever's pulling his strings has other ideas."

"You heading into Nuecestown?"

"Likely as not we have a few days, but I'd better ride in and warn the folks in town. I'll send Dan to Corpus to let Sheriff Whelan know. George has an interest in this for sure."

"George? What interest?"

"Dang," thought Luke. He'd just about let the proverbial cat out of the bag. "Well…er…he did capture her and then bring her to Nuecestown while she has that baby."

Elisa sensed that Luke wasn't telling her the entire story. Should she press him? Why not? "Lucas, darling, what are you not telling me?" She made one of those squinty-eyed expressions and swaying motions accompanied by a wagging finger that some women do when they know their man needs to cough up the answer to some mystery.

"It's a secret."

She stood and put her hands on her hips and gave him one of those looks that only wives can give. "Lucas Dunn."

Her standing there pregnant with hands on hips and a tell-me-the-story expression was too much for Luke. "There's even money the child is either Dirk Cavendish's or George's." There, he'd said it.

Elisa was quite naturally taken aback. To her seventeen-year-old thinking, this was simply not the way things were supposed to be. "Oh my, Lucas." She didn't know whether to feel sorrier for Scarlett or for George. The two of them certainly faced a dilemma. Now their problems were being compounded by this Colonel Rucker.

"Hopefully, I can reason with Colonel Rucker. I wish I knew who he was getting his orders from."

"Would Scarlett be safer if you brought her out here for a couple of days?"

"Lisa, I know you're a fearless fighter and a hard-working wife, but you're also carrying our child. I don't want to risk putting you in harm's way."

"Let me be the judge of that, Lucas Dunn." She had strong feelings about this and wasn't about to let a matter of pregnancy get in the way. "It might make it easier to deal with Colonel Rucker."

It also meant they wouldn't be bringing Mike out to the ranch just yet.

SIX

Caballeros Negros II

Every time he answered nature's call, Carlos Perez was reminded of what that Laredo whore had done to him. The scar in his chest from Three Toes' arrow and the lost eye were almost forgotten compared to the loss of his manhood. By his measure, she would pay dearly. Rape and torture would be incidental to her ultimate agony. Had he known she was with child, he would have been incentivized to a higher-fevered pitch.

He was nearly ready to pursue his prey. Hours had been spent riding more aggressively by the day and regaining his shooting skills. Marksmanship was especially daunting for a man with one eye, as he had no depth perception. At long range, the odds were against his achieving much accuracy. The rifle wasn't much use to him, so he carried two pistols and a large knife. They were early model Walker Colts, serviceable but a bit less reliable than more recently manufactured versions.

He and his four *Caballeros Negros* mapped out a plan to ride back to San Patricio and pick up the trail of the red-haired Laredo whore. He also wanted to repay the whore he'd hired to bring Scarlett to him in the boarding house. He was convinced that she'd been involved in setting the trap that gave Scarlett the opportunity to cost him his manhood. He had strong feelings she had double-crossed him.

"*Caballeros, obtener dos paquetes de mulas. No vamos por la mañana.*" They'd head out in the morning with a couple of pack mules. "*Vamos a San Patricio.*"

His men were excited at the prospect of finally getting started on their quest for revenge. It would be a hard ride and highly dangerous. Had they known what was happening in Nuecestown, they'd likely have had greater concern. All Perez had talked about was getting even with the Laredo whore and the others who'd caused him so much pain. But their fight was to avenge the loss of brothers and fathers. The nexus of their collective purposes worked for now.

The *Caballeros Negros* obtained fine horses for the trek to San Patricio. They even managed to find a saddle with extra padding to ease Perez's ride. They'd considered a wagon, but all agreed it would be far too slow.

Three Toes and his two remaining warriors were hot on the trail of whomever had killed and scalped Eagle Eyes. Their prey was certainly savvy, leaving false sign and doubling back to make tracking challenging. It fully tested their skills.

On the second day of their pursuit, they found Eagle Eyes' scalp pinned to a live oak branch. They were being taunted; laughed at. It was all Three Toes could do to keep his warriors from yielding to their seething anger. Their frustration was palpable.

The trail was drawing them ever westward toward Fort Inge. While they remained in the Comancheria, Three Toes nevertheless was concerned that to go further west took him farther from the farms and ranches he aimed to attack.

They were still traveling along the Frio River. The trees and rocks along the river afforded plenty of cover for their prey. They continued to walk their ponies, yet couldn't help but feel vulnerable. This was proven a valid fear soon enough.

A shot rang out. Another of Three Toes' warriors fell mortally wounded. The chief and his remaining warrior stood back to back surveying the surrounding area. A tell-tale wisp of smoke lingered near some live oak trees a hundred or so yards away. They moved toward the smoke. They didn't arrive soon enough. Whoever had fired the shot had disappeared.

"Quick, go back!" Three Toes realized they'd reacted as expected, having been drawn away from the dying warrior. They raced back to the spot and found him dead and scalped.

Three Toes was beside himself with frustration. Was this the work of the Great Spirit punishing him? Had he been impetuous in leaving his family at Fort Cooper? Had his ego led these warriors on a death mission? Who could this enemy be to escape unseen? Was it even human?

The rifle was a concern. The Comanche used lance and bow and arrows. It led Three Toes to think the enemy might be an Anglo or Mexican. Perhaps it was a woodsman, a trapper, or buffalo hunter, someone used to regularly working from camouflage in the wilds.

Those types of men might take scalps and would certainly be excellent marksmen. Now that he was learning this enemy's technique, Three Toes decided to turn the tables a bit and be the one leaving false sign and doubling back to set ambushes. He took the dead warrior's moccasins and put them on the ends of live oak branches. His thought was to lay back in hiding while his warrior went forward laying a second track. A savvy tracker would recognize the trick but not necessarily right away. His plan was to stay concealed long enough to spring the trap.

It wasn't long before he heard a live oak branch scrape against something or someone behind him. A dark figure stealthily snuck past his hiding place. It was one of the black skins. He was dressed in buckskins and a felt cap and carried an old musket.

Three Toes sprang from his position, shoving his war lance deep into the man's back. The victim gasped and then lunged forward with the effect of ripping the lance from Three Toes' grasp. This was strong prey indeed. A knife was in the black skin's hand faster than an eye could blink. Three Toes pulled out his own knife. As they faced each other, feinting with their knives, the remaining warrior with Three Toes nocked an arrow and sought an opportunity to take a shot. A mere ten yards separated him from the black skin. He shot an arrow, burying it deep into the black skin's shoulder.

Now wounded a second time, the man turned toward the warrior with the angry glare of a wounded mountain lion. Ignoring Three Toes, he was on the warrior before another arrow could be fired. His knife ripped deeply into the warrior's belly.

Three Toes attacked from behind, plunging his own knife deep into the black skin's back. Its blade split muscle and bone and went deep into his enemy's heart. The black skin staggered back. The pain evidenced in the grimace that spread across his face bore testament to hurts from long past. Now, in his final agonizing torment, he fell in a heap at Three Toes' feet. He lay on his back and breathed his last. His chest lay bare, exposing many scars from whippings.

Three Toes would never know the black skin's story. Nary a word had been spoken. Now, the Comanche chief stood alone in the midst of his own story. He'd been tested, but for what? He bent down, thinking to scalp the black skin, but couldn't grasp the man's hair. The chief spit on the black skin in disgust. It had not been a good day.

Thaddeus Brown was in a quandary. Winter weather was not far off, and he needed to make another circuit of the forts and reservation camps up near the Texas panhandle. He assumed the agencies had been resupplied by now, and he could deliver their share of their ill-gotten gains. He hoped to get at least as far as Fort Chadbourne and, with luck, Fort Phantom Hill.

Roughly a half-day into the trek northward, a hard-riding courier caught up with him. He pulled up to the wagon on his well-lathered mount and handed Brown an official-looking envelope.

Brown broke the seal and read the message. He sighed resignedly. A couple of generals from Washington, D.C., along with some congressmen, were touring the northern Texas forts and reservations. It wouldn't do for Brown to be anywhere close to those dignitaries.

It looked as though it would be a lean few months without skimming supplies from those northern camps and forts. He turned his wagons south and thought about next steps. The forts on the Nueces Strip weren't flush with supplies for Comanche or Apache, but there were resupply lines that posed potential. It would be riskier, but he did have his high-placed protector in Austin.

He also figured that he could rendezvous with the hiders. He'd heard that there were plenty of cattle to the south, as well as the buffalo. The hides brought top dollar, so it made sense. The Comanche and Apache threats had been reduced and the U.S. Army was working to eradicate the Mexican hiders that crossed the Rio Grande regularly to work their thieving ways. Brown's own hider recruits seemed immune from the soldiers. He attributed that to General Truax's influence. The only lawmen that might be a challenge to their activities would be the Texas Rangers, and no companies were currently authorized. What could possibly go wrong?

He even began to consider the forts in West Texas in what they'd begun calling the Big Bend. Life was good; business was good. Indeed, what could possibly go wrong?

Colonel Rucker had rested for a couple of days at his Austin ranch before heading south toward Corpus Christi. He didn't yet know that Scarlett was in Nuecestown, but he planned to visit with Luke so would find out soon enough.

Time at his ranch meant dining with his wife and talking with his sons about their future military careers. Rex was packing to leave for New York City and its nearby military academy. Stephen would help his mother care for the ranch while Rucker went south.

He wanted to share with Mrs. Rucker his fear of receiving some assignment fighting Sioux in the northern plains. The wild countryside and brutal winters would not appeal to her genteel sensibilities. Unless he chose to resign and end the future military careers of his sons before they'd even begun, he was committed to bringing Scarlett to General Truax. She had little choice but to agree. Austin wasn't the glittery Washington, D.C. social scene she'd hoped for, but no social life would be total anathema.

Rucker eschewed his officer's uniform, given the nature of the mission ahead of him. It wouldn't do to have the good name and reputation of the U.S. Army sullied with the kidnapping of a common prostitute. This time, he even traded his blue campaign hat with gold braid for a nondescript broad-brimmed, well-weathered brown felt hat. He was fully armed with pistol and rifle and had loaded up a pack mule to carry his supplies. After all, creature comforts were still important to him.

He set out in the morning after a hearty breakfast with his family. While they didn't know the specifics of his mission, his son Stephen had his suspicions. Rex headed for West Point, and Stephen saluted as the colonel rode out on the trail leading from the ranch. There was a sort of bitter-sweetness in the air. Had his career come to this? After all, the choices had been his.

At a steady pace, it would take between eight and nine days by horseback to Corpus Christi. It'd give Rucker time to think, though his stress would undoubtedly build as he approached his destination. He had no idea what he might be dealing with from the Texas Ranger or the sheriff. He knew they were not to be underestimated. Had he known that they knew he was coming to get Scarlett, he'd have had greater cause for serious concerns. Captain Luke Dunn, especially, had begun to establish a wide reputation as a highly effective lawman.

Luke figured that they wouldn't have to take in Scarlett at the ranch for another few days. Meanwhile, he'd sent Dan to Corpus Christi the day before to alert Sheriff Whelan.

"I'm heading into town, Elisa. I need to…" His words trailed off as the sound of an approaching horse caught his ears.

Sheriff Whelan pulled up in front of the cabin. "Luke, Elisa," he tipped his hat to Elisa, "I came as soon as I heard from Dan. What's going on?"

Luke explained that Rucker was on his way. "I think we'll be able to protect Scarlett, but I'm more concerned about who is pulling the strings, so to speak. Who's in charge?" An idea dawned on Luke. "Say, George, you have any more on that Thaddeus Brown fella that Crawford mentioned?" It was mostly a rhetorical question. Crawford was merely a pawn in the game. "Seemed like he needed to catch up with Thaddeus Brown."

Whelan shook his head about Brown. "But I did ask Colonel Kinney about Colonel Rucker. Seems he reports to General Truax in Austin."

"Truax?" Luke stood thoughtfully. "What's his command?"

Elisa went into the cabin to pour some coffee. Luke and Whelan might be chatting for a bit.

"Colonel Kinney says the general has quite a reputation. He's well-connected in D.C. He's sort of in charge of the military in Texas. I say sort of, as he has few direct support staff. He's supposed to have amassed a considerable fortune."

"Hmmm. How's he doing that amassing, George?"

Whelan smiled. "Rumor has it he's more like a crime king. It's said he runs a couple of brothels, makes money in cattle trading but doesn't run a ranch, owns a couple of trading posts with questionable inventory sources, and trades in cattle and buffalo hides…" George's voice trailed off. He saw that Luke was connecting Truax's activities with what they were dealing with on the Nueces Strip.

"I've got a feeling, George…mind you, it's just a feeling, that there's a connection with this Thaddeus Brown fellow. I'd also bet the general covets Scarlett, not for a brothel, but for some power broker in Austin."

"Could be, Luke. But why hasn't anyone else figured this out?"

Elisa overheard the tail end of the conversation. "Maybe there are folks placed higher than the general." It was far too easy to figure out. She felt almost smug. "He may be like one of those puppets on strings."

Luke smiled. "Like a marionette. But who might it be?"

Whelan looked worried. "In my experience, the more powerful the lawbreaker, the more dangerous the mission to get justice."

"I'm thinking we need to capture Colonel Rucker and question him." Luke was formulating a strategy to lure Rucker in and capture him. A few days in the Nuecestown jail might loosen his tongue. Of course, Luke had no idea that Rucker had already attempted to turn in Truax and was now being threatened to ensure compliance.

"Day after tomorrow, let's bring Scarlett here to Heaven's Gate where we can guard her more closely. I've already established a bit of a mutual respect with Colonel Rucker, and we might intercept him and have a peaceful capture. We can head him off in Nuecestown."

"You of a mind to meet him before he reaches the town?"

"I'm thinking there's less chance for shooting if we are able to waylay him in the town. I judge him too much the officer to risk innocent citizens."

Elisa smiled. She loved the way Lucas thought. "I'll set up a place for Scarlett to sleep."

The *Caballeros Negros* were making good progress across the prairie from Laredo. The younger men were surprised at Perez's energy despite his ailments. Their camaraderie transcended that of the original gang, so Perez was pleased. He found the modified saddle reasonably comfortable.

As they pulled into San Patricio, their first act was to find the unofficial *alcalde de el barrio*. Perez remained mounted while one of his men knocked on the *de facto* mayor's door.

It was early in the day, and the mayor groggily opened the door, squinting in the sunshine. He blinked and shielded his eyes. What he saw threw him into panic.

With the bright sun behind him, Perez was essentially a silhouette to the *alcalde*. "*Señor Garcia, me recuerdas.*"

The *alcalde* could never forget that voice. "*Señor Perez, bienvenidos.*" He offered the welcome in a shaky voice. "*Cómo puedo ayudar?*" What had brought Perez back here? How helpful could the *alcalde* be? As helpful as necessary to stay alive.

"*Donde esta la puta?*"

Of course, he sought the prostitute. "*Pelo rojo o negro?*" Which whore was Perez referring to? Intuitively he figured it was the red-haired whore who'd shot him. He did not want to put the black-haired whore into harm's way. After all, she was his daughter.

"*Negro primero, luego rojo.*" Perez thought to savor the torture and killing of the Laredo whore. First, he'd deal with the black-haired whore he thought had set him up.

The alcalde paused and looked pleadingly at Perez. "*Misericordia, por favor, señor.*" He begged for mercy.

"*Donde la puta?*"

The alcalde pointed to the saloon up the street. "*Misericordia.*"

"*Y la roja?*"

He responded hopefully, as though it might go better for his daughter. "*La llevaron a Nuecestown.*"

"*Gracias, Señor Garcia.*" Perez turned his horse and led his *Caballeros Negros* to the saloon. He ordered the men to fetch the black-haired whore and bring her into the street. The stagnant morning air reeked of the odor of evil.

She struggled desperately in their grasp. By this time, a small group of onlookers had begun to gather. "*Atarla a la publicación!*" On his command, the men tied her to the post. Perez swaggered alongside her and motioned to strip her. The men eagerly ripped off her skirt and petticoat. The crowd gasped. "*Follarla.*" They gasped again. They didn't know whether to look or run away. None dared intervene at the horror about to befall the *alcalde*'s daughter.

Each *Caballero* in turn had his way with the whore. She struggled and strained at the ropes that held her. Perez laughed through the entire ordeal. Then the cold reality hit him. He could not have her. He could not join his men in their lust. He could never again have a woman. A shroud of evil blackness descended upon him

The *alcalde* stood with the crowd and continued to plead for mercy. "*Por favor, por favor.*"

Perez looked coldly at him with his one eye. The evil cut like a black knife through the morning air. He raised his pistol. The crowd gasped. Perez turned, aimed, and shot the *alcalde* through the heart. "*Via con Dios, senor. Adiós.*"

The men cinched their belts, mounted up, and followed Perez south in a cloud of dust. They could be heard laughing as they rode into the distance. A merciful citizen untied the mayor's half-naked daughter, who rushed to her dying father's side. Her rape had been a horrid form of vengeance indeed.

Perez figured to cover the twenty miles to Nuecestown in less than a day. They'd camp north of the town to reconnoiter and lay a plan of attack. They were excited at the prospect of torturing the Laredo whore. For Perez, he knew his other enemies weren't far away. He was confident that he'd soon have his revenge and reveled in the mere thought of it. His chase was nearing completion.

Luke calculated that he and Whelan had at least a day of cushion before Rucker arrived. Had they known about Perez, they'd have been

far more concerned. Luke was confident he could reason with Rucker. That wouldn't be the case with the Mexican hider.

"What do you think, George? My thinking is for you to set up at the jail, while I take Scarlett to Heaven's Gate."

"Works for me, Luke. We should alert Doc, too. Hell, we may need his services before this business is done."

"I'll go see Doc; you head over to the boarding house and get Bernice and Agatha to help get Scarlett ready to travel. I'm thinking you may want to get a buckboard from the livery. Scarlett might not sit a saddle too well."

"Okay, Luke. Let's rendezvous at the jail."

They split up and hastened to prepare the town for what might be coming.

It was late afternoon before Luke pulled up in front of the cabin and helped Scarlett from the buckboard. Elisa had arranged space for her, enough to be comfortable for at least a couple of days.

"Thank you so much, Elisa. I'm sorry to be such trouble."

"Think nothing of it, Scarlett. We wouldn't have you falling into the clutches of Colonel Rucker."

Luke carried in Scarlett's bag. He was impressed at the lengths Elisa went to in making their very pregnant guest comfortable. "Lisa, sweetheart, I'd best be heading back. George and I will be taking turns standing watch."

She handed him a sack of dried venison, biscuits, and some sweets. "Be safe, Lucas. By all means, be safe."

He swept her up and kissed her fully.

She felt secure caught up in the strength of his arms, a stark contrast to the emptiness when he stepped away.

"Mind the ranch, Lisa. Keep the rifles handy." There was an urgent plea in his words. He knew she could defend herself, but she had Scarlett to protect as well. This is what made for the hardy women of the Texas frontier. He mounted the big gray and was soon headed back to Nuecestown.

Rucker saw the campfire off in the distance as he approached the town. He figured to rest at the boarding house before continuing on to Corpus Christi. He was also of a mind to stop by and see Captain Dunn along the way.

Curiosity was getting inside his head. What, or more specifically, who was that campfire about? He rode just close enough to make out several men with horses and pack mules. He was downwind so it helped him to barely make out the sound of their voices. Mexicans. Intuitively, he decided to skirt wide of their camp and continue on into Nuecestown.

As he pulled up to the boarding house, he noticed the light on in the sheriff's office. After he checked in, he determined he'd have to pay a visit.

After a meal of Bernice's usual over-cooked roast, Rucker strolled over to Whelan's office.

"Who is it?" Whelan heard the knock and peered from the window. At first, he was put off by Rucker not being in uniform.

"I'm Colonel Rucker. May I come in?"

Whelan didn't figure to make Rucker overly suspicious, so slowly opened the door. "Come on in, Colonel." He motioned to a bench under the front window and about six feet from the desk. "How may I be of service, sir?"

"I'm spending the night across the street and noticed your lighted office. I'm headed to Corpus in the morning. Would you know whether Captain Dunn is at his ranch?"

Just then, Whelan heard the buckboard rig drive by. "I think he just pulled in, Colonel. He's returning a wagon to the livery, and I expect him to come by in a moment or so. You're welcome to set a spell. I'd sure like to know what's happening in Austin."

Rucker seemed to relax for the moment. "Austin's a busy place, Sheriff. We have a fast-growing state."

"How's soldiering going for you? Luke told me one of your sons is headed to West Point."

"Oh, Rex. Yes. He'll make a great officer."

Whelan couldn't help but hope the son would be a better man than the father. "I'm sure you're very proud."

Luke heard the voices as he neared the office, and recognized Rucker's. He chose not to announce himself.

Rucker was startled as Luke opened the door and strode in. He gathered himself and extended his hand. "Captain Dunn, good to see you again."

"Why, Colonel Rucker, what brings you to Nuecestown?" It was all he could do to keep from throwing the colonel into a cell right then and there.

"Actually, I have business in Corpus Christi, Captain."

"Can we be of any help?" Luke knew that Rucker knew of Whelan's ties to Scarlett. This little ruse had quickly run its course.

"Well, Captain, before we discuss my business, are you aware that a handful of Mexicans are camped just north of this fine town? From the look and sound of them, I think they may be up to no good."

Luke was taken aback. Memories of Carlos Perez rushed through his head. "Mexicans?"

"I dared not get close enough to hear anything of value, but they didn't seem to be intending to make nice in these parts. I got just close enough to see that one of them wore a patch over his eye."

Luke silently acknowledged the increasing chance that these men might actually be led by Perez himself. "I appreciate the information, Colonel. I'll have to check them out." He looked over at Whelan. "But, back to your business here, Colonel. Are you looking for something or perhaps someone?"

"You do get right to the point, Captain Dunn."

"It's likely the Irish in me, Colonel. Blarney isn't in me today." Luke glanced again at Whelan.

Whelan shrugged. "I think what Captain Dunn is getting at,

Colonel Rucker, is that we all have a mutual acquaintance that we understand you're looking for."

Rucker's eyes grew wide and his eyebrows lifted for a moment. He'd been made apparently, long before he arrived in Nuecestown. "Seems we have no shortage of loose lips in Texas, gentlemen."

Luke shook his head. "It's less about loose lips than about intentions, Colonel. I can tell you here and now, she's not for the taking and you'd best not force your hand."

Whelan placed his Walker Colt on the desk with the muzzle pointed at Rucker. The threat was veiled, but not thinly veiled.

"Let me get you off the hook, Colonel. Miss Scarlett is not only going to give birth very soon, but she's married."

Whelan nearly fell back in his chair.

"Your General Truax wouldn't be wanting a married woman, now, would he?"

Rucker slumped in his seat. "I'm ruined," he gasped.

Smiling, Luke offered Rucker an out. "You could work with us, Colonel."

"What do you mean?" He had Rucker's full attention.

Luke got up from the bench and stood with a thoughtful expression as his fingers stroked at his mustache. "I understand Rip Ford has it on good authority that General Truax is…well, to understate it…corrupt. We captured a hider recently who gave us the name of a trader named Thaddeus Brown. Go figure, but this Brown fellow apparently travels with his wagons from fort to fort helping quartermasters dispose of extra merchandise. 'Course, we know there are Army supply shortages, so this doesn't make sense, does it?" Luke watched Rucker's face intently as he let this sink in. "A source in Austin tells us there's some connection between Thaddeus Brown and General Truax. Doesn't that just beat all, Colonel?"

"The Texas Rangers seem to do excellent work even when they're not official, Captain." Rucker was amazed at what Luke already knew.

"You had no idea this was going on, did you, Colonel Rucker?"

"And if I did?" The colonel's face paled a bit with the realization that Luke had him figured out.

"There's a thing that folks of faith call redemption, Colonel. I suspect that turning on the general would put your family and the future of your sons at some significant risk. If you were involved, we'd do all we could to protect them. 'Course, there are no guarantees."

Rucker sat and thoughtfully considered Luke's offer. He really had no choice. "You looking for a confession?"

Luke shook his head. "Don't need one...yet."

"Okay, Captain Dunn, let me know how I can help."

Whelan slipped the revolver back into his holster.

Perez was so confident that he didn't bother to set any watch over his camp. No one around Nuecestown knew he was coming, much less that he was still alive. His imagination was filled with graphic images of what he would do to that red-haired whore that had stolen his manhood. She would regret all she'd done as she died an agonizing death. The images kept turning in his mind.

SEVEN

The Chase

"Colonel, I suggest that you and I do a bit of scouting of what may be an enemy preparing to cause us a bit of trouble."

"Lead the way, Captain." Rucker had heard a bit about this Texas Ranger and the reputation he was establishing. He'd get to see him work first hand.

"George, you hang out here at the jail in case we need to beat a hasty retreat. If you hear us shooting and riding hard, be ready to cover our rear."

With that, Luke and Rucker fetched their horses and were soon riding out to where the colonel had seen the Mexicans. They'd ridden no more than a mile out when they saw the glow of the fire. There was cloud cover, so the moon and stars didn't light the landscape to near-daylight brightness as was often the case on the Strip.

"They figure they're above suspicion, Captain, as no one around these parts would be expecting them. In my experience, that often breeds over-confidence," Rucker whispered. "Let's circle to the east and get downwind."

Luke nodded. After a short way, they dismounted and began their attempt to get closer on foot. It became obvious that the Mexicans' carelessness was being fueled by booze, likely rum or whiskey.

"Looks like there's five of them," Luke whispered. "Let's wait a bit and see if we can even the odds."

Two of Perez men started to walk away from the campfire to answer nature's call. They were joking and carrying on. As chance would have it, they came to within twenty feet of Rucker's and Luke's positions. Luke nodded over at the colonel.

Their two pistols discharged nearly simultaneously. Both Mexicans fell.

There was a commotion in the camp as Perez and his remaining men bolted for their horses. "*Andele Caballeros!*" There was shouting and confusion.

Luke and Rucker leapt into their saddles and galloped toward Nuecestown with Perez giving chase. Despite the darkness, Luke quickly led the way to the road.

Perez, on the other hand, had no idea where the road was. His horse tripped and fell in the darkness as he tried to cross a shallow arroyo. The cloudy night added to their woes, becoming another enemy. His men, realizing they were leaderless, ended the chase. They returned to Perez, who was lying in the dust cussing his horse. He was nearly ready to shoot the poor animal, but his *Caballeros Negros* held him back.

Perez went back to find his other two men. He heard groans and soon came upon them. One was wounded; the other was dead. Attrition was once again beginning to work against Perez. "*Malditos gringos!*" he shouted to no one in particular. These setbacks served to further fuel his frustration and his anger.

"*Por la mañana, nos montamos, Caballeros.*" They'd head to Corpus Christi at the crack of dawn.

The reality of the loss of one of their own served to sober the *Caballeros Negros*. They'd gone from the perverse pleasures of rape to drinking and carrying on only to be confronted by the truth of their vulnerability. They'd built a cocoon of vengeance only to have the chrysalis torn asunder.

It was a relief when Luke and Colonel Rucker arrived at the Nuecestown jail. The two smiled at each other, pleased at having succeeded in their mission. It'd been Luke's way of testing Rucker.

"Pleased y'all returned safe, Luke." Whelan stood on the front steps. "I expect they'll give Nuecestown a wide berth in the morning."

Luke turned serious. "If it's Perez, they'll know I'm here. They won't be doing any bypassing."

For three days, Three Toes lifted his being to the Great Spirit. He meditated, sitting alone, immovable, under sun and stars. He came to realize that he'd failed to listen to the Great Spirit. Had his vision quest been for naught? Had he learned nothing? His anger at the Indian agency and frustration with how his own people had capitulated gnawed at the deepest reaches of his soul. Three Toes had failed to exercise the cool patience of spirit and action that he'd striven to cultivate. He had abdicated his duties as leader of his people. His Comanche essence had been seriously compromised.

He finally stood. His joints were stiff from sitting so long. His pony stood by dutifully. Three Toes looked down at the already decomposing corpses. Scavengers and carrion beetles were already taking their fill of the remains. He'd be taking no scalp from the black skin. He'd meditated on how his very soul had been corrupted just as the bodies were rotting. He'd lusted for a return to the old ways and had paid a price for wrongfully seeking to quench his craven hopes. He'd paid the price for ignoring the master of his soul.

He now felt that the Great Spirit told him to renew his vision quest, that it was unfinished. With still-aching joints, he slowly mounted his pony and headed eastward toward Nuecestown. He felt led to find his friend Ghost-Who-Rides. He concluded that the Texas Ranger held the answers to his vision quest.

Lieutenant Belknap led his little entourage into Fort Inge. He was confident that he had enough evidence to convince the commanding officer to support his strategy. He and his soldiers had experienced the barbaric results of the Comanche attack on the homesteaders. His strategy transcended mere logic. It had become personal...and an emotion-laden mission.

"Lieutenant Belknap reporting, sir." He saluted smartly.

The major deferentially offered a sort of half-salute while seated at his desk and half-paying attention. "Can I help you, Lieutenant?"

Belknap dropped a piece of paper in front of the major. He grudgingly lifted his gaze to look at it. "Three names? What is this?"

"Those are the names of the homesteader families killed by Comanche a couple of days ride east of here, sir."

"So?"

"I have a strategy for eliminating those Comanche, sir."

The major leaned back in his chair. Belknap had gotten his attention. "What strategy?"

"It's about setting a trap, sir. We send out a couple of wagons, disguising them as homesteaders. In the wagons are soldiers set to ambush the Comanche when they attack the seemingly vulnerable wagons." Belknap offered his most enthusiastic delivery of his plan. "We know roughly where the Comanche are headed, sir. We estimate they'd find us and attack right soon, sir."

The major finally got up from the desk. "Follow me, Lieutenant." He ushered Belknap onto the gallery of the commanding officer's house. He waved his hand at the horizon beyond the fort. "This is big sky country, Lieutenant. They call it the Nueces Strip. From here to the coast is mostly flat, grassy prairie. Wiregrass 'bout as far as the eye can see. Your Comanche could be most anywhere out there." He shook his head in dismay. "You'd be searching for a mere speck on that enormous expanse. Frankly, I'm not the least inclined to risk men and material on such a strategy that's unlikely to succeed." He sensed Belknap's disappointment, but crossed his arms to indicate that this was his final decision.

Belknap's shoulders slumped. "With permission, sir, I'll be pleased to rest my patrol here for a day and then resume pursuing the Comanche."

"You can chase them so long as you want, Lieutenant. You've got your orders. But, I suspect you're on a fool's errand. I urge you to call off your mission and head back north."

Belknap saluted, not nearly so smartly as earlier, and excused himself to rejoin his men. Most of them were secretly pleased that Belknap's plan had been rejected. They were outdoors in beautiful surroundings, didn't have to endure the chores of camp life, were convinced that it was unlikely they'd encounter any Comanche, and had a leader that was just learning the ropes of Indian fighting. They were also blessed with a sergeant who knew what needed to be done.

The next day, Belknap led his patrol from Fort Inge and headed north. He'd resigned himself to coming up with a new strategy.

Most of the forts on the Nueces Strip didn't have Indian agents associated with them, so Thaddeus Brown's mission shifted to connecting with the hiders and scamming the soldiers at the forts to acquire tobacco, whiskey, and dry goods that could be resold at inflated prices to homesteaders. With all this in mind, he rolled into Fort McIntosh outside of Laredo.

He decided not to engage the commanding officer just yet. He needed information on his local contact, and that would most likely be found in Laredo proper. He and his men set up their camp on the outskirts of the town and decided to ride in shortly before sunset and check out the local color. He'd heard about a well-supplied saloon and a brothel. Little more was needed.

The sun sat like a glowing coal on the horizon. Brown and two of his men rode into Laredo. The streets were surprisingly busy, mostly with Mexicans that trafficked back and forth from Nuevo Laredo. They stopped at the livery stable, as they didn't expect to need their horses for a few hours yet.

Brown and his men were a picture of trail-weary but mission-focused and very well-armed travelers as they walked to the saloon. Each man had two revolvers and a Bowie knife. So armed, there'd likely be few that would want to engage them in any sort of trouble.

As they walked through the front door of the saloon, there was a pregnant pause among the patrons as they took notice of the newcomers. Brown sidled up to the bar, while his men found an empty table and sat. Notably, they sat with their backs to the wall, a natural inclination in this environment where death could be too easily delivered from behind.

"Mister barkeep, some whiskey for my friends over there." He placed a gold coin on the bar.

The barkeeper reacted as expected. Gold had a certain allure. He figured there was likely more where that came from. He had a bottle of whiskey and glasses sent over to Brown's men.

"Where are the ladies tonight?" Brown had taken a quick inventory and noticed their absence.

The barkeep smiled broadly. "They're busy. But we can make arrangements."

Another gold coin dropped on the bar. "That would be appreciated." Brown smiled almost patronizingly. "Who would I talk with about some merchandise?"

"What sort of merchandise?"

"Just about anything you might think of. I buy and sell merchandise, barkeep." He emphasized the last word. "Tobacco, whiskey, guns, ammo, hides…you name it."

"This isn't the time or place, Mister…"

"Brown, Thaddeus Brown. Perhaps we can talk in the morning?"

"That would be fine, Mr. Brown. You're new to these parts?"

"I mostly trade quite a bit north of San Antonio, up as far as the Red River. I have some profitable arrangements that I'm looking to expand."

He'd now gotten the full attention of the barkeep. "I expect you'll be wanting to meet Colonel Higgins at Fort McIntosh and Marty Garcia here in town. They pretty much control what moves in and out of Laredo. Oh, and there's Sheriff Stills, but he's lost a lot of credibility since Carlos Perez escaped from his jail."

"Wasn't Perez once a hider?"

"Once. Long past now. He ran into a Texas Ranger Captain Luke Dunn and came out the loser for it. Cost him an eye, among other body parts."

"Dunn, you say?"

"He's not one you want to have on your trail. He served under Callahan on that Apache campaign back in '55 and has been collecting bounties ever since." The barkeep shook his head knowingly. "Nope, stay clear of Luke Dunn, Mr. Brown."

"I appreciate the advice." Brown started to walk over to the table his men were sharing but paused. "You heard of a man named Cord Crawford?"

"Crawford?" He scratched his chin. "Some drifter passed through a few days back and mentioned that name. You know him?"

Brown wasn't about to mention the context. "Drifter offer any more?"

"I think he was in the Corpus Christi jail. That's 'bout all he said."

That left Brown wondering as to the condition of his hider operations on the Nueces Strip. He'd have been more concerned had he known that it was Luke who'd jailed Crawford. Brown joined his men at the table.

Before long, three attractively dressed young women entered the rear of the saloon. The barkeep sent them over. Brown would have to wait to learn more about Higgins and Garcia.

Perez and his men moved at a brisk trot toward Nuecestown. He recalled that the last time he visited the town he'd ridden into an ambush and was fortunate to escape unharmed but for his pride. He'd been chasing that red-haired whore from Laredo. The ambush had eliminated the remainder of his *Caballeros Negros*. It was not a pleasant memory at all. He'd eventually tracked her to San Patricio, and it cost him his manhood.

Whelan and Rucker took positions behind buildings on either side of the road by which Perez would enter the town. Luke waited near Doc's place, crouched behind a water trough.

Perez rode to the ferry landing before dismounting. He intended to be far more cautious entering Nuecestown this time. "*Detener! Hay peligro!*" he uttered in a low barely audible voice. He'd seen the sun's glint on a rifle barrel. "*Es un enboscada!*" He wasn't about to walk into another ambush. He motioned his men to mount, and they spurred away.

Luke saw their dust and ran to the stable to get his horse. "George… Colonel! Let's go!"

By the time they got horses saddled, Perez had ridden several miles north toward San Patricio. Luke started to give chase, but then thought better of it. "He knows we're here. Whether he's heading toward San Patricio or Corpus, he'll circle wide around us."

"What do you have in mind, Luke?" Whelan looked to Luke.

"I'm betting he's not going back to San Patricio. Normally, I'd say we set a position in Corpus. If he circles west of here, he could run into Heaven's Gate. That would put our women in serious danger."

"They'll be doubling back to the south. I'd say we take a track that keeps us between them and the ranch," Whelan suggested.

"There's a bluff a half mile from here. We can get a decent sighting if, in fact, they're moving south."

The chase was on.

They didn't have to wait long, as they soon saw Perez's reconstituted *Caballeros Negros* riding far to the west and southward toward Corpus Christi. At the pace they were traveling, Luke calculated they'd arrive in a couple of hours, discover that Scarlett had moved from Corpus to Nuecestown, and then double back. He figured Perez would waste no time in Corpus once he'd learned what he needed to know.

Meanwhile, George had recruited the stable boy, Dan, to increase their firepower. Dan had performed well the first time Perez came charging through Nuecestown into their ambush. Four against four made better sense.

"What do you think, Colonel? Where shall we set our defensive perimeter?"

"To be straight, Captain Dunn, I'd remain staked out on this bluff. It isn't especially high, but high enough to offer an advantage. We might spread out a bit to give the impression of more men and greater firepower."

"Works for me, Colonel. Keep in mind that Perez needs to engage in close quarters. With only one eye, he can't hit anything at distance except maybe a barn. He's got to get to where his pistols will give him an advantage."

Luke rode out to serve as lookout so as to give advance warning of Perez's approach.

Perez's anger had by now soared to unimaginable heights. His dreams of vengeance knew no bounds, encompassing nearly all living things around him. He promised himself that after he wreaked his revenge on the Laredo whore, he'd burn the town to the ground. Then, he'd turn to that damnable Texas Ranger and, if he could find him, that god-forsaken Comanche.

He pulled up to the sheriff's office in Corpus Christi. His men aimed their rifles at the place. If anything moved, it'd be hit with a fusillade. Perez dismounted, drew his pistols, and proceeded to crash through the front door. "*Maldita sea! Esta vacio!*"

It was indeed quite empty...of life. Cord Crawford's lifeless body hung from the top bar of the cell door. He'd torn the mattress apart to make a rope of sorts. Perez shook his head condescendingly at the dead man. "*Débil*," he muttered. The man was a weakling to have taken his own life. Perez turned in frustration and left the sheriff's office. This wasn't helping him find his quarry.

He gathered his wits and strode across the street to the bank. He screamed at the teller, "*Donde esta el pelirojo?*"

The teller thought the bank was being robbed and ducked down.

Perez went around behind the window and put a pistol to the man's head. "*Donde esta el pelirojo?*"

"Redhead? There's lots of redheads. How would I know? Maybe Nuecestown?"

"*Esta puta.*"

The bewildered teller was clueless. He knew that *puta* meant whore. Then it struck him. He recalled the red-haired woman held briefly in the bank for extra protection. "You must mean Scarlett. She's in Nuecestown."

Perez winced and gritted his teeth in frustration. He'd half a mind to blow the teller's head off. There it was. That damnable town thrown up at him again. He'd just been there, and they'd set a trap. For the moment, all he did seemed to point to Nuecestown. He pushed the teller to the floor and dashed out of the bank.

"*Caballeros, rapido vamos a Nuecestown!*" He thought to leap into his saddle, but the reality of his still-tender condition slowed him just a bit. He scowled as though to warn his men not to laugh. Then he managed to climb onto his horse, turn the beast, and lead his gang back toward Nuecestown.

Luke raced back toward the bluff. "They're coming! Get ready!"

He reached the far side of their defensive position, dismounted, pulled the Colt rifle from its scabbard, and took his place near a live oak.

"Gotta believe they're not very happy," Whelan called over to Luke.

"Those horses will be well lathered." Luke smiled. "Let's hope Perez is enraged beyond reason."

Perez and his men got to well within fifty yards when the ambush was sprung. Luke and his men laid down a withering fire before Perez could return a single shot. Two *Caballeros Negros* flew from their saddles, hit multiple times and likely dead before they hit the ground.

Perez veered to the left, keeping at a full gallop while taking a westward track. His remaining *caballero* was hot on his tail. Both stayed low in the saddle, hoping their horses wouldn't be shot from under them.

"*Malditos gringos!*" Perez hollered. "*Malditos Nuecestown y Luke Dunn.*" Too late, he'd seen Luke's tell-tale gray horse. Self-preservation trumped vengeance…at least, for now.

"Come on, Luke. Let's chase them down and be done with them." Whelan pleaded to go finish the job. "Let's go!"

Rucker mounted and was ready to join the chase.

Perez was already out of sight. Luke knew they'd have to pull up and rest, as the horses had already been ridden hard. There wouldn't be much left in their mounts, and they'd be forced to dismount and set some sort of defense. It seemed foolish to give them a chance to have any advantage. "Easy, men. Let's keep our heads."

Whelan was unhappy with Luke's reluctance to pursue Perez. "Come on, Luke. Let's not give him any more chances to come back."

Luke knew it would make everyone feel far more secure if Perez was disposed of once and for all. "George, I hear you. It's not worth the risk. He could set an ambush for us." There was no point in risking all their lives. "Let's cool off and make a plan. Their horses are tired. We can catch up easily enough. Maybe you could go back to Corpus and get a couple of volunteers for a posse."

"That makes sense. No point in getting us all killed." Colonel Rucker agreed with Luke, and that had the effect of cooling Whelan.

"What was that?" Scarlett had heard the shooting off in the distance.

"Sounded like shooting, but it's a long way off. Didn't last very long, either." Elisa seemed unconcerned. After all, she'd faced Comanche, so facing a one-eyed crippled hider didn't seem all that tough.

"How can you stay so cool?" Scarlett had been through a lot herself, but this pregnant young woman seemed far too nonplussed for her years.

Elisa knew enough about Scarlett to appreciate the question. "I expect we've both been through a lot, Scarlett. We've both suffered loss. Guess I've learned to rely on God's providence."

Scarlett didn't understand. "Providence?"

"Most times things happen that you can't control. Think how I might feel when Luke goes away to chase some lawbreaker. I'd be worried sick if I didn't have my faith to fall back on."

"Would you stay if something happened to Luke?"

"No question," Elisa smiled, "and I'd likely have children to care for, too."

Scarlett was impressed with Elisa's confidence. The God business wasn't for her but, if it helped Elisa, that was fine. She changed the subject. "Do you think George might be taking a shine to me?"

Caught off guard by the question, Elisa had to pause and think a moment. "It's complicated, isn't it?"

"I expect so." Scarlett knew there was a wide gap between love and obligation. Her greatest fear was that her baby would look like Dirk Cavendish. She had a fighting chance to make a family if it resembled Whelan.

"As Luke tells it, you didn't come west until a few years ago.

How'd you wind up in Laredo?"

"Laredo? That wasn't the life I dreamed of growing up in Richmond. My parents died in a flash flood in a rainstorm when I was young, and I was raised by my grandparents. I expect I became bored. A soldier home on leave from some duty station out west caught my eye. He worked his charms on me and persuaded me to run away with him. We made it as far as a riverboat on the Mississippi when I discovered I was pregnant and he lit out like a scared rabbit. A gambler on the boat befriended me. He took advantage of me all the way to New Orleans. It turned out he owed some folks money and was on the run. I followed him to Texas and eventually to Laredo, where he was shot dead after a game of poker went terribly wrong. I had the fortune, or misfortune, to miscarry." Scarlett stared absent-mindedly off into space. "What's the secret, Elisa?"

"Secret?"

"You and Luke appear to be so happy. What's the secret?"

Elisa felt for Scarlett. She had no family, no close friend to fall back upon. She'd led a lonely life, its irony being her compensating by whoring. Scarlett had chosen her men unwisely.

Elisa opened her Bible. "As my mother taught us from the Bible, Scarlett, in Ephesians, God tells us to 'submit to one another in the name of Christ.' And then it tells us, 'Husbands, love your wives, just as Christ loved the church and gave Himself for her to make her holy, cleansing her with the washing of water by the word.' I'm not going to preach to you, Scarlett, but it's about finding the right man. God says husbands are to love their wives as their own bodies. He who loves his wife loves himself. For no one ever hates his own flesh but provides and cares for it, just as Christ does for the church, since we are members of His body. If you don't love yourself, how can you love anyone else? That's what Luke and I believe. Certainly, my family that I grew up with was a product of that view. I do think George will come to love you, Scarlett. Give it time and have faith." As she took Scarlett's hand to comfort her, there were noises outside the cabin.

Elisa ran to the window and carefully looked outside. It was Luke.

He dismounted and hitched the big gray. "Lisa! I'm home."

She came rushing from the cabin and threw herself into his arms. "Thank God, you're okay."

"I'm not stopping long, sweetheart. George has gone to recruit a posse. We've got Perez on the run with only one of his men left."

The air went out of Elisa's hope for resolution of the Perez problem. "I...I understand, Lucas."

"Can Scarlett stay here 'til we return? I don't think we'll be too long."

"We're getting to be friends. She can stay." What could Elisa really say? It would have been awkward to send Scarlett back to Nuecestown with Perez still on the run.

EIGHT

Comanche Surprise

Lieutenant Belknap was nothing if not totally frustrated by the lack of support for what he saw as his innovative approach to fighting the Comanche. Disguising his soldiers as homesteaders seemed like a great way to entrap the savages. Instead, he was engaged in a dusty, dogged pursuit of his elusive enemy. Little did he know that Three Toes was now by himself.

He was about two days out from Fort Inge when he came upon a familiar set of wagon tracks. He wasn't a tracker, but he remembered the wide tread of Thaddeus Brown's wagons. They carried heavy loads so had been built accordingly. What was Brown doing this far south?

He didn't have any especially logical reason, but he decided to follow Brown's track. He'd heard of the man's less-than-savory dealings. Belknap thought he might catch Brown up to no good. On the other hand, the lieutenant was a long way from his home fort. Dare he stay the course? The Comanche scheme was over. Perhaps he could yet salvage the mission.

"Private Carlson!" The trooper rode forward to Belknap's position. "Yes, sir."

"You are to carry this message back to Fort Mason." He handed a folded piece of paper to the soldier.

The sergeant joined Belknap and the trooper. "If I may, sir?"

Belknap nodded. He both valued and endured the sergeant's advice. Fortunately, the lieutenant wasn't a prideful man. "Go ahead, Sergeant."

The sergeant looked at Carlson. "Soldier, the lieutenant and I need to talk privately." Once the trooper was out of earshot, he turned his attention back to Belknap. "Sir, we have no idea what we might encounter. Given the high value of his cargo, Mr. Brown usually travels with heavily armed escorts. I simply suggest that it might not be the best decision to engage in any pursuit, sir."

Belknap locked eyes with the sergeant. He knew the non-com was pretty savvy when it came to these sorts of things. He took the note back from the trooper and ordered the patrol to turn north.

They'd gone no more than a few hundred yards when they came upon a grisly scene. A black man was laid out in the sun, and a Comanche had been ceremonially bound and wrapped in traditional ritual fashion nearby. The bodies were far along in decomposition and scavengers had been at work.

Belknap could readily identify Three Toes and could see that the dead Comanche was not the Indian he so wanted to pursue. It made him long to find the chief, but the sergeant was right. He'd already exceeded his mission and needed to return to the fort. The major might be wondering what happened to his freshly-minted lieutenant.

An unseasonably cool breeze washed across the prairie west of Corpus Christi. Perez was so angry that he actually remained calm. He sat in the shade of a live oak on the edge of a dry stream bank, trying to decide his next move. With just the two of them, it would be foolhardy to go back to Nuecestown. He also figured that that damnable Texas Ranger knew he had him on the run and was likely to pull together a posse to come after him. Perez was playing a fool's game.

He sighed heavily. "*Volvamos atrás a Nuevo Laredo.*" He mounted his horse and turned westward. He'd live to fight another day. He'd need reinforcements, and they'd best be found back in Nuevo Laredo.

He realized they'd lost their supplies, so it would be necessary to obtain food. They dared not shoot anything until they were farther ahead of any posse. The prairie being so empty of civilization, they'd need to keep watch for lone travelers or perhaps a mail station. He considered the Corpus Christi to Laredo road through San Diego, but decided it didn't offer enough cover for anyone on the run from a posse.

"*Vamonos.*" He began the ride back to Nuevo Laredo. They looked for fresh horse or wagon tracks that might lead them to the supplies they needed.

They'd barely ridden a day and a half when they found their prize. A fast-moving horse had passed through, likely a postal rider headed to a station. "*Caballero, sigamos est pista.*" He picked up their pace. "*Vamonos, Manuel.*" Thoughts of the station translated into much-needed supplies and even fresh horses.

Reaching the top of a rise in the trail the postal rider was following, they spotted the smoke from a chimney. They were close. Now, they needed to scout the place to ensure a successful raid. It was late afternoon, and dusk would descend soon enough.

They snuck to within fifty yards of the cabin and its corral. There was a lantern lit inside and two men's voices mixed with at least one woman. Perez recognized that he had the element of surprise. They needed to create a diversion, perhaps confusion. He handed Manuel a blanket and pointed up at the roof. "*Manuel, mete esto en la chimenea.*" His intention was to smoke them out into the open.

It didn't take long for the small cabin to fill with smoke. The inhabitants came staggering out, coughing and flailing about. Perez and Manuel calmly gunned them all down at close range. Even the one-eyed Perez couldn't miss at a distance of only a couple of feet.

It took nearly an hour for the cabin to clear of smoke after the blanket was removed. Perez got Manuel to swap out their horses and pick a third as a pack horse. They gathered as many supplies as they could carry. As they were about to leave the cabin, Perez noticed a box they'd failed to inspect. As he lifted the lid and gazed inside, he broke into a broad toothless grin. "*Mire, Manuel, whisky!*" He scooped up four bottles and stuffed them securely on the pack horse. "*Vamos de fiesta esta noche!*" At that, he decided they'd spend the night at the mail station. There certainly would be no more visitors this day.

Despite hangovers, Perez and Manuel were headed west by mid-morning. They took a final look at the three bodies lying in the dust of the Nueces Strip.

Nuevo Laredo was to be their next destination, and he'd yet seek his revenge.

Belknap was focused on returning to Fort Mason. He made sure he had a man riding point well ahead of the patrol so as to avoid any ambushes. He sent Private Carlson ahead to take a first turn at that forward position.

Carlson never knew what hit him. The arrow passed through his eye and deep into his brain. It was several minutes before Belknap caught up to his point man. His first image was of the soldier's horse standing riderless. The troopers approached cautiously, scanning their surroundings. Belknap wondered why his point man had dismounted. Then, their worst fears were realized as they came upon the trooper's body lying in the dust. It conjured memories of their battle with the Comanche not long before.

The sergeant dismounted and examined the arrow. "Sir, this doesn't look like a Comanche arrow."

Belknap looked at him as if to wonder that there was any difference in arrows from one tribe to another. "How can you tell?"

The sergeant winced reflexively as he pulled the arrow from

Carlson's head. He examined it carefully. "Shape of the arrowhead, length of the shaft, placement of the feathers, sir. This seems to be Kiowa, sir."

"You look concerned, Sergeant."

"I didn't realize they'd come this far south in the Comancheria. They've been known to ally with Comanche, but I don't understand this attack." The sergeant was dumbfounded as to why Kiowa would make such an unusual attack so far from their normal habitat. Most importantly, where had they gone?

"We'll need to stay alert, sir. It may make sense to head back to Fort Mason and see what they know about Kiowa activity."

"Sounds like good advice, Sergeant." They placed Carlson's body over the saddle of his horse, and Belknap turned the patrol eastward toward Fort Mason. He found himself fully dismayed at the encounters with Indians. He wondered at the final solution to the dilemma. The only thing that seemed to work against the Indians was continued settlement into the western territories, pushing the Indians continually westward and eliminating their sources of sustenance, their hunting lands. What gradual frontier expansion didn't achieve, the white man's diseases surely would. Belknap had heard of the plight years earlier that befell the cannibalistic Karankawas in eastern Texas. Disease had devastated the tribe.

Three Toes had been traveling southeast, taking care to avoid the U.S. Army forts. Now that he was alone, he was able to travel more swiftly. He felt that the Great Spirit must have spared him for some greater quest.

So it was that he came upon the mail station the day after Perez vacated it. He recalled that his Penateka Comanche warriors under Long Feathers had destroyed the station and its previous occupants months ago. Now, the rebuilt station had suffered a similar fate, at least to the extent that the operators of the station had been killed.

Unlike their predecessors, these victims had not been mutilated.

He entered the cabin and saw that it had been stripped of much of its food supplies. He observed that the people who did this deed weren't likely to be much different from his own people, other than the lack of mutilation. The inhabitants had most likely been killed by bandits of some sort, not an unusual occurrence on the Nueces Strip. Then he recalled Luke Dunn's show of respect for the Comanche warriors killed back near Nuecestown. Three Toes found a shovel, dug three graves, and buried the bodies. He recalled that the white man's ritual included fashioning a cross, so he made three and planted them at the head of each grave.

An unusual feeling swept over him. He found himself repulsed by what the attackers had done. He who had scalped and mutilated many victims found himself offended. Perhaps Luke Dunn was rubbing off on him, at least a little.

Three Toes mounted his pony and began to follow Perez's trail west. He wasn't certain what he might do if he found this new prey. He'd worry about that as he got closer. From the evidence, he judged that there were only two enemy.

The sign left by Perez was easy to follow, likely because he felt no one was following him.

Rucker and Luke had taken Scarlett back to the boarding house, as any immediate danger from Perez seemed to have passed. Rucker stayed back at the town while Luke returned to Heaven's Gate to have a bit of time with Elisa.

"Luke!" George Whelan rode up to the cabin with his horse well-lathered. He flew from his saddle and banged on the door. "Luke!"

Luke slowly opened the door. He didn't especially appreciate the interruption. "Dang, George. What's up?"

"Crawford...it's Crawford! The sonofabitch hung himself!"

Luke's mouth gaped. "Wasn't anyone watching him?"

"Luke…we don't have those sorts of resources. When I'm not there, there's an old man who brings food to any prisoners. He found Crawford hung yesterday morning. Looked as though he tore the mattress apart and used the cover to make a noose."

"Does Colonel Kinney know?"

"Yeah, he's gonna have the man buried. Kinney's headed back to Austin and will let Rip Ford know." Whelan relaxed a bit. "I'm sorry about this, Luke."

"It's all right, George. Nobody knows what he did or didn't tell us and that might work to our advantage."

Elisa walked out of the cabin. "George, I heard. I'm sorry." She sidled up against Luke, her face just a bit flushed.

Whelan suddenly realized he'd interrupted them at an ill-chosen time. "Uh…I think I'll head into Nuecestown and see Scarlett. We can talk later about what we do next. I expect that Perez fella has put some distance from here." With that, he swung into the saddle, tipped his hat, and rode off to town. He thought on how he'd been unable to muster a posse to pursue Perez. It was frustrating.

It didn't take long for Three Toes to close the gap with Perez. The sign had been all too obvious, and Perez wasn't moving as fast as he might have. Three Toes was surprised when he saw who he was tracking. The Mexican should have been dead long ago, by hanging, if not by his wounds.

As he considered the best way to kill his quarry, his thoughts were interrupted by the noise of wagons. He dismounted and hid behind the shelter of a live oak motte. He watched as the people with the wagons encountered Perez.

"*Buenas días.*" Perez raised his hand in greeting. "*Como se llama?*"

"Uh…Mexicanos?" Thaddeus Brown feigned surprise. He outgunned his visitors, but wasn't going to take any chances. These two looked to be quite swarmy. "You speak English?"

"*No entiendo Inglés, señor.*" Perez hesitated to reveal that he knew any English.

"Sam, Pete, show them how we deal with Mexicans." Two of Brown's outriders aimed their Sharps rifles in Perez's direction.

"*Un poco, señor, un poco Inglés.*" Perez didn't like the look of those guns.

"You're traveling?" Brown stated the obvious. "Where you headed?"

"*Nuevo Laredo, señor.*"

"What's your business...*trabajo?*"

Perez had already noted the cattle and buffalo hides in the wagons. "*Cazamo pieles de Ganado*...hides, *señor,* we hunt hides."

Brown smiled broadly. "You need some work? My name is Thaddeus Brown, and I do much trading up north."

Perez wasn't so sure. He'd given up the hider life not long after Luke Dunn cost him his eye. "*No, pero se cen*...I know others who will."

"I'll send a man to Laredo to sign your men up. Be ready in a month." Brown tipped his hat. "By the way, what's your name...*su llamo?*"

"Carlos Perez."

The name sounded vaguely familiar to Brown, but he couldn't recall what it was associated with.

Three Toes observed that the men seemed to be acting in a friendly manner. This was concerning. He was seriously outnumbered. He wished he had his warriors with him, but that was not to be.

When he saw Perez and his man depart, it gave him pause to rethink his strategy. The wagons also seemed a worthy prize, but his recollection of Perez's attack on Three Toes' friend Luke Dunn weighed heavily on his thinking. He had his pride as a Comanche chief, as a strong warrior who had counted many coup and taken numerous scalps. The wagons could wait. Besides, there were four heavily armed men protecting them.

He waited in hiding until the wagons had passed into the distant prairie.

He began to track Perez. The horses were easy to follow, and it took about a day to close to within a half-mile. Three Toes dared not get closer on the wide-open vastness of the prairie. Of a sudden, he noticed a faint sound coming from north of his position. The source was upwind, or he might not have heard it so soon. He squinted off to his right to try to better see what was making the sounds.

"Three Toes, why are you here alone?" He spun his pony to face the voice. It was Calling Bears, a Kiowa chief, long-time friend and occasional enemy.

"Calling Bears, it is good to see you, my brother. I am on a quest."

"You have no warriors?"

"All are with the Great Spirit."

"You are welcome to join with us. We joined with three of your Penateka Comanche brothers, and there are now six of us chasing the Indian agency thief. He has wagons filled with our gifts from the agency."

"Have you seen any bluecoats?" Three Toes asked.

"We saw a small patrol a day north of here and killed one of their soldiers."

Three Toes nodded. He knew very well how naive the soldiers could be. "The wagons are guarded by heavily armed men, Calling Bears."

"Their leader is named Thaddeus Brown. He has been stealing from the agencies and taking buffalo and cattle hides. We must kill him."

Three Toes understood. He decided that he could find Perez easily enough on another day. This was an opportunity to fight with his Kiowa and Comanche brothers in common cause. Once again, he found himself compromising his vision quest.

"The wagons are not far off," he said. "Let's prepare ourselves." Each warrior painted himself. Three Toes applied the customary Penateka Comanche broad black band across his forehead and another across his cheeks. He decided the Great Spirit would likely be pleased with his decision to join Calling Bears.

They would make a full frontal assault aimed at surprising Brown's wagons and enabling warriors to count coup.

The small band of allies headed out at a canter, with Three Toes and Calling Bears in the lead. They were as fearsome a band of Indians as ever rode the frontier. Not a word was spoken, nor was any needed.

At a little more than a hundred yards from the wagons, they hadn't yet been discovered. They jammed their heels into their ponies' ribs and were instantly at full gallop. They were on the caravan in a blur. The first outrider barely saw them coming. He turned and shot a Kiowa from his horse before catching several arrows himself. Three Toes' pony leaped onto the rear wagon, and he counted coup by striking his lance on the shoulder of the wagon driver. As his horse bounded from the wagon, Three Toes turned and fired an arrow at the man.

By now, Brown's men had begun to gather their wits. All were fighters trained in battle, and they began to pour a hail of lead at the attackers with Colt revolvers and repeating rifles. Three Toes saw Calling Bears get shot from his pony. Men and horses seemed to be everywhere. Three Toes sounded the retreat, as he and two wounded Comanche escaped. All of the Kiowa had been killed. Calling Bears had seriously misjudged the strength of his opponent.

Three Toes brought his pony to a halt nearly a mile from the battle scene. They needed to take stock of their situation. One of the Comanche warriors was bleeding profusely from bullets to the stomach and leg. He would not live long. The surprise attack hadn't worked out very well.

The chief pondered what to do next. He could afford no more disasters like the raid on Brown's wagons. It seemed like the time of the Comanche was drawing to a close. He realized that he had recently begun traveling around Texas with no clear direction or purpose. He was beginning to doubt his abilities as a chief, a leader of warriors in life and battle.

Thaddeus Brown looked around. Apparently, they'd driven off the attackers. He'd lost one man and three were wounded, none seriously. They counted four dead or dying Indians. One of his men went from one to the other delivering kill shots as needed. As much as anything, the kill shot put a dying man out of his misery.

Brown gave careful consideration of their present situation. "The savages are gone, men. Let's camp here for the night. We need to care for our wounded." He was stating the obvious, but his words had a calming effect on his remaining men.

They moved the wagons together to afford protection in case of another attack. Brown hadn't encountered an Indian attack in months. He realized he'd gotten careless and would have to be more careful. He also rightly figured they might be on borrowed time so far as the law was concerned. He half-expected Texas Rangers to be tracking him.

NINE

Choices

Luke and Elisa sat quietly on the gallery he'd built across the front of the cabin. They didn't seem to get so much of this sort of quality time these days. She was about halfway into her pregnancy and, from the activity stirring in her womb, she was increasingly convinced she'd be having twins. Elisa had even sought Bernice's thoughts on the possibility one day when she'd visited. In her all-knowing way, Bernice predicted that twins could indeed be possible.

Luke knew he needed to fulfill his obligation to Rip Ford and to Texas. These sorts of choices seemed a given so long as he divided his time between lawman and rancher. While Carlos Perez remained a serious irritation, a danger to himself and others close to him, Luke necessarily focused on the Indian agency scandal. He had already connected the dots between Thaddeus Brown and General Truax. He still hadn't figured out who the general was getting his marching orders from.

"Lisa, sweetheart, I've got to go investigate this Indian agency scandal business. I may be gone a few days or it could be a few weeks. Depends on what I find out."

She tilted her face downward just a bit and let her lower lip protrude a little more in a pouty manner. "Lucas Dunn, just don't you dare miss the birth of your children!" Oops! There, it was out.

"Children?" Luke smiled so big, he nearly popped the mustache off his upper lip.

"Bernice thinks I'm carrying twins."

He couldn't suppress his grin if he'd wanted to. "Hell will have to freeze over to keep me from here when your time comes, Lisa."

"I don't give a hoot about hell, Lucas Dunn. Just please stay safe and be here to welcome your children into our lives."

"I promise." Luke never promised something he felt he couldn't deliver on. The firmness of resolve in his voice gave Elisa a strong sense of assuredness.

"I'll be riding out tomorrow, sweetheart. I expect Colonel Rucker will be accompanying me. He's got a special interest in bringing down General Booker Truax. I'll talk with George about him watching over everything around here. Besides, I think he's growing more partial to Scarlett and maybe she to him." He smiled at the thought of Whelan settling down with the comely red-haired former prostitute.

"Well, go do what you must do, Lucas Dunn. I'll have dinner waiting and gather victuals for you and the colonel for your leaving in the morning." She figured they'd take one of the horses they'd recently purchased to serve as a pack horse. Riding out on the Nueces Strip at this time of year meant being well-supplied. The weather would be chancy, especially the likelihood of storms and flash floods.

They had stored plenty of feed for their growing herd of longhorns that would fatten up over the winter. Fattening up as concerned longhorns was a relative term, as they tended to be on the lean side as far as cattle went. Hopefully, the reward from resolving the Indian agency scandal would enable them to acquire more land and continue building their stock of cattle.

Morning arrived too soon. Luke was up early enough to greet Colonel Rucker. They all shared a delicious breakfast with all the home fixins'. Elisa had by now established her reputation for great cooking. It was enough that some gossip in town was devoted to how long it would take for her to fatten up Luke. The only things that might keep him on the leaner side were his forays pursuing lawbreakers on the wide prairies of the Nueces Strip.

"Colonel, the word I got from Colonel Kinney's office was that Thaddeus Brown had headed south due to federal inspections of the northern forts. I understand he was seen at Fort McIntosh outside Laredo. He did some whoring and his usual business before heading east."

Rucker thought on that. "You thinking of heading west?"

"Might intercept him. He's got a couple of heavy wagons, so there are only a couple of trails he can take. I'm betting he's headed due east toward Corpus on the road through San Diego."

"He's supposed to be heavily armed, Luke."

Concern began to manifest itself in Elisa's manner. She dropped a dish.

"Fret not, Lisa. I'm not figuring to attack him. I just want to get acquainted, to let him know we're around...give him something to chew on." Luke tried to appear reassuring. "I don't want him to think folks might be on to him."

"You certain we shouldn't get a couple of more men, Luke?"

"Don't want to threaten the man just yet. These sorts of vermin tend to be always looking over their shoulders. We're gonna give him something to think about by letting him know there's a Texas Ranger presence on the Strip." Luke stared thoughtfully at Rucker. "I gotta believe that General Truax is aiming to take you down, Colonel. Didn't he give you three weeks to bring Scarlett back?"

"What's on your mind?"

"Just wondering whether there might be a way to draw the general out of Austin."

"He's pretty careful, Luke."

"Do you know where he stores his loot?"

Rucker quickly picked up on where this was headed. "Matter of fact, I do." He smiled broadly at the sheer simplicity of what Luke was thinking. "It's in a barn."

"What if the barn caught fire and he heard that someone from Nuecestown set it afire?" Luke looked off into the distance, trying to imagine Truax's reaction. "You think that might get him angry enough to come south? The man seems to have a lot of pride, likely too much."

"I know someone who is up for getting back at the general. I could get him to set the fire and leave a note from you."

Elisa was taking in the conversation. She never would have imagined coming up with such a scheme. It just might work.

Luke saw her wide-eyed look of admiration, and it gave him a warm feeling. Having a wife's respect was second only to her love.

Belknap limped into Fort Inge. While the deeds he'd seen from the Comanche and Kiowa still weighed heavily on him, he saw the Army as seriously limiting any retaliation. He had discovered that the Army way failed to live up to his own high expectations. The environment left no room for innovative strategic thinking. The dreams of success fighting Indians that he'd harbored upon leaving West Point would likely never come to reality.

The major in command at the fort heard the lieutenant's entourage arrive and stepped out to greet him. "How did your hunt go, Lieutenant?"

Belknap's look spilled the entire story. He offered a less-than-smart salute. "Lost one man, sir. Didn't engage any Comanche." He rode up to the major and dismounted.

"How'd you lose your man, Lieutenant?"

"Kiowa ambush, sir. Sort of strange. They only attacked our point man."

"You sure it was Kiowa? They're not known to be in these parts."

"Sergeant, show the arrow to the major," Belknap ordered.

The sergeant dismounted dutifully, pulled the arrow from his bedroll, and presented it to Belknap to show the major. "Begging your pardon, sir. I'm familiar with the designs used by different tribes. This one is definitely Kiowa."

The major absorbed the news. "I appreciate the news, Lieutenant Belknap. I suggest you and your men get some rest. I'm sure you'd like to eventually return to Fort Mason."

Belknap knew it was the Army way. He craved being reassigned to where some action was. Other than the incident with the Kiowa and his previous forgettable engagements with Three Toes, he had yet to be involved in any offensive maneuvers against the Indian threat.

It was slow going across the rough road with heavily laden wagons. The gullies and arroyos of the prairie, formed mostly by heavy rain storms, made for occasionally difficult passages, especially as bridges were mostly non-existent. The grasses served to pretty much hold the mostly sandy soil in place. Occasional mottes of live oak and mesquite dotted the landscape.

The flatness of the land enabled travelers to see a long distance. Thus, it was no surprise when Brown first spotted Luke and Rucker moving across the prairie toward his wagons.

By now, Rucker had grown a full beard and acquired a civilian hat. Coupled with being out of uniform, he had a fairly effective disguise in the event Brown suspected anything.

Judging distance on the prairies was deceptive. It was an art form to practiced trackers. Everything was farther away than it appeared. It took a couple of hours before the wagons closed the distance between them and Luke and Rucker.

Luke rode out front with Rucker following closely behind. By now, it was late in the day, and Rucker's disguised appearance was even more effective. Luke closed the final hundred yards quickly. "Howdy, traveler. Where you headed?"

"Who's asking?"

"Captain Luke Dunn, Texas Rangers. Just making sure all is well out here." Luke was letting Brown know that he wasn't a threat for the moment.

"Name's Brown, Captain. We're on our way to Corpus Christi to do a bit of trading." He took in Luke's imposing figure. He looked every inch the quintessential Texas Ranger, tall, broad, erect in the saddle, and heavily armed. "Don't mess with me" emanated from every pore of his being.

"Must be valuable cargo you've got there," Luke offered, as he scanned the heavily armed drivers and outriders. He noted that Brown was well-dressed for traveling across a barren prairie. He appeared to have a single pistol and possibly a knife. Given the frilly lace at his shirt collar, he could be mistaken for a high-stakes saloon gambler. Clearly, he relied on his hired hands to do any serious fighting.

"Yes, sir. We don't trade in poor quality or ill-begotten goods," Brown said. "We don't seek trouble, but must be ready when it comes. We're on our way from Laredo."

Luke made the obvious connection to Fort McIntosh but chose not to pursue that query. "I've been looking for a couple of Mexican bandits. You happen to see any come by?"

"Matter of fact, Captain, we did see a couple of Mexicans in a hurry to get to Nuevo Laredo. One had lost an eye." Brown figured to offer up Perez as a good faith gesture.

"Appreciate that, Mr. Brown." Luke circled Brown's wagons, taking in the contents. He noticed a couple of arrows stuck in one of the side boards. "You seen some Indians lately?"

"Oh, the arrows. Yes, sir, Captain, but we run them off. Killed all but two."

"Did you recognize the tribe?"

"It was a mix of Kiowa and Comanche. Didn't expect to see Kiowa this far south."

Luke wondered whether Three Toes might have been involved, but knew that Brown would have no idea who he was. "Well, you fellas have a safe journey to Corpus. Be extra careful, as there's supposed to be some hiders active in the area." By now, Luke had taken a good measure of Brown's situation in terms of goods and armament. "See you boys down the trail." With that, he turned and rejoined Rucker. The two took a wide berth of Brown's wagons as the sun began to set and Rucker's face remained in the shadow of his hat.

Brown turned to his lead driver. "Wonder what the hell that was about? I didn't like that second man out there. Something familiar about him, but I couldn't figure it."

"Boss, I got a feelin' we were being scouted."

Brown chewed on that a moment. "Maybe we should ride into Nuecestown, leave the wagons, and a couple of us ride into Corpus to see what's happening." He pondered that a bit more. "Yeah, that's what we'll do."

Luke and Rucker rode northward out of sight of Brown's wagons before turning eastward back toward Nuecestown. "What do you think, Colonel?"

"I think he was tryin' to figure out who I was, for one thing. You unnerved him a bit by inspecting his cargo. You were right that lawbreakers are a suspicious lot."

"Let's follow at a distance." Luke dismounted to walk his horse for a while. "The wagons are slow, Colonel. Might as well save our horses as much as we can."

"By now, my man ought to be heading to Austin to fire the general's barn."

"Whew, Colonel, won't be long before things will be getting very interesting." Luke thought a moment. "It still concerns me that the general must have someone he reports to who knows what's going on."

"I know his direct report in Washington, Luke, but so far as I know, that man is unsullied."

"I'm thinking it might not be a military man."

Rucker hadn't considered that. "Damn, Captain. There are some very powerful people in Austin. Politics can be ugly. But that's a possibility." A worried look crossed Rucker's face. "I hope they haven't done anything to my family." He recognized that, by now, Truax would have figured out that Rucker wasn't coming back to Austin with Scarlett Rose.

That night, they saw Brown's wagons set up camp. Feeling assured that Brown would continue on to Corpus, they decided to ride back to Nuecestown by the light of the moon. They planned to share what they knew with Whelan and plan for a possible fight with Brown and his men. Had they known the thief was headed first to Nuecestown, they'd have been far more concerned.

Three Toes and the remaining Comanche warrior headed eastward. The warrior was not seriously wounded, but his condition slowed their travel. Three Toes had treated the wound with an old poultice recipe from one of his wives. With any luck, they'd get to Nuecestown and reconnect with Ghost-Who-Rides.

The chief kept the two of them well fed, stalking and killing a couple of deer. He saw some buffalo, but his supply of arrows had dwindled, and he decided he didn't have enough men to feed with such a large animal.

TEN

Gathering Clouds

In the dark of early morning just before sunrise, the sky east of Austin was set ablaze. The secretly hidden merchandise, including gunpowder, went up in a tremendous conflagration. Explosions rocked the area. The roaring inferno wreaked utter destruction.

Truax was alerted by a watch officer but, by the time he was awakened, it was too late to save the barn and its contents.

An orderly brought him a sealed envelope, handed it to him, saluted, and slinked away. Truax noted the singed edge. He smelled what seemed to be a lamp oil derivative that he'd recently heard about. It was called kerosene. In any case, the envelope likely would contain a clue as to the arsonist. He tried to contain his anger, nearly cutting his hand as he used his knife to cut open one end of the envelope.

He held the note up to better read it by catching the dim light of the sun as it inched up on the eastern horizon. The note was cryptic, to say the least.

"General,
The barn is only the beginning. You have trouble on the Nueces Strip.
Texas Justice"

He couldn't help but be frustratingly curious as to what had concerned him on the Nueces Strip and who "Texas Justice" was.

While the general was pondering the mysterious fire that had destroyed his merchandise, Rip Ford received a hand-delivered secret note from Luke Dunn explaining what was known thus far. He was cautioned not to share it with Truax's inside man, O'Rourke.

General Truax called for his staff officers. They rushed to headquarters, arriving in various states of disorderly dress. It would never do to keep the general waiting.

"Sit down, gentlemen." Truax was still trying to work out how best to explain the rationale for sending a troop to Corpus Christi. He couldn't reveal the fraud he was perpetrating on the Indian agencies, even though most of his staff had their suspicions. Fortunately, many of them had partaken of at least some portion of the general's largesse. With that as a sort of blackmail, it was highly unlikely that they would risk their careers to betray him.

"We've received a threat against U.S. Army property in Corpus Christi. We will send a troop of twenty-four soldiers to investigate."

The staff looked one to the other trying to figure out who would be in command of the troop.

Truax ended the guessing promptly. "I will head this troop, with Colonel McDougal accompanying. We must be able to respond quickly and effectively to any threats."

This was highly unusual. A troop was the command purview of a lieutenant and, at rare times, a sergeant. It was rather easy for Truax's staff officers to figure out that this mission concerned his fraudulent ventures. Why else would he accompany a mere troop, especially given that it had been four or five years since he'd engaged in any battle.

"We will march out tomorrow morning. Please prepare field support accordingly." The general looked around the room, as if trying to catch someone smirking. "Dismissed."

Truax pondered what had become of Colonel Rucker. Given the

previous contact with O'Rourke, he knew Rucker was likely betraying him. If the man was still in Corpus Christi, revenge would be sweet. He decided not to bother Rucker's wife and son just yet. Besides, he had a greater problem. A certain high-placed, wealthy Texas plantation owner was going to be extremely unhappy. The man had his heart set on that increasingly notorious Laredo whore. He was certain she'd never forget him, such was his narcissistic view of his sexual prowess. Obsessed? Maybe.

Luke and Rucker arrived in Nuecestown to coordinate with Whelan. "George, have you recruited some men for our defense?"

Whelan grinned. "Found eight men, Luke. Most of them are fairly decent with pistol and rifle. I have them encamped a couple of miles east of Corpus. I just hope Kinney is prepared to pay them the money I promised."

They headed toward the sheriff's office to discuss strategy. "How's Scarlett doing, George?"

"Pretty good, considering all that's been going on. I think she may have that baby sooner than later."

As they pulled up chairs around the desk, there was a soft knock on the window at the back of the building. Luke drew his Walker Colt and carefully peered out. He stepped back in surprise. "Dang! It's Three Toes!" He threw open the back door and motioned the Comanche inside. "Where you been, my friend?"

"Ghost-Who-Rides, it is good to see you." He looked at Rucker and Whelan. Rucker looked familiar, but he couldn't place him without the blue uniform. "I have seen trouble."

Whelan and Rucker sat back silently. Neither had been this close to a Comanche chief outside of battle. All their experience had been toward killing Indians, especially the savage Comanche. They didn't quite know what to make of it, but had to trust Luke. They reflexively ran their fingers through their hair as if to ensure that it was there.

"My warrior was wounded in a battle with men that stole from the agencies. We killed one of them, but all but the two of us died in battle. They killed all of our Kiowa brothers."

Luke gave a nod of recognition. It was another case of rifles in trained hands being significantly more effective than arrows. This accounted for the arrows he'd seen embedded in Brown's wagon. "These men are headed to Corpus Christi."

Three Toes shook his head. "They are headed here, my friend. They fear a trap in the city." He looked over at Rucker. His eyes widened in recognition. "You were at Camp Cooper."

"I visited there. I am Colonel Horace Rucker, U.S. Army. I'm helping Captain Dunn and Sheriff Whelan stop the agency thieves."

His answer seemed to satisfy the chief. "I am Three Toes, war chief of the Penateka Comanche. Many of my people lived at Camp Cooper with Buffalo Hump. The Indian agency did not keep its promises."

It took deep soul-searching for Rucker to become humble in the face of a man whose race he'd been sworn to hold in contempt. The words were difficult. "I regret what my people did, Chief Three Toes."

"We are likely going to be outmanned and outgunned," Luke stated, expressing his overriding concern. "There is a mounted Army troop of two dozen soldiers not more than a two-day ride from here. Our friend, General Truax, has decided to take our bait."

"Bait?" Three Toes had no clue what Luke was talking about.

"We burned the barn where the general stored his stolen goods and dared him to come and get us on the Nueces Strip." Luke suppressed a feeling of satisfaction. "Now, we've created a challenge for ourselves. We have a dozen defenders against the general's twenty-four men and Brown's four." He pondered that a moment. "Perhaps our best defense is to go on the offense."

Three Toes liked that idea. He admired Luke's penchant for being the aggressor, not to mention his success at it.

Luke had a motley group on his hands. It was the typical ragtag sort of assemblage that characterized posses of the day. The two

Comanche were a different sort of addition. He pondered how to use Three Toes and his warrior to advantage.

"The wagons are close," Three Toes commented. "We should attack them first."

Luke could tell that Three Toes' mind held far more than he was revealing. He tried to get inside the chief's head. "If we take Brown out of the action, can we use his wagons to trap the general?" he asked.

Three Toes nodded. As white men went, Ghost-Who-Rides had the Comanche chief's deep admiration. He still thought Luke talked funny, but that didn't matter much. He often seemed to think like a Comanche as far as strategies went. Luke's respect was powerful medicine to the chief.

Whelan was fascinated by the exchange between Luke and Three Toes. He'd thought of the Comanche as savages, and that they did not possess the intelligence for this sort of strategizing. "If I were Thaddeus Brown, I'd camp here and then go scout the situation in Corpus Christi," he commented.

"We could take advantage of him separating from his men. He has no idea we're waiting for him here." Rucker was beginning to get into the thinking. Like Whelan, he was gaining respect for Three Toes. "Once we've defeated Brown, we can set a trap for the general."

Luke stepped back, and his eyes engaged each man in the room. "It's settled then. First, we eliminate Brown. Let him go off to scout Corpus as George suggests. Depending on whether he goes alone, the colonel and I will pursue him. Once he's out of earshot, the rest of you can attack and capture the wagons." He smiled. It was a good plan.

Manuel, one of the Caballeros Negros, rode well ahead, much like a point man. There was a high price on Carlos Perez's head. It tempted Manuel a little, but not enough to risk Perez's wrath if the man escaped again. Perez was no longer the tough physical specimen that had been the scourge of the Nueces Strip just a couple of years earlier, but he was not to be trifled with. They swam the horses across the Rio Grande and rode into Nuevo Laredo.

"*Necesitamos reclutar hombres.*" Recruiting more Caballeros Negros was a top priority. Perez wanted to get his revenge while there was still life in his bones.

Manuel would have to carry the logistical load. They needed to either steal some supplies, or the money to purchase them with. Recruiting an additional man or two would help, so they settled on visiting a local cantina.

The *tabernero* was surprised to see Perez walk through the door. He immediately poured a couple of drinks in anticipation as Perez and Manuel sidled up to the bar.

"*Hola, Carlos. Genial verte!*" He'd given the man up for dead, as had most of Nuevo Laredo. Apparently, Perez had the nine lives of a cat. "*Tienes la vida de un gato, amigo.*"

Perez forced a toothless smile. The cat metaphor amused him. He had certainly established a reputation as a survivor. "*Muchas gracias.*" He gazed around the room.

The tables were full, but the *tabernero* chased off a couple of customers to make room for Perez. "*Te gustaria mujeres, señor?*" He'd momentarily forgotten Perez's condition.

Perez cast a steely eye at the man, wondering whether Sheriff Stills was still looking for him. "*El Sheriff Stills todavía me está buscando?*"

The *tabernero* smiled. He'd apparently been forgiven for his faux pas. "*Si, el te esta buscando.*" Sheriff Stills was still on the lookout for Perez. The embarrassment of Perez escaping from his jail weighed heavily on him.

Perez nodded. "*Gracias. Necesito dos buenos luchadores rudos.*" Did the barkeeper know a couple of tough fighters to join him? Perez's recruiting was underway.

"*Si, Carlos. Conozco tales hombres.*"

"*Tráelos aquí esta noche.*" Perez would meet the recruits that night at the saloon.

The *tabernero* was relieved to be able to help Perez. No one wanted to be on the bandit's bad side. "*Mujer?*" He nodded toward Manuel.

Perez smiled again. "*Dos mujeres, pero despues.*" They'd avail themselves of the whores after they finished their recruiting. It remained to be seen how Perez might deal with a whore given his condition.

Thaddeus Brown's wagons came to a halt on a bluff overlooking Nuecestown. As he gazed out toward the town, he saw that the town looked peaceful enough. There were no signs of unexpected activity that would trigger alarms for him. "Set camp here."

Brown's men placed the wagons side by side and tethered the horses close so as set up as much of a defensive perimeter as they could. The wagons were heavy with booty and tended to sink in the sandy soil. It wouldn't do to have them slowed down any more than necessary. The weight had made the last couple of miles especially slow, even on the man-made road.

Brown appreciated his men's work. "I'll ride on alone to Corpus Christi. You men lay low. Do not go into the town. We don't want to stir up any unnecessary trouble." He scanned the horizon one last time looking for anything troubling. "Be on alert. Set up camp, but keep our fire low. I'm not sure what to expect here." He knew there was a ready market for his goods in Corpus if there was no trouble.

Brown grabbed a rifle and a pistol and mounted one of the outrider horses. He stuck the pistol in his belt and turned the horse southeast toward Corpus. He decided to skirt wide of Nuecestown. Little did he know what a fateful decision that would be.

Riding his horse at a brisk pace, he calculated that Corpus lay only a dozen or so miles ahead. He'd gone about five miles when he sensed that he had company. Two riders were approaching at a gallop. It was clear they were coming after him.

He had choices. Should he turn and flee back toward the wagons?

Should he try to outrace them to Corpus Christi? Should he simply await his fate? It was two against one, and he quickly recognized the riders as the men he'd encountered a couple of days earlier. He was outgunned in any case.

Once they got within rifle range, Luke and Rucker slowed down and approached cautiously. They were quickly within hailing distance and had their rifles at the ready. "Thaddeus Brown? Thaddeus Brown, you are under arrest."

"What charges?" It seemed like a logical question to buy time for the thief.

Luke smiled. "Theft, of course. Now drop your weapons on the ground real easy like."

Brown had no choice. It was surrender or die. "You've got me, Ranger." He placed his pistol and rifle on the ground and then raised his hands. He kept his small vest pistol just in case he got the opportunity to use it.

Rucker knew this man all too well. "Thaddeus Brown, I figured you for a smarter man. Drop that little peashooter, too."

Brown complied, tossing the derringer to the ground. Now, he recognized the colonel. "Why, Colonel Horace Rucker! I'll be damned!" He aimed a rueful look at Rucker. "I shoulda recognized you the other day, dammit."

"You're right on that, Mr. Brown."

Rucker kept his rifle aimed at Brown while Luke approached him and manacled his wrists behind his back. All the while, Brown stared at Rucker with hate-filled eyes. Luke attached a rope to the halter of Brown's horse, and the three headed to Corpus Christi.

Back outside Nuecestown, Sheriff Whelan slowly approached the two wagons. His pistols remained holstered and his rifle stayed nestled in its scabbard. He wasn't going to tempt Brown's men into shooting if he could help it.

The heavily armed men saw him coming and at first thought he was alone. "Halt! Who goes there?" The wagons bristled with rifles aimed at Whelan.

Whelan brought his mount to a halt. "I'm Sheriff George Whelan from Corpus Christi. You men are under arrest. If you resist, you will be killed."

The men laughed at his confident manner.

Five armed men rode up behind Whelan to reinforce him. Unlike Whelan, they had their rifles at the ready. Whelan shook his head resignedly. "Perhaps y'all didn't understand. Y'all are under arrest."

One of the men in the wagon stood tall and aimed his rifle as if to shoot. He took a Comanche arrow through his back and a second shaft as he fell. The other two men dropped their weapons like hot potatoes.

"Now y'all have gotten some sense. Men, get their weapons." Whelan's posse moved forward and quickly disarmed Brown's men. "Let's get them bound and take them to the Nuecestown jail. Leave the wagons as they are."

Three Toes moved forward, knife in hand. He was aiming to scalp the man he'd shot.

"Ignore the Indian, men." Whelan looked away as Three Toes put the knife to the man's scalp.

As Three Toes began to make his cut, he stopped. In the back of his mind, he recalled Luke's respect for the Comanche dead many months before. Perhaps it was time to change. He pulled back his knife. "Sheriff, I do not need this man's scalp."

The Comanche warrior with Three Toes stepped forward, but the chief held him back.

Whelan tipped his hat to Three Toes. "Men, throw the dead man over a horse, and let's get him back to Nuecestown."

It was late afternoon when General Truax decided to camp outside the abandoned site of Fort Merrill near the Nueces River. The old fort with its log cabin headquarters was still in good shape, despite lack of daily upkeep. The Army had sporadically used it as a base, but finally gave it up. It was about a day-and-a-half ride from Corpus Christi.

The mysterious note still gnawed at the general. He wanted to meet the man who had the temerity to have his barn burned down. It went without saying that he'd already concocted a story by which the traitor would be arrested for interfering with U.S. Army business.

Truax hated not knowing what to expect in Corpus. He prided himself on knowledge of his enemies and having good scouting reports on the nature of enemy armament and how they were deployed. O'Rourke had told him about Luke, so he quite naturally attributed the mystery note to the Ranger. This man Luke Dunn baffled him. He knew the lawman had established a reputation for always getting his man and that, according to O'Rourke, he had the trust of Rip Ford.

Another worry was Colonel Rucker. Where was the man? Could he have joined forces with Dunn? The man would have hell to pay if he had.

The time was at hand for the general to send out an advance scouting party. He wished he still had the Cherokee scout he used back in the Mexican-American War, but he'd have to work with what he had.

"Major Thompson, choose two men and follow the road down through San Patricio and Nuecestown. See what you can find. We'll be heading out early, so we'll meet you late tomorrow afternoon. I expect a full report of any unusual activity." Truax had worked with Thompson before and trusted the officer to bring back reliable information about any enemy. The general yearned to know whether he was facing a single Texas Ranger or a sizeable force of men.

Thompson recruited two privates he felt were fairly practiced at scouting. They mounted up and headed southeast on the San Antonio to Corpus Christi road. They'd reach San Patricio by dark, make camp, and head to Nuecestown in the morning.

★

Luke and Rucker rode into Nuecestown at dark after having deposited Brown in the jail in Corpus Christi. They'd gotten Colonel Kinney to place round-the-clock guards on the jail. This was far too valuable a prisoner to allow him to escape. They also didn't want Brown to suffer Crawford's fate.

They were pleased to find the Nuecestown jail occupied with Brown's remaining two men. The third had been buried in the Nuecestown Cemetery. Thus far, the plan had gone exceptionally well.

They found Whelan over at the boarding house dining with Bernice, Agatha, and Scarlett. "George, you lucky man," Luke exclaimed. "How'd you attract so many lovely ladies?" Everyone had a good laugh. They needed a bit of humor to relieve the stress that was building over what they might face in the next day or two. "May we join you?"

"Luke, Colonel Rucker, by all means. Have a seat." Bernice was always the gracious hostess.

Scarlett was now looking very pregnant. She had been on the petite side, but was obviously heavy with child. She was taken aback as Rucker walked in behind Luke.

Luke tipped his hat to Scarlett as he and Rucker grabbed seats at a nearby table. Rucker had a second thought and went over to Scarlett. "Miss Rose, I apologize for the way you were treated in Austin and the trouble my sons and I made during your travel to Corpus Christi. I have no ill intention toward you."

Scarlett smiled nervously. This was the man who had threatened her. But now, he was treating her like a lady, not like a common whore. "I do accept your apology, Colonel Rucker."

Rucker gave a look of relief, as though a burden was lifted from his conscience.

Luke turned to Whelan. "I see you captured Brown's men. What happened to the third one?"

"Three Toes." Enough said.

"Did he?" Luke didn't want to mention taking a scalp in front of the ladies.

"Strangely enough, he chose not to." Whelan smiled approvingly. "How'd it go with Thaddeus Brown?"

"He's in a cell under round-the-clock guard."

Luke eased back in his seat as Bernice placed plates featuring her notorious roast before he and Rucker. "We've got to set our trap for the general."

Scarlett listened intently, as she dared not fall into the clutches of General Truax.

"I suggest that George take the lead at the wagons. Other than Brown himself, I doubt the general has ever met Brown's men. In fact, I'd be surprised if he didn't send a scouting party ahead. If we can engage them into thinking the approach to Corpus is safe, it'll give us an edge. We can get the general to ride right into our trap."

Whelan and Rucker nodded agreement.

Whelan looked over at Scarlett. "Don't you be worrying," he reassured her. "Everything will be all right."

Scarlett blushed at Whelan's concern. "Why, thank you, Sheriff Whelan."

"You can call me George." He smiled sheepishly.

For Scarlett, this move to familiarity gave her a faint glimmer of hope.

ELEVEN

Versus the U.S. Army

General Truax's troop broke camp at the crack of dawn. They mounted up in columns of twos and headed south along the San Antonio to Corpus Christi road. Truax expected to encounter his scouts a few miles past San Patricio. In keeping with a general commanding the troop, the men were properly outfitted in regulation uniforms with blue tunics, blue trousers with yellow stripe, campaign hats, and yellow kerchiefs. The lead trooper carried the U.S. flag while a second carried the unit colors. If they could fight as well as they appeared, they might do well in battle. At least half the men had some battle experience, though most had never fired a weapon in battle.

Truax rode with the bearing most folks might expect, erect in the saddle, sword dangling at his side, brass buttons glittering, epaulets with a general's stars reflecting the morning sun…indeed, the textbook picture of a commanding general.

Notably, it was wickedly hot and humid. The men sweltered in their uniforms. Each mile incrementally fed the men's worsening discomfort. Truax sat straight in his saddle at the front, looking cooler than he was and seemingly oblivious to the condition of his men.

No one had the temerity to mention the energy-sapping effect. The general was focused on meeting his scouts. He dared not enter any engagement without a sense of the environment he was facing.

Major Thompson had joined Truax's command back during the Mexican-American War. He knew what the general expected. He was vaguely aware that the general had certain business interests, but had been kept clear of any involvement. As with other officers in Truax's command, he'd been kept mostly ignorant of his commander's activities to lessen the likelihood of anyone being able to testify against the general in the event of legal trouble.

The major and his men had ridden at a brisk pace, finally arriving about a half-mile north of Brown's wagon encampment. He had seen Thaddeus Brown a couple of times but never met the man personally. He understood that Brown was a no-nonsense trader and savvy fighter. Thompson was surprised to see the wagons and didn't realize at first whose they were. He did know by his map that Nuecestown and its ferry crossing were just beyond the wagons.

There was plenty of activity around the wagons. There appeared to be no security concerns, as the men had posted no guard. "Private Reynolds, stay here and observe. If there is any trouble, head back to General Truax on the double."

Thompson headed forward to investigate the wagons. As he came to within hailing distance, he caught the attention of the men in the encampment. He noted with reassurance that they were well-armed.

George Whelan stood in one of the wagons. "Halt! Who goes there?"

"Major Thompson, U.S. Army. I'm from General Truax's command. Identify yourselves." Thompson had a rifle at the ready. It was hot, and Thompson could feel a rivulet of sweat run down his back inside his tunic. Damned wool uniforms weren't made for Texas heat.

"Dang! Don't go shootin'! This is Thaddeus Brown's rig. Is the general heading here?" Whelan's attempt at familiarity had its anticipated effect.

The major let his guard down and approached. "Where's Brown?"

"He went into Corpus. Should be back later today. Can we help you?"

The major wasn't certain as to how much he should reveal but, after a moment's thought, figured he was among a friendly crowd. "Do you know the whereabouts of a Texas Ranger name of Luke Dunn?"

"Dunn?" Whelan acted as though he was trying to recollect. "Oh, yeah. Long Luke Dunn. We ran into him about a day's ride east. He was curious about our cargo. I'm thinking he was headed to Corpus Christi." He paused for effect. "You have business with him?"

"Maybe. Much obliged for the information. If you could be here tomorrow when we travel through, it'd be appreciated." He yearned to order them to stay and hoped that Thaddeus Brown would be with them.

"See you tomorrow, Major." Whelan tipped his hat and smiled broadly. "Oh, by the way, Major, what sort of firepower did y'all bring south from Austin? Mr. Brown may want to know." He hoped he'd established just enough trust with the major that he'd reveal this key information.

"Twenty-four soldiers, all well-armed. Standard issue rifles, sabers, and pistols." The major didn't even hesitate.

"See y'all tomorrow, then." Whelan quickly did the math. He'd be outnumbered by two to one. He, Luke, and Rucker needed to get their heads together as soon as possible.

Carlos Perez had to find a means to fund his revenge. He wouldn't survive long existing on the petty thefts of Manuel and his cronies. Patience wasn't a virtue he normally ascribed to, but it had become clear to him that emotion-driven strategies were not working. He was mostly healed physically. He even began to feel fortunate that Scarlett's shot with the revolver hadn't done more than castrate him.

Manuel could be a true asset, given properly channeling of his youth and energy. Perez felt it was time to change strategy. "*Manuel, ven aca.*" When Perez was nervously excited, his mustache twitched on the left side. It was twitching madly.

"*Si, senor Perez.*"

"*Esta noche, nos encontramos con hombres nuevos. Tengo un nuevo plan.*" Perez was going to share his new plan with these candidate *Caballeros Negros*. "*Voleremos a despellejar Ganado.*" They'd be returning to Perez's specialty: skinning cattle. They'd once again be hiders. It would be like not so long ago, when they'd establish basecamps with clusters of men and even families they loosely called ranches. They'd herd rustled cattle to the ranches and skin them at leisure.

Manuel enthusiastically supported Perez's plan. He didn't especially like sneaking across the border into Laredo to steal supplies for him. This at least had the aura of a legitimate business operation, despite the cattle theft part of it. He knew hides brought good money on the black market.

Major Thompson rejoined his men and rode as hard as he dared, knowing that he'd eventually connect with General Truax's command on the San Antonio to Corpus Christi road. He felt confident that the general would appreciate his scouting report. There was no sign that any defensive perimeter had been set up by the Texas Ranger, and the presence of Thaddeus Brown's men boded well for eliminating the lawman's threat.

General Truax had set a brisk pace since breaking camp that morning. He'd already led his men past San Patricio and was well on his way to Nuecestown. He stopped to rest men and horses about ten miles east of the town.

It was at this rest stop that Major Thompson rode into the camp. He rode up to where the general was relaxing under the shade of a lone cypress along the bank of the Nueces River. He dismounted and saluted. "General, I bring good news."

Truax could use some good news. A dozen days on horseback did little for his constitution. He had a couple of nagging saddle sores and vowed to spend more time riding in the future to prevent any recurrence. "What good news do you bring, Major?"

"I encountered Thaddeus Brown's men and wagons encamped outside Nuecestown, sir. They said that the Texas Ranger was last seen heading alone to Corpus Christi. Brown had gone into the city to reconnoiter. There was no sign of any defensive perimeter, sir."

"So you're telling me that we can simply ride right on into Corpus, Major?" Truax was just a tad apprehensive. "Did you travel beyond Nuecestown?"

"No, sir. We took the word of Brown's men." As he thought about it, they never said anything about the territory between Corpus and Nuecestown. He'd simply drawn an assumption.

"Well, we'll proceed forward with caution, Major. Next time, check the potential battlefield yourself. Never rely on civilians, especially men that run with the likes of Thaddeus Brown."

"Yes, sir. Understood, sir." Major Thompson saluted.

"Oh, Major, we'll spend the night here and ride out in the morning." Truax saw this as an opportunity to give his saddle sores a break.

His troopers saw the Nueces River as a much-needed opportunity to cool off. Truax, for his part, didn't dissuade them.

Luke, Whelan, Rucker, and Three Toes met at the stable in Nuecestown. With Brown's men locked in the jail, it wouldn't do for the prisoners to have any inkling of the plans to take on Truax's force. If they escaped, it could doom any hopes for success. Importantly, Luke still maintained the element of surprise while having reduced the strength of the enemy by eliminating Brown's men.

"Thaddeus Brown chose just about the best defensive ground around Nuecestown to camp on." Luke stated the obvious. "Colonel, do you have any thoughts as to strategy?"

"You seem to have a natural affinity for this sort of fighting, Captain Dunn. If I were a betting man, I'd sense that you were thinking of an aggressive defense. It's what we call counter-intuitive."

Luke smiled. "You're learning, Colonel." He winked respectfully at Rucker. "I'm thinking George will set up in the shelter of the wagons with four heavily armed men. Since the soldiers think they're facing Brown's men, they'll come very close…likely right up to the wagons…before they realize anything is amiss." He looked from face to face around the gathering. Everyone seemed approving.

He continued. "Now, I have to admit that, regardless of the general's ill intentions, there are worthy soldiers under his command. I cannot in good conscience kill U.S. Army soldiers. We need to get them to surrender, and that will require setting a trap from which fighting might be hopeless. The colonel and I will each have three mounted men to act as cavalry in a pincer move to threaten the general from his flanks. We move forward at the moment the general realizes he's been duped. With the element of surprise and a superior strategic position, we should even the odds or even gain an advantage from which they'd likely choose not to fight." Luke let the strategy sink in. "If we must resort to fighting, they'll likely resort to pistols and sabers, so we'd best be accurate with our shooting."

"What about the general? I assume we want to capture him. What do you have in mind?" Whelan asked.

"This is where Three Toes' special talents may come in. General Truax is no young man. He'll order his men to attack, but he hasn't seen a battle in quite a long time. If he decides to try to escape, I leave it to Three Toes and his warrior to capture the general. I expect he'll be scared to death at what the Comanche might do, so we must be careful that he doesn't kill himself."

Rucker joked. "He may even pass out at the prospect."

"What's this major like, Colonel? If something happened to the general, would he go on fighting or be likely to surrender? Might he have a conscience as to fighting an officer of the law?" Luke turned to Rucker.

"I don't expect he enjoys Truax's command. The general has a way of belittling his officers. He's condescending. The major won't be enjoying any fight over a mission he likely doesn't support. He'll follow the general's orders until the general is captured or killed. I expect he'll surrender if he's not shot and killed first."

"Let's pray this all works, gentlemen," Luke said. "We dare not fail."

The area where Brown had parked his wagons was slightly elevated compared to the surrounding area. Looking north, roughly a third of a mile toward the Nueces River, was a stand of cypress that afforded a modicum of cover for Rucker and his posse to hide from Truax. Luke's flanking position to the south was more exposed and downhill. He found a gully that was deep enough to almost hide the horses. Unless Truax was looking to the south, Luke would be okay. They hoped the general would be fully focused on the wagons.

They set their trap a bit after dawn and waited. The ground that Truax had to cover would likely take about three hours at a brisk ride, so the sun would be high to the southeast and in the general's eyes as he approached the wagons.

It's said that waiting is hell. That was certainly true for Luke and his men. The sun had not yet brought to bear the full intensity of its heat, but it was warm enough that, in combination with anticipation of battle, the men were sweating. Bandanas were the order of the day. Soaked in water and wrapped round each man's neck, they provided a certain level of cooling. The horses sensed the nervousness, pawing at the ground.

They judged that it was around mid-morning when the flags of Truax's troop appeared on the horizon.

"Wait until they're close to us, men. We mustn't spring our trap early. Don't fire unless I fire. We must give them a chance to surrender." Whelan reminded his defenders that surprise was the essence of their trap. Rucker would move in from the north and Luke from the south into the flanks of Truax's troop. With any luck, there would be no battle and, if there was, it might be brief.

Closer. The general's troop was oblivious to everything but the wagons they saw in front of them. The troopers could be seen bantering carelessly as they rode into the trap. They trotted in a loosely aligned formation. The major waved a greeting of familiarity. Ever closer. They were closing the distance to their possible fate. They picked up their pace. Three hundred yards, two hundred, one hundred. At about twenty-five yards, Whelan could easily make out the relaxed expressions on the faces of the general and the major. Fifty feet. Whelan and his men stood with rifles aimed at the troop.

"Halt! You are under arrest!"

The move was designed to force the general to take action. "What? You're not Brown!" Truax was totally surprised. He pulled his saber. "Prepare to attack!" His troop was already confused. No soldier had been ready to do battle, and Truax's desperate command wasn't even the proper one. Major Thompson drew saber and pistol, but it was too late.

With the hostile reaction of General Truax in immediately shouting a call to arms, Luke and Rucker began to move in. The general was effectively caught in their snare.

Truax turned his horse and waved his saber about before quickly pointing to the rear. "Retreat! I say, retreat!" There wasn't even time for a bugle call. The colors fell. The troop had just begun to turn when Rucker's and Luke's men closed in tightly from the general's flanks. Not a shot had yet been fired.

"Dismount! Form a defense!" the general yelled.

It was too little, far too late. In fact, it was downright laughable. The major was embarrassed.

Truax stood in the center of a ring of soldiers, including the major. The general held his saber, but then Three Toes entered the circle at a gallop and the saber was immediately struck from his grasp by a forceful whack of Three Toes' lance. Having counted coup, the chief was on Truax in a heartbeat. His fellow Comanche warrior held the major at bay with a nocked arrow in his bow. No soldiers moved to aid the officers. Truax's remaining soldiers stood about the scene in utter disarray, not having a clue as to what to do. The general had become Three Toes' prisoner. Three Toes had forced the general to his knees and held him by his hair with his knife poised as though ready to scalp him alive. Truax was in such a fearful panic that he peed in his trousers. Three Toes brought his warpaint-bedecked face to within inches of the general's and smiled.

Luke rode up. "General Booker Truax, you are under arrest."

The general gave a momentary thought to protesting the validity of a Texas Ranger arresting a federal officer, but he was relieved to be free of Three Toes' grasp and decided to save it for another day. He was, after all, at a decided disadvantage. He and the major were escorted from the troop. That in itself was an embarrassment. He looked at Luke resignedly but respectfully. "I'm your prisoner, Captain Dunn."

As Luke placed manacles on the general, Truax tossed Colonel Rucker a contemptible look dripping with sentiments of son of a bitch and turncoat.

Whelan dismounted and took Truax into custody. "General, our jail here in Nuecestown is a bit full, so we're taking you to Corpus Christi. I'm sure you'll enjoy the hospitality of our fine city. I understand you're to be turned over to federal marshals. It seems you may get your wish of a transfer to the nation's capital." He uttered the last sentence with a wry grin. He felt some sense of relief that Scarlett would be safe for the present.

Luke took stock of the scene. By any measure, the general had suffered a disastrous defeat without a shot having been fired. "Sergeant, you are in charge. Your orders from Colonel Rucker are to return to Austin."

General Truax nodded appreciatively at Luke. It was his fate that he'd engaged and been defeated by an honorable man.

Three Toes for one would have liked to have taken the general's scalp. He'd counted coup, but had come away empty-handed.

Luke noticed the chief's plight. He took the general's saber and dutifully presented it to Three Toes.

"Thank you, Ghost-Who-Rides. I am honored, but not sure what to do with the long knife. It rattles so much, I could never sneak up on my enemy." He handed the weapon back to Luke, hoping it would not be taken as an insult.

Luke looked the general up and down. At last, he fixated on the general's shoulder bars. Three Toes nodded. Luke tore them from the general's shoulders and handed them to the Comanche. The general fully appreciated that he'd encountered a Comanche chief and managed to keep his scalp.

"I will stay here, Ghost-Who-Rides." Three Toes didn't feature the prospect of being an object of curiosity and derision in Corpus Christi.

Luke understood and nodded his assent.

"George, once the general and major are in jail, I suggest you deputize some reliable citizens and have them bring this stolen merchandise to Corpus Christi."

TWELVE

The Plot Thickens

The single file line of horses moved slowly and silently on the road to Corpus Christi. It seemed almost funereal. Whelan led the way, with the two captives behind and Luke and Colonel Rucker following. The posse strung out behind them. Two members of the posse stayed behind to guard the men in the Nuecestown jail.

The ride to Corpus wasn't long, and soon the mostly silent procession pulled up in front of the jail.

Luke dismounted and cautiously entered the jail. Thaddeus Brown stood as the door opened and wrapped his hands around the bars of his cell.

"Good afternoon, Mr. Brown," Luke said. "We have some temporary company for you today." Luke glanced at Brown, but his eyes were distracted to the desk where two men arose upon his entry. From their badges, they looked to be U.S. marshals.

Brown's curious look changed to wide-eyed surprise as Truax and the major were ushered in behind Luke. Colonel Rucker followed. Rucker, after all, was a material witness.

"What the…" Brown was now dumbfounded. Everything seemed

to be crashing around their scheme.

Truax followed the major into the only empty cell. He turned to Luke. "I've got to relieve myself, sir."

Whelan smiled and pointed to the hole in the floor. "Help yourself, General."

"You must be Captain Dunn." The larger of the two marshals extended his hand. "We're certainly impressed, sir. When Mr. Ford assured us that you'd show up with the general, we had our doubts."

"Well, these things never end so well as they appear."

"Deeply sorry about that, Captain. I'm Marshal Stodgkins and my partner here is Deputy Marshal Johnson. If you don't mind, given the late time of day, we'll leave the prisoners here overnight and begin their little trip to Washington, D.C. in the morning."

"No problem with that, Marshal Stodgkins, so long as the sheriff doesn't mind these men soiling his jail for one night." Luke seized the opportunity to grin.

Stodgkins glanced over at Rucker. "Colonel, we have orders for you from Army Command to join us in Washington, D.C. in three weeks. As a material witness, your testimony will be important, sir."

Rucker looked from Luke to Whelan and then to Brown and Truax. "I guess I'd best be heading back to Austin and get my family affairs in order. I would like to take this opportunity on behalf of Major Thompson here to let the marshals know that he can be trusted, that he was not involved in the scandalous doings. And, Captain Dunn, I am grateful for the trust you placed in me."

Luke nearly blushed. Yet he knew the Indian agency scandal investigation was far from concluded. There were still hiders on the Nueces Strip with links to Brown, and there was at least one high-placed person pulling Truax's puppet strings. "If you gentlemen don't mind, I'm going to take a couple of days and see to my wife and ranch." He headed toward the door.

"Captain Dunn?" Truax called out from the cell. "Sir, I hate to lose, but must admit that your strategy was brilliant. And you're a damned honorable man." These were extremely difficult words for the ego-centric, prideful general to get out. He nearly choked on the admission. He'd lost fair and square.

Luke stopped cold. "General, you are a fraud and a coward. It's a sad day that your actions cost so many people so much in both lives and money. May you forever roast in the hell you sprang from."

Whelan had never heard such impassioned feelings from Luke.

Luke strode from the jail, mounted the big gray, and headed out toward Heaven's Gate.

Whelan meanwhile was pleased that Kinney had seen to it that payment was ready for the members of the posse. Everything seemed to have come together well.

Three Toes camped about five miles outside Nuecestown. He figured to give Luke a couple of days before paying a visit to the ranch. He had only a couple of arrows remaining in his quiver, and that was a major concern. He needed the materials to replenish his supply. He had arrowheads, but needed shafts and feathers. If he couldn't make more arrows, he'd have to consider changing his choice of weapons. The idea of acquiring a rifle had begun to work on his psyche.

The ornate desk was outsized, even for a man as physically imposing as Horatio Thorpe. He'd drawn the curtains, throwing the walls of mahogany shelves filled with all manner of books and expensive statues into darkness. At six-foot-three and close to three hundred pounds, Thorpe was not a man to be overlooked. He tended to test the limits of the seams of his three-piece white suit, but no one dared mention that to him. He owned one of the largest cotton plantations in eastern Texas, and he exercised the outsized influence appropriate to his money and his girth. Nobody messed with Horatio Thorpe.

So it was, then, that Thorpe found himself fully distressed at the news that his key man in Austin, his lynchpin for his highly profitable military supply racket, had been lured into a trap and was headed to Washington, D.C., where he'd surely implicate Master Horatio Thorpe. The man with two thousand slaves suddenly found himself vulnerable. His aspirations of running for governor of Texas could quickly become history. His travels around the state from Austin to Houston to San Antonio to the Nueces Strip would be wasted. He even thought for a moment about whatever became of that red-haired whore in Laredo that was his obsession. Truax had failed him there, too. The answer to his distress was straightforward; simply eliminate the problem.

"Samuel! Samuel, get in here."

The black man got up from the only slightly less ornate desk outside Thorpe's office. He was dressed with a stateliness that reflected the way folks thought Thorpe should look; trim and well-tailored. He strode into Thorpe's office. "Yes, sir, yes, sir, Master Thorpe." Samuel knew where his bread was buttered, so to speak. He had a good situation going compared to his fellow slaves. Thorpe even took good care of his family. It might not compare to freedom, but it beat being in some cotton field and feeling the overseer's lash.

"Samuel, get hold of Roy Biggs. I need him to do something for me." He scribbled a few lines on a piece of paper. The only evidence of attribution was Thorpe's bold signature with its tell-tale paraph.

Samuel knew Thorpe was up to some serious business. Roy Biggs was arguably the meanest, baddest, most-evil, most cold-hearted killer living in Texas. The master definitely had some sort of wicked task in mind. It certainly was not likely to end well for the person who'd crossed him. Nobody double-crossed Horatio Thorpe and lived to tell about it.

Samuel knew just how to get the word to Roy Biggs. There was a sort of informal chain of communications that permeated the seamier side of Texas…and most anywhere, for that matter. The folks around Austin knew Samuel and knew who he belonged to. He had privileges that many white folks never enjoyed. In this case, it was access to that craven, sin-laden side of the law. He needed only tell one person, and the message would travel with incredible speed. Even a secretive message such as this would never be compromised lest the breaker of the code of secrecy be ready to meet his maker.

It took Samuel a mere five minutes to walk to the back of the Bullock House Hotel. He passed only one saloon and one brothel along the way. Samuel could have done without seeing those, but he knew that Thorpe loved to frequent them. There was sometimes no escaping inevitability. He passed Thorpe's note to a local roustabout named Chunk Egan. No words were spoken, nor were they needed. The name on the envelope was enough…just a name…no address.

Thorpe knew he had to get to Truax and Brown before they left Texas. Once they were on a train moving closer to Washington, D.C., they'd be more difficult to eliminate. Of course, he'd first try to rescue them but, failing that, elimination equaled death.

Luke and Elisa passionately celebrated his return to Heaven's Gate. He dared not tell her of the risks he'd taken, as it would have caused her far too much anxiety when he undertook his next foray into the inner soul of the lawless Nueces Strip.

Soon enough, the aroma of frying bacon permeated the air of their little cabin. With Scarlett back in Nuecestown, it was just the two of them, for at least this moment.

"You hungry this morning, Mr. Ranger?" Elisa laughed as though she'd been storing up laughs for the past several days, which she had. She'd begun to accept that her life would bounce from his being husband and rancher to his being a lawman. She awaited Rip Ford's next message with lingering trepidation.

"I've missed you, Lisa, but I've especially missed your fine cooking. You're going to turn me into a fat Texas Ranger." He laughed back at her. "Not that I'd mind."

Luke was dealing with his own conflict, being torn between the two worlds of ranching and Rangering. Seemed that, so long as there was lawlessness on the Strip, there'd never be a resolution, never a ceasing. He strove to put it out of his mind, watching in wonder as she stood at the stove frying up eggs and bacon. The feel of her soft skin yet lingered on his fingertips, his lips. Who'd have figured that he'd have found and married such a wonderful woman after his rough years growing up in County Kildare? Ireland had been a different life, a decent life, but it sure couldn't hold a candle to the life he'd found in Texas. "Sweetheart, how far along did you say you were?"

"Been 'tween four and five months now, Lucas." She smiled. "What makes you ask?"

"You sure have grown more than I'd have expected." He walked over and wrapped his arms around her, placing his strong hands gently around her growing belly.

"What are you suggesting, Lucas Dunn?"

"You might double check with Doc. I'm thinking that Bernice might have made a good guess. In fact, I feel pretty sure there's three of you in my arms."

Elisa dropped the spatula into the greasy pan. "Oh, my. I'd thought of that, Lucas, but not seriously. What if?" She turned and held him tightly. "Just so they're healthy, Lucas, just so they're healthy."

She still held visions of the hemorrhaging miscarriage that took her mother. It had been the beginning of the end of her family. Comanche had killed her father and youngest brother. Her brother Mike lingered ever closer to death's door from the debilitating sickness brought on by a rattler's bite. Luke and the child or children in her womb were her hope for the future.

The too-recent recollections brought her to thinking of Mike's deteriorating condition. "Lucas, Mike's not doing well. Doc says the end might be near."

Luke had known this time would arrive. The effect of the rattlesnake's venom had a long-term effect, often destroying a victim's renal system. Mike's kidneys were failing. "I understand, Lisa. You'd have him spend his last days at the home he loved?"

Her eyes said yes even before he'd mouthed the words. "Let's make him comfortable here at Heaven's Gate."

Marshals Stodgkins and Johnson awakened early. They had a long day ahead escorting their prisoners to the railhead in San Antonio. They'd be heading to St. Louis to catch a train to Washington, D.C. It'd be a four-day ride via the Corpus Christi to San Antonio road.

They'd visited Luke's cousin Peter in Corpus. The renowned smithy made three special sets of manacles for the marshals. They could be taking no chances with these prisoners.

"Morning, General. You ready to travel?"

One by one, each prisoner was invited from his cell and duly manacled. Stodgkins held a shotgun aimed at the prisoners, as Johnson chained each prisoner in turn. Soon enough, they were led out to waiting horses.

"You going to feed us, Marshal?"

"You complaining already?" He yanked extra-hard on the general's manacles, pulling him out the door. Truax almost fell. "We'll get you fed." He contemptuously avoided using the general's military title, as he saw it as a denigration of the military service.

Brown and Truax exchanged concerned glances. Would they be rescued from this seemingly ignominious fate? Desperation hung in the air. They'd look for a chance to escape, but it was already clear that these marshals were not to be trifled with.

The major noted their silent communication. He was like an unwitting pawn in their game. He could only hope that he'd not be dragged down by their deeds.

They were soon riding north single file. Johnson led the way with Stodgkins in the rear. They placed the major between Truax and Brown to inhibit any talk.

Carlos Perez had made a convincing case to set up a new hider ranch in the southern bowels of the Nueces Strip. Given that his last two adventures toward Corpus Christi had ended in the tragic demise of two incarnations of his *Caballeros Negros*, it was a wonder that anyone would follow him. But his passion was infectious. Revenge seemed to attract certain men though, so far as Perez was concerned, feeding on it had made for a very sparse meal. The *Caballeros Negros* would be headed to a place about eighty miles north of Fort McIntosh. That made for a three-to-four-day escape path to Mexico if needed. More importantly, it placed the growing ranching industry of the eastern Nueces Strip within easy reach.

With fully loaded wagons across rough prairie terrain, the trip from Nuevo Laredo to the ranch would take at least ten days. The *Caballeros* would get to know each other well. Perez would be feeding their camaraderie to better prepare them for when there'd be gunplay. They'd need to be forged into a team, not simply to rustle cattle, but to help Perez achieve his life ambition. It remained to be seen just how patient the man could be.

The seven men and four women with household items made for a quite noticeable caravan, and noticed it was as it lumbered past Laredo. Sheriff Stills could only watch longingly. He had no idea that these were Perez's men. Perez's escape from his jail had been an embarrassment to him and to Laredo. It wouldn't be forgotten. Stills felt that he'd eventually have the sweeter revenge. Meanwhile, he prayed that the Texas Rangers would be reauthorized by the powers in Austin. The U.S. soldiers had already been pretty much pulled from the Strip, leaving it vulnerable to the likes of Carlos Perez.

THIRTEEN

Ambush

R oy Biggs was average height with dark brown hair. He was slim, reasonably fit, and had disproportionately large hands. They easily handled the Colt Walkers that were his weapons of choice. He was unremarkable in almost every respect, save for his hands and his eyes. Ah, those dark, vacant, unfeeling eyes set wide and deep between a pronounced brow ridge and unusually high cheek bones. Pure evil oozed from every pore. Biggs' eyes made a rattlesnake's eyes seem almost human. He lacked only fangs and a forked tongue to complete the picture of the pure vileness of soul that he embodied.

He pocketed the message from Thorpe. Time was of the essence, yet he dared not be careless. Thirty-eight men plus a few women had met their ends as spewed from the muzzles of Biggs' guns. Most had been ambushed. Face-to-face confrontations did not lend themselves to survival on any lawless frontier, and the Texas Nueces Strip was no exception.

He wasn't certain what he'd face, and he was tempted to bring a couple of his men. In the end, he decided to do this job alone. All he could be certain of was that U.S. marshals were moving prisoners along the road from Corpus Christi to San Antonio. He knew from experience that there'd only be two marshals. That was their modus operandi, and he could count on that. They preferred not to be hung up with large entourages. This also meant there would be only two prisoners of importance. Yes, he'd handle this by himself. Thorpe was a generous employer, and Biggs would share a portion of the bounty with his men at the hacienda, simply to maintain their loyalty.

He took a stroll round his hacienda to be certain all was in order. He'd named the place Twin Creeks for two nearby streams that came together and eventually fed into the Nueces River. He was a meticulous man; everything had its place. He expected it to be every bit as clean and well-ordered upon his return. It was a substantial structure with thick walls and four parapets designed to facilitate defense. There was a clear line of sight for perhaps a half-mile. This discouraged potential attackers, as they'd be easy targets for Biggs' security. There was on the order of five thousand acres upon which Biggs raised cattle and grew most of what fed him and his men. It was a self-sufficient operation.

Biggs unlocked the door to his armory. It was more like a vault and was purposely kept cool and dry. It contained all manner of weaponry, including guns, knives, swords, bows and arrows, and even a small cannon. It was quite a collection indeed. He was partial to Colt firearms, and chose a pair of Colt Model 1851 Navy revolvers and a brand-new Burnside carbine featuring a .54 caliber percussion round. The rifle packed plenty of wallop. As a backup, he picked out a Sharps Model 1853 rifle, which was becoming popular with buffalo hunters. His thinking was that he'd not get closer to his quarry than a couple of hundred yards and would need to get off multiple shots in a short span of time. In addition, he sought the stopping power that larger bores ensured.

Given Biggs' profession and his reputation, it might not be expected that he was married, but he had a beautiful, dark-haired wife and two young children, a boy and a girl. Counter-intuitive for certain.

Roy Biggs was an educated man, schooled at a boys' school back in Massachusetts. However, his wanderlust was embedded deep within his bones. He had chaffed at the bit to be free of his strict parents and the school. Upon graduation, he spurned his father's business and headed for the gold fields of California. He managed to be one of the lucky ones that struck it rich. But the experience netted him trouble, too, as he got caught up in gambling, boozing, whoring, and the like. It was a short leap to cheating at cards, some gunplay, and a stint in a local jail for shooting an itinerant miner that tried to jump his claim. He managed to escape and thence began a crime spree that took him further eastward. Each move was an escape.

He was street-smart and, despite his waywardness, had been careful with how he spent his fortune. His mind became numbed to killing living things, whether animal or human. He fell in love twice, but both times wound up killing the women's jealous husbands. He shunned relationships and sought solitude. This led him to build his hacienda. There he felt protected from the harsh realities of the world, though the loneliness tended to make his evilness fester like an infection of the soul. His wife was the consequence of one of his more lucid moments of holding human feelings. Despite his own terrible upbringing, he wanted to have a family.

This day, he left Twin Creeks with two horses and enough grub and ammo to meet his needs for the job. He'd switch mounts every ten miles or so to give the horses a break. He didn't ride at a full gallop but did set a fast pace. With any luck, he would arrive just south of San Antonio ahead of the U.S. marshals. If he arrived late, he'd have to deal with them being on a train. This posed far greater risk, as passengers could get in his way and ambush would be more difficult. Plus, Thorpe wanted these prisoners taken alive if at all possible. Biggs' thoughts hung on the "if possible" phrase. This was his challenge, as Thorpe's money didn't really matter so much. It was about the thrill associated with accomplishing a mission that entailed some risk.

A warm breeze wafted in from the west as little Mike sat comfortably on the gallery. His skin had taken on a sallow tone. His once-dancing blue eyes seemed to be dimming. Elisa tried her best to make his final days as best as could be hoped for. His frail body had put up a long battle against the after-effects of the rattlesnake's venom.

In the distance, he could see the creek that spilled into the Nueces River. The yellow flowers were still blooming on the prickly pear cacti. Just to his right was the live oak motte where his mother, father, and brother were buried. He could hardly remember the Comanche arrow that nearly took his own life, nor the arrow gifted to him by Three Toes. He couldn't remember much, though he hung onto his sister's love. And he'd never forget the big Texas Ranger.

Luke rode in from checking cattle and hitched the big gray stallion in front of the cabin. He could hear Elisa rattling pots and pans inside. Mike had fallen asleep in his chair on the gallery.

"Hey, Mike, how's my cowboy?" Luke called.

Mike didn't stir.

Elisa heard Luke's voice and quietly opened the cabin door. "Shhhh, Luke. He's sleeping." She smiled and went to give her man a hug.

Luke rushed past her and over to Mike. "Lisa! He's stopped breathing!" He was at a loss. Mike was already beginning to turn that tell-tale blue of death. The rattlesnake had finally had his way with the child.

Elisa held Mike in her arms while Luke embraced them both. Mike was Elisa's last tie with her birth family. Tears flowed freely. They sat for the next hour on the edge of the gallery holding Mike. There were no miracles for the little guy.

"It's time." Luke spoke the words quietly.

They wrapped Mike in a blanket and placed him gently into the grave Luke had dug. He'd lie with his family under the sheltering shade of the old live oak motte. Luke recited an old Irish prayer and joined Elisa in sprinkling flower petals over the grave. The length of time Mike had dealt with the consequences of the rattlesnake's venom in no way diminished the impact of the loss. The frontier had taken another life, but seemed set to increase God's bounty with the two children Elisa was carrying.

"Scarlett? Scarlett, are you okay?" Whelan and she had just finished dinner at the boarding house. The expression on her face was unlike anything he'd ever seen.

"George, call Doc." She sounded quietly anxious. "I think the baby's coming early."

"Bernice, get Scarlett to a bed. I've gotta fetch Doc!"

Bernice helped Scarlett to a bedroom in the back of the boarding house. Agatha, an old hand at this sort of thing, having had six children herself, filled a pan with water and began warming it.

"Ohhhh. It's coming. I know it's coming."

The ladies knew better. The tough part was just beginning.

Doc threw some instruments in his bag, grabbed Whelan's arm, and staggered mostly sober over to the boarding house. He'd delivered a few babies in his life, but this one seemed especially important, given the doubtful paternity. He hoped for Scarlett's sake that it bore some resemblance to George Whelan and not a lick to the deceased ne'er-do-well Dirk Cavendish.

Scarlett was proving to Bernice and Agatha that they didn't know better. The baby in her womb was determined to get out sooner than later.

Doc worried. This child was coming a lot sooner than expected. He'd known very few to survive the ordeal.

Whelan paced outside. He could hear Scarlett moaning and occasionally screaming. He heard Bernice's and Doc's exhortations to push harder. Little wonder they called this "labor." Thankfully, his own labor only consisted of pacing and waiting. The air seemed still. There'd been a breeze earlier, but it had stopped. He shrugged. Not much he could do.

Scarlett pushed, moaned, sweated profusely, cursed, and pushed some more.

"A head…keep pushing, Scarlett. Keep pushing," Doc encouraged her. She might be one of the lucky ones to beat the odds with premature birth.

A piercing wail reached Whelan's ears. He half-collapsed on the doorstep. The door creaked behind him.

"You just gonna sit there, or do you want to see your daughter?" Bernice asked.

Whelan rushed the first few feet into the house, and then nearly stopped. Was this his child? He walked into the room with trepidation.

Scarlett lay exhausted with a bundle in her arm. "You going to just stand there or come hold your daughter?"

Whelan leaned over and picked up the baby. He pushed back the blanket and was greeted by unforgettable eyes. They were his mother's eyes. She was indeed his. "What shall we name her?" He smiled at Scarlett.

"Margaret?"

Whelan smiled. "That's a pretty name." He lay Margaret back in Scarlett's arms. He reached into the pocket of his vest.

Scarlett watched him inquisitively. He got down on one knee. "What are you doing, George?"

"Will you marry me?"

She had mixed feelings. Would he have asked if the child wasn't his? Did she want to marry him? Did he love her? Could he be a one-woman man? She tried to shake the questions from her head. She was so tired. Now, she had the responsibility of raising a child. He'd been by her side protecting her. She looked over at Bernice and Agatha, standing in the doorway.

Bernice gave Scarlett an "it's up to you" look. Agatha was even less help. She shrugged with a "why not?" expression. Meanwhile, Doc took a swig from his whisky flask.

Whelan was still on his knee offering the ring. It finally struck him why she was conflicted. "Scarlett Rose, I do love you. I'll always be here for you." He took her hand.

"No."

Doc dropped the flask, Bernice and Agatha gasped, and Whelan's jaw dropped. Then he smiled an understanding smile. "I'll be around, Scarlett." He pocketed the ring, nodded to everyone, took a loving last look at baby Margaret, and left the boarding house.

The ground south of San Antonio consisted mostly of rolling hills. It wasn't so hilly as the Comancheria, but its ravines and arroyos offered plenty of places to set an ambush.

Marshal Stodgkins and Deputy Marshal Johnson were increasingly vigilant as they negotiated the countryside. The road was helpful for traveling, but was concerning, given the plentiful cover along their route. Nevertheless, they continued to ride in single file formation.

The nights were a challenge. They chained the manacled prisoners to available trees and took turns standing watch. They managed to cook up enough grub to stop Truax's whining. The prisoners were a bit challenged in answering nature's call, but the marshals had decided against removing the manacles.

The morning of the third day out of Corpus Christi found them a bit past two-thirds of the way to San Antonio. They'd pushed their pace and figured they were now a little more than three days out.

Thaddeus Brown, always the wheeler dealer, had been pretty much silent up to now. He was disappointed that General Truax had said little that mattered other than to complain. As they drew closer to San Antonio and the train ride to his own fate, he began to think he had nothing to lose. "Say, Mr. Marshal?"

"Keep it shut, Brown."

"What you gonna do? Shoot me in the back?"

Stodgkins rolled his eyes. He hadn't liked this assignment in the first place and was surprised it had taken this long for Brown to say something. He was ever the con man, so nothing would really surprise the marshal. "What's on your mind, Brown?"

"Do you really think you're gonna make it to San Antonio?"

"You think otherwise?"

"Just sayin,' Marshal. You could live to see another day. You just gotta let us go free."

Stodgkins knew there was far more to the Indian agency fraud scheme than embodied in the trio he was escorting. There had to be some high-placed powerful forces that would as soon not be discovered. A trial in Washington, D.C. would surely result in uncomfortable revelations. The fact that they were even going to the nation's capital meant that this was a highly significant matter. He could set the prisoners free, but he'd never get a job as a lawman again. "Can't do it, Brown."

"You know this is bigger than you or us."

"I expect so. Wouldn't surprise me none." Stodgkins remained resolute.

"You ain't gonna see San Antonio, Marshal."

"Could be you won't either, Brown. Maybe they don't want you to sing." He smiled to himself. Killing a U.S. Marshal would be another federal offense added to all they were already being charged with, assuming everyone lived to tell about it. Stodgkins began to wish he'd recruited a couple of more men.

Brown shrugged. The marshal had a point.

Truax had been listening but resisted stepping into the conversation. In between he and Brown, the major was resigned to whatever the fates held in store for his association with Truax.

Luke was thoroughly enjoying Heaven's Gate and preparing the ranch for the vagaries of winter on the Nueces Strip. They might even have a snow or two, though it always melted away quickly. He was thinking about his soon-to-be family as he curried the big gray stallion. Of a sudden, it occurred to him that he'd never named the horse. He'd immigrated from County Kildare all of five years ago, and this big horse had been his first purchase, even before his guns. He was a wonderful steed, great for riding across the vast grasslands of the Strip. They'd become fast friends. He recalled that Three Toes nicknamed him Ghost-Who-Rides. Rides what?

Elisa appeared in the doorway to the stable. She looked around and was impressed. "You sure keep a clean stable, Mr. Dunn. The mules are living better than us." She smiled at her little joke.

"Thinkin' about finally throwing a name on this big stallion."

Elisa barely thought a moment. "I'd name him to describe what he is. Simply call him Big Horse." Folks on the frontier were sometimes reluctant to name their animals for fear of becoming overly attached.

"Ghost-Who-Rides-Big-Horse." Luke chewed on the phrase a moment. "What do you think, Big Horse?" The big gray snorted.

"He likes it." She smiled at him. "You hungry, Lucas?" She stood beside Luke and Big Horse, reaching high to stroke the horse's muzzle. She caught Luke's eyes scanning her as she stretched upward to reach the animal's nose. The bump in her belly didn't seem to matter to him so far as her allure. She stroked his cheek and looked into Luke's eyes. "Hungry?"

"Only for you, Lisa. Only for you." He winked.

She pushed him off playfully. "You'd better wash up in any case." She loved that her man had an insatiable appetite for her. She'd always dreamed that would be the way her forever man would be.

Luke watched her walk to the cabin. Actually, it was getting to be more of a waddle as her belly grew. He prayed that he'd get to see his child or children before Rip Ford threw another assignment at him.

His Irish intuition told him something was brewing. After all, they'd not found the head of the Indian agency fraud scheme.

He released Big Horse into the corral, and the steed circled spiritedly as if to show off his freshly cleaned coat and new name. Luke drew water from the new cistern, sprinkled it on himself, and attempted to wash away the dust and stable muck of the morning's efforts from his big frame. He rubbed some flowers on himself in an attempt to hide any lingering odors. He hoped Elisa would appreciate his efforts. He made a joke to himself at how ranchers smelled of livestock and Rangers of gunpowder. He performed both roles admirably. He'd been building an enviable reputation on the Nueces Strip as a savvy cattleman and lawman. His Irish accent was even taking on a bit of Texas twang.

About this time, Whelan came riding up.

"George," Luke called, "what brings you out this way?"

"I'm headed to Corpus. Gotta witness against Thaddeus Brown's hiders standing trial."

"What's wrong?" Luke could sense something was amiss.

"It's Scarlett. She...we...had a baby girl. Named her Margaret."

Elisa heard the conversation and stepped out into the gallery. "Congratulations, George."

He dipped his chin to his chest. "She won't marry me."

Luke's eyes went wide. "Really?"

Elisa looked disconcertedly at Luke. "Men." George looked up at her. "What do you expect, George? You kill her lover and rape her in the jail. Is she supposed to instantly fall in love with you, just because the child is yours?" Elisa realized she'd revealed the secret of the jail escape that Luke had shared with her. No matter, she needed to pound some sense into Whelan's head.

"Did she tell you to leave, George?"

"No."

Luke was quick to respond. "I hear tell that sometimes women say no when they mean yes. I expect you're gonna have to work on courting her."

Elisa laughed. "He's right, George. You need to show her that you truly care for her. Show her love and respect."

Whelan's spirits lifted a bit. "I'd best be getting to business in Corpus. Thanks for the advice." He mounted up and was on his way.

"You're a wise man, Lucas Dunn."

"You mean for agreeing with you?"

She smiled and pulled him inside.

Horatio Thorpe paced the periphery of his office. His knees hurt. He knew he needed to lose weight. He assumed Roy Biggs had received his message and was already taking action. He hated anxiety. It led to eating, which increased the pressure on his tender knees. He passed by the full-length mirror in the corner. He paused just long enough to realize he needed a better-fitting suit. As he passed his desk, he picked up a slice of buttered cornbread and stuffed it in his mouth. A little melted butter dribbled out of the corner of his mouth. He kept on walking. He stopped at the office door. "Samuel, are you certain he got my message?"

"Yes, Master. I'm sure, Master."

"How can you be sure, Samuel?"

"I've already heard that he's accepted your offer and is on the road toward San Antonio, Master Thorpe."

Thorpe exhaled a puff of air in his frustration. He'd stopped smoking cigars, but this seemed like a time to resume the habit.

"Thanks, Samuel. You can go. I won't need you this afternoon."

Samuel knew what that meant. There was little that relieved the master's stress more than a choice prostitute from one of his brothels. He'd delay his departure out the back door so he wouldn't cross paths with the wench of the day.

"Ah, Monique. How good of you to come." Thorpe had already shed his coat and unbuttoned his vest. "Would you care for a drink? I've got some fine whiskey that just arrived from Kentucky." Thorpe wasn't especially refined except for his taste in whiskey and whores.

Biggs arrived at the San Antonio to Corpus Christi road roughly twenty miles south of the city. He turned southward, calculating that he'd arrived comfortably ahead of his prey. From this point on, he'd have to be especially vigilant. It simply wouldn't do to meet unexpectedly around some bend in the road. He began to scope out a place for an ambush. He had been along this stretch of road a couple of times, but the landscape seemed to be as changeable as the weather.

There it was. The spot he was looking for came into view. It was elevated and offered a clear line of fire for at least five hundred yards. Importantly, it featured a motte of live oak with branches upon which he could steady the Sharps rifle. He'd practiced shooting the Sharps at what seemed like extraordinary distances. Certainly, he'd impressed a few of his contemporaries with his marksmanship at those long ranges. He'd employed the Sharps a couple of times toward enhancing his record of killings. He was invariably surprised by the initial look of surprise on a victim's face as the deadly .50 caliber slug seemed to come silently from nowhere.

He set up a little campsite, tethering his horses just out of sight on the other side of the hill. He'd avoid building a fire, as he didn't want to tip off his location. Besides, he didn't imagine he'd have to wait but a couple of hours at most.

A lone rider approached. Biggs toyed with the idea of a practice killing to better gauge wind and distance, but decided not to chance the noise giving away his position. He watched the potential victim ride on by, oblivious of the fate that could have been.

He only had to wait another hour. He heard the approaching clopping of several horses on the hard, dirt road surface. From the volume, he judged them to be nearly within sight. He planned to get off two quick shots. He leaned the Burnside carbine against the tree. It was cocked and ready to fire. The barrel of the Sharps nestled in the crotch of a sturdy live oak branch. He slipped a round in and aimed carefully. His plan was to shoot the last rider. That would throw the riders toward the front into confusion and perhaps make them think the shot had come from behind. The rifle report would echo about enough through the low rolling hillside to make placing its direction difficult.

Biggs took careful aim and squeezed the trigger. Stodgkins' head exploded.

Biggs quickly picked up the Burnside, aimed, and fired. Johnson had a hole where his heart had been.

The prisoners were confused. Truax turned toward Brown. "What the hell is going on, Thaddeus?"

Biggs slipped another round into the Sharps, aimed, and fired.

The major would have fallen from the saddle but for the fact that he was tied in. Blood seemed to be everywhere.

"Who the hell is out there?!" Truax was scared to death. "Who…" Another bullet ended his distress. Two dead men were tied to horses that circled aimlessly.

Prisoners…if possible…thought Biggs. One prisoner might be manageable.

Brown was looking about in sheer panic. The confusion of the other horses threw his own mount into turning circles. The marshals' horses had already run off. There had to be an army out there somewhere. A train to Washington, D.C. suddenly didn't seem so bad.

Biggs calmly fetched his horses, put the rifles away in their scabbards, mounted, and headed down the hill to the road.

Brown soon enough spotted the solitary figure approaching. In moments, the two were within earshot. "Hello? Who are you?"

"Your worst enemy or best friend, depends on you, pilgrim." The vacuous steeliness of his eyes brought Thaddeus Brown to a halt. "You are now my prisoner." Biggs tied a halter line to Brown's horse.

"Where are you taking me?"

"A very safe place, Mr. Brown."

That this man knew his name took Brown by total surprise.

This had obviously been planned by someone that knew what was happening. The general and major had simply been loose ends. Brown was apparently perceived as having some value. He was about to ask another question.

"It you care to live, Mr. Brown, you will not utter another word." Biggs rode up next to Brown. They stared eyeball to eyeball. Brown blinked first. Biggs wrapped a blindfold over the man's eyes.

They began the trek westward back toward the hacienda. Biggs would await further directions for the disposal of Brown.

FOURTEEN

Evil Ends

L uke was out on the ranch herding some stray cattle when a rider approached at a full gallop. The Walker Colt quickly found its way into Luke's hand.

"Captain Dunn! Don't shoot!" The rider came to an abrupt stop. "I've got a message from Mr. Ford."

This was a dreaded moment for Luke. He'd had a couple of weeks of re-familiarizing himself with Heaven's Gate and fattening up on Elisa's cooking. "Come in slowly." He holstered the revolver.

"Yes, sir." The rider approached and extended an envelope to Luke. He was taken aback a bit by the Ranger's size. "Now I understand why they refer to you as Long Luke back in Austin," he commented.

Luke cocked his head. "Long Luke, heh? I've gotten used to what the Comanche call me." He took the message.

"What's that, sir?"

Luke absent-mindedly opened the envelope and began reading. "They call me Ghost-Who-Rides." He finished reading. The assignment was to capture or kill Roy Biggs. It briefly explained that Biggs had killed two U.S. marshals and all their prisoners two weeks earlier but for Thaddeus Brown, who might have escaped or been taken prisoner.

"Must be the horse, sir." The man offered a friendly smile. "You're certainly no ghost."

"Tell Mr. Ford that I'll take care of this. Ask him how many Texas Rangers he'll give me." Luke knew it was a rhetorical question.

"Sir?"

"Just joking. But do give him my regards." Luke had heard rumors of Roy Biggs' hacienda and knew of the man's reputation. This would entail a far different strategy than tracking outlaws like Bart Strong and Dirk Cavendish across the Nueces Strip.

With Colonel Rucker returned to Austin and George Whelan tied up with sheriff duties in Corpus Christi, Luke was in a bit of a dilemma. In the first place, no one knew where Biggs' hacienda actually was. It was surely heavily fortified. It had been nearly two weeks since Biggs' successful ambush up near San Antonio, so any trail would be stone cold.

He resigned himself to having to tell Elisa in any case. She'd be none too happy.

Thaddeus Brown tried to memorize the sound of the horse's hooves on the terrain along which he was being led. He soon realized that Biggs was making wide circles every few miles designed to confuse his prisoner. All Brown could be certain of was that the countryside was fairly hilly. He tilted his head back in an attempt to peek under the bottom of the blindfold. Biggs saw him try that, rode over beside him, and didn't say a word. Brown could feel Biggs' horse alongside. The outlaw rapped the side of his head with a pistol butt. Brown felt the warmth of blood tricking down from his temple. He wouldn't try peeking again.

The ground eventually seemed to level out. He could feel the sun bearing down on him from his left, so he knew they were heading west. He sensed that they might be on the northern edge of the Nueces

Strip, part of what some folks called the Wild Horse Desert.

They'd ridden for three days. Biggs had spoken nary a word. The nights were getting cooler as appropriate to the coming onset of winter. Biggs had given Brown occasional chews of dried beef and drinks of water during the ride. The prisoner had already wet his trousers. Brown couldn't know that Biggs laughed inwardly at so humbling a situation.

At last, Biggs brought them to a halt. He rode up beside Brown's horse and lifted the blindfold. "Damn, but you stink." He offered up a venomous smile, barely hidden by the bandana he was holding over his nose. "By the way, my name is Roy Biggs." He pulled away and pointed ahead of them.

Brown blinked as the sudden light nearly blinded him. Before him was a massive structure. So this was the famous hacienda of the notorious Roy Biggs.

"So, Thaddeus, my friend, did you bring the key to those manacles?" It was Biggs' idea of a joke. He rode over and began unlocking Brown's shackles. "Welcome to Twin Creeks. You're going to be here for a few days, Thaddeus. Feel free to explore, but stay out of the living quarters. If you go in there, you will surely die."

He offered a wry, almost diabolical grin, as though it would be his pleasure to kill Brown. "Oh, and don't even think of escaping." He pointed down toward a ravine to Brown's left. There, bones bleaching in the sun, hung the crucified remains of what were apparently previous attempted escapees. He counted eight skeletons in various stages of decomposition. One was fresh. Clearly, part of Biggs' income was derived from detaining those deemed undesirable by his powerful employers.

Brown had heard of Biggs and his reputation. He figured that whoever Truax got his orders from saw some value in keeping him alive.

"Do you know who General Truax worked for?" It was a simple question.

"No."

Biggs believed him. Brown was vulnerable. There would be no point in his lying. He pointed Brown to the livery. "You can stable your horse over there. Dinner will be in a couple of hours. You'll eat with my men. The stable boy will direct you." It was all quite well-ordered.

Biggs might have seemed a madman to many, but he was not crazy in the sense of being a loose cannon. He may have been heartless and cruel in his chosen profession, but he also managed an organization. As if in blatant contradiction, he had a family that he apparently cared for and even loved, at least within the limitations of whatever love he could offer. He certainly protected them, at least so far as it suited his ends.

Brown watched as Biggs rode over to an outbuilding and began to talk with one of the men loitering outside. Whatever he said caused the man to immediately run to the stable, saddle a horse, and ride out.

Lieutenant Belknap was getting frustrated. It was so obvious that his men could readily see it in his day-to-day demeanor. He was going through the motions. He itched to get back out chasing Comanche. He hadn't joined the Army to hang around doing chores at a frontier fort.

"Sir, the commandant has requested you report to him." The corporal was just a little hesitant, given the lieutenant's recent mood swings.

Belknap thought about snipping at the poor messenger, but thought better of it. It was close living quarters at Fort Inge, and they all had to live together at some level of military civility. He half-saluted the corporal, grabbed his saber and revolver, put on his campaign hat, strode over to the commandant's cabin, and knocked on the door.

"Come in, Lieutenant."

Belknap walked in, came to attention, and saluted. "Reporting as ordered, sir."

"At ease, Mr. Belknap."

The more familiar address threw Belknap off a bit. He relaxed his stance.

The major was holding an official-looking brown packet. "I received these orders today from U.S. Army Texas Headquarters. Upon consideration of you being obviously quite anxious to be out scouting for trouble on the Comancheria, I am giving you this assignment. It will truly test your mettle, Lieutenant Belknap."

Belknap fidgeted. He was getting impatient to know what the major was proposing.

"Lieutenant, you are to assemble a troop of twenty-four men. Requisition a cannon with appropriate ammunition and three weeks of rations. You will hunt and capture a man named Roy Biggs and his captive, Thaddeus Brown. Brown is a federal fugitive and Biggs is wanted for killing two U.S. marshals and two U.S. Army officers." Belknap's eyes grew wide. This was a career-making assignment. "You will rendezvous with Texas Ranger Captain Luke Dunn in San Diego." He had Belknap's undivided attention. Then, he dropped a bomb. "Captain Dunn is in charge of this mission."

The air audibly escaped from Belknap's lungs.

"There's more. You may be joined by a certain Penateka Comanche chief you are intimately acquainted with."

"Three Toes, sir?"

The major smiled. "Perhaps you can learn his ways." His smile broadened. "But not all of them."

"Thank you, sir." Belknap was apprehensive at the thought of working under a Texas Ranger, but had heard about Luke's reputation. On the upside, this would be an experience in living on the edge danger-wise. His pulse quickened at the thought of it. He returned the major's salute and hurried out to gather a troop. He did wonder what the cannon was for.

FOURTEEN | EVIL ENDS

"I heard from Rip Ford."

The words sent a chill through Elisa. She knew what the phrase meant. Luke would be away. It conjured many questions, but two were most important. Would he return safely? Would he return before she gave birth? "Must you go?" It was the first time she'd offered even a hint of resistance.

Luke was deeply conflicted. He knew this might very well be his toughest assignment yet. "I'll make it back in time." He tried to be reassuring.

Doubt hung in the air. Elisa didn't have a good feeling about this. A rapping on the gallery post interrupted their conversation barely after its beginning.

Luke peeked out from the window. "Dang, Lisa, it's Three Toes."

Sure enough, there he was in his full Comanche splendor, lacking only the warpaint. He was tapping his lance hard against the post trying to get a response. "Ghost-Who-Rides, come out."

Luke shrugged and stepped onto the gallery. "Chief, you're making a lot of noise." He gave a friendly grin. "Welcome, Three Toes. Are you hungry?"

"It is good to see you, brother." Three Toes dismounted and jumped up onto the gallery. "Yes, I'm hungry." He grasped Luke's hand, and then proceeded to sit on the edge of the gallery. "I eat here."

Like many of his race, Three Toes had an aversion to being enclosed by solid walls. The outdoors was vastly preferable.

Elisa glanced out the window. "Luke, let's eat outside."

Luke caught her drift. "Great idea." He pulled over a couple of chairs. "So, what brings you here, Chief? And where is the warrior who was with you?"

"I was called to be here." He ignored the second question. There wasn't any point, as the warrior hadn't been able to accommodate Three Toes' spiritual journey, his vision quest, and went back to Camp Cooper.

Luke wasn't surprised. "Your return is well-timed." He stared intently at the chief. "I was getting ready to try to find you." He reflected a moment on how difficult that was going to be on the vastness of the Nueces Strip prairie.

Elisa appeared with coffee and three plates stacked with eggs, bacon, and biscuits. "Hope you brought your appetite."

Three Toes' eyes grew wide at the sight of Elisa's growing belly. He looked back over at Luke. "You going to have two."

She smiled. The chief's word was like a final assurance. He had further confirmed the increasingly obvious.

"Where do we go, Ghost-Who-Rides?"

He hadn't even shared the mission with Elisa. "We are meeting with a troop of U.S. Army soldiers from Fort Inge. We'll be bringing Roy Biggs to justice."

The name was lost on the chief.

Even Elisa had not heard it before. "Who is Roy Biggs?"

"As I understand it, he's likely the most evil outlaw on the planet. He's killed more than forty people that we know of. Most recently, he killed two U.S. marshals and most of their prisoners. That's a federal offense. The prisoners were being escorted to stand trial for cheating the government."

Elisa asked the obvious. "Why so many men?"

"He lives in a large hacienda called Twin Creeks somewhere north of Laredo. It's very well defended and almost impossible to get close to."

"How do you propose to defeat him?" she asked.

Luke looked just a tad perplexed. "Working on that. We'll need to lure him out."

That didn't allay Elisa's concerns. She silently dug at her breakfast.

"We'll meet the soldiers at San Diego day after tomorrow."

"Who is in command?" Elisa and Three Toes asked nearly in unison.

"Mr. Ford assured me that I'll be in charge." It was the only way the mission had a prayer of succeeding with a wet-behind-the-ears, fresh-out-of-school officer leading the troop. From what Luke had heard, there wasn't a single U.S. Army officer in Texas that was the measure of a Comanche or a strong civilian force. It boiled down to style. The military fought a certain way, and the outlaws and Indians fought another way. The military were painfully slow to adapt to guerilla-style battle strategies.

"What you know about this man Biggs?" Three Toes was beginning to get into the challenge of the hunt.

"He's not a very big man. I understand he's an excellent marksman. He mostly works from ambush. He's said to be heartless, except that he has one vulnerability. He has a wife and children."

That got Elisa'a attention. "I wonder whether they spend all of their time in the hacienda?"

Three Toes understood where her thinking was going. "If we could capture his family…"

"We need to find the hacienda first." Luke gave an apologetic glance to the chief for interrupting him. "We are time-limited. At some point, he's going to move the prisoner…or kill him."

Elisa had resigned herself to her lawman husband's mission. "Let me help get you ready to travel." She took the empty plates and went back into the cabin. She leaned with her back against the door and had herself a bit of a cry. Then she began loading Luke's saddlebag.

Too quickly for Elisa, Luke had Big Horse ready to travel. He brought the horse around to the front of the cabin and went inside.

She was standing in front of the bed with his saddlebags hanging from her hands. He turned her toward him. He could see the faint trace of tears on her cheeks. "I love you, Lisa." He took her in his arms, and they kissed deeply. The saddlebags dropped to the floor.

Too soon, Luke and Three Toes were headed westward toward San Diego. With any luck, the soldiers would have arrived.

Biggs' wife was growing restless. "Roy, when are we going to San

Antonio again?" She had been getting more demanding lately.

He figured she must be pregnant again. "Soon. I must finish this business." He knew being dismissive wasn't a great strategy, but he was impatiently awaiting word from Thorpe on what to do with the prisoner.

"You never pay attention to me anymore."

He'd endured this prattle before. But for the children, he'd be done with her when she was like this. He was uncomfortable with this side of his life, as it required that he at least fake being vulnerable. He hated being vulnerable. He'd built his reputation on being cold, calculating, and utterly invulnerable. Everything he touched was touched with death, except for his family. "We'll get to San Antonio, Maria. I promise."

She shook out her dark hair. It was naturally curly and hung in rippling waves to her waist. She was full-bodied, exuding an allure that had fully penetrated his hard exterior. She loved and hated what he was, yet he drew her like a magnet. She dropped the filmy negligee and stood exposed before him.

He didn't disappoint her.

He'd barely fallen asleep when he heard a commotion in the courtyard. He pulled on his trousers and boots, grabbed his guns, and hurried in the direction of the noise.

He flung open the door from the living quarters. "What's going on?"

Brown was being held by two men who were taking turns punching him.

Biggs gave an inquisitive look. "Stop. What's he done?"

"Got too close to your space, Mr. Biggs."

"Well, stop hitting him. I haven't heard what to do with him, and I don't want to ruin this merchandise. String him up outside at the pole."

Brown took a couple of deep breaths. If he didn't know before that Biggs meant business on what was off limits, he certainly knew now.

This post sounded better than being beaten.

"And strip him."

The men smiled. "The usual, Mr. Biggs?"

"Honey on his balls? No. Not this time."

Brown's eyes grew especially wide. It wasn't hard to envision what ants attracted by honey would do to him. This Biggs fellow was not to be underestimated.

A lone rider was permitted entry to the hacienda. He had a message for Biggs. His mount was well-lathered.

Biggs was concerned about taking good care of his horses, so hoped the rider's message was worth having abused the beast. The rider drew his attention from Brown, who was dragged off to the punishment post in the courtyard. "What's your news?"

"Mr. Biggs, I saw a troop of twenty-four soldiers with cannon marching to San Diego."

Biggs knew that was a couple of days' ride from the hacienda. "Why should I be concerned with this news?"

"A friend at Fort Inge told me they'd be hunting for you."

Now that was news. "Hunting for me?" He laughed. Nothing new there. Many hunted for him, but to see the hacienda was to die. Only Biggs' most trusted men knew the location. The skeletons bore silent testament to the uninvited who'd found the hacienda. "Thank you." He looked over at the now strung-up Thaddeus Brown. The ignominy of his situation had been fully borne out, as Brown relieved himself there and could do nothing about it.

Biggs had second thoughts. Brown had surely learned his lesson. "Let him loose and give him his clothes. Be sure he cleans his mess." He turned to go back into the living quarters, while speaking to Brown over his shoulder. "Oh, Mr. Brown, the next time will be much more unpleasant. Know your place."

"Lieutenant! Riders approaching." Belknap's troop had barely begun to set up camp just west of San Diego when the two riders were seen approaching.

"Let them pass, soldier. Let them pass."

"But one's an Indian, sir."

"I can see him. And the Texas Ranger."

Luke, with Three Toes beside him, soon pulled up to where Belknap was standing. Luke tipped his hat, as was the custom on the range. "Lieutenant Belknap, I presume?" Luke dismounted. He noted the soldiers unloading equipment. "Lieutenant, we've no time to be making camp."

"You must be Captain Dunn." He didn't know whether to salute or offer to shake hands. He did the latter. "My men are tired, Captain. I thought to give them some rest."

"We don't have time to rest, Lieutenant. Roy Biggs isn't resting."

"Do you know where this hacienda of his is, Captain?" He looked round. The Comanche had disappeared.

"See that tumbleweed over there tumbling west?"

Belknap looked at Luke with utter incredulity. "You can't be serious."

"Just joking, Lieutenant. Got a rough idea where the hacienda is. My friend Three Toes has been through the territory where it's supposed to be located. He's a fine tracker." Luke paused for effect. He read the disconcerted look on Belknap's face. "Don't worry. He won't scalp you."

"He's had his chances, Captain." Belknap ordered the sergeant to have the men repack their gear.

"Ride lead with me, Lieutenant. I'll tell you what I have in mind."

Within a few minutes, the soldiers were moving forward in a column of twos. There was a little grumbling, but mostly out of concern for whom this Texas Ranger was and a touch of fear over the prospect of what might lie ahead.

"What's our plan, Captain?"

"First, lose all your notions of what makes a fair fight. We may resort to methods that would make a Comanche blush. Roy Biggs is a very evil man who has been successful at his craft because he's meticulously careful. However, we understand that he's got one important vulnerability."

"Captain?"

"His family." Luke let that sink in. "The next question you might ask, Lieutenant, is how do we get to Biggs' family. I don't know yet."

That answer didn't give Belknap any sense of confidence. "You don't know, sir?"

"Trust me, Lieutenant. These things have a way of working out. First, we want to capture Thaddeus Brown. Since the man didn't show up in Austin, we have been led to understand that he's being kept in Biggs' hacienda." Luke looked off into the distance, where he could barely make out Three Toes' silhouette waving him on. "We're gonna fool him, Lieutenant. We're gonna fool him." End of conversation. He spurred the big gray to pick up their pace.

Three Toes found himself about a mile and a half ahead of Luke and the soldiers. He shook his head at the thought of the bluecoats' cannon that was slowing them down. The chief rode to the crest of a rise above a meandering dry creek bed.

Off to his right, he spotted a lone rider. From the pace and westerly direction, he judged that he could continue westward and easily intersect the rider's path. He drove his heels into his pony's flanks and galloped ahead toward setting a trap. He found several mottes of live oak on either side of the trail and quickly discovered a pair that would be perfect. He strung a line across the trail and waited. He wouldn't have to wait long.

Only a couple of minutes later, the rider came into sight. He was riding hard, and it was too late when he saw the rope across his path. It hit across his chest, knocking him clean off his horse. He hit the ground hard enough to knock the wind from him.

Three Toes was on him in a heartbeat, tying the man's hands behind his back.

The horse came trotting back. The man was beginning to get his wind back. Three Toes reached the man's horse and began to open the saddlebag.

The man gasped. "No, please, no." It hadn't yet dawned on him that he was dealing with a Comanche chief, and his scalp was at risk.

Three Toes looked back at the man and scowled. He made a cutting motion across his own hairline. He turned back and reached into the saddlebag. He pulled out an envelope.

The man became nearly apoplectic. It was readily obvious to Three Toes that the envelope must contain something very important. This man was clearly some sort of courier.

The man struggled to get up, but Three Toes pushed him back down. "You stay." The chief climbed back onto his pony, pointed his lance at the courier, and waited for Luke to come into view.

Luke and his military entourage had been riding nearly nonstop for two days and were beginning to enter countryside that was a bit more hilly. He had begun to worry that they were too visible. The soldiers with their flags and blue uniforms with yellow accoutrements stood out too well.

"Lieutenant, I've been thinking. We have far more men and firepower than I think we're going to need. I don't anticipate a frontal assault on Biggs' hacienda. In fact, my hope is to accomplish this mission without losing any of our men." He had Belknap's undivided attention. "I propose that we divide your troop, leaving half of them back here. The cannon are slowing us down, and I don't think we need them." He gave Belknap an earnest look. "Lieutenant, do your men have any clothing other than those bluecoats?"

"No, sir. Why do you ask?"

"I thought not. Guess we'll just have to deal with it." As he finished the sentence, he saw Three Toes off in the distance motioning for Luke to join him. The chief was mounted with a riderless horse beside him.

"Stay here, Lieutenant." Luke galloped the five hundred yards or so over to where the chief was waiting.

"What's h…" He looked down. The chief had a nervously shaking captive who was obviously quite frightened.

Three Toes handed Luke a large envelope.

He opened it with great care and anticipation. Inside was money and a note. "Seems we've gotten lucky, Chief. This man is a courier to Roy Biggs with instructions as to what to do with Mr. Brown. I wonder who is connected with the initials H.T.? Let's see if the courier will help us."

Luke dismounted and looked down at the courier. He appeared to be of Mexican descent. *"Como se llamo? Comprendo Inglés?"*

"My name is Bill." That answered the second question, too.

"Will you lead us to Biggs?"

"You can't be serious. He'd kill me certain."

"So will we." Luke held a gun on the man while Three Toes drove stakes into the ground. The man watched with considerable trepidation. He'd long since gotten his wind back, but he was helpless in the face of Luke's gun. He was soon stripped and tied spread eagle to the stakes. "Do you know what Comanche do to captives, Bill?"

About this time, Belknap caught up with Luke and Three Toes. Upon seeing what they were doing, he was horrified. "You can't do this, Captain."

"I told you this wasn't going to be a fair fight, Lieutenant. Stand down."

Luke nodded to Three Toes, who pulled out his knife and made a superficial but painful cut down the center of the man's chest from throat to navel. "Ever seen a longhorn bull castrated, Bill?"

The now wild-eyed man strained at his bonds. "If you help us, we'll spare you this fate and even let you go when we get close to Biggs' hacienda."

Belknap winced and turned away as Three Toes' knife hovered over the man's privates.

"Yes! Yes, I'll help!" The man looked pleadingly at Luke.

"Get dressed." Three Toes cut the ties and threw the clothes at him. They tied his hands again and put him on his horse.

"Was that necessary, Captain?" Belknap had nearly thrown up at the sight.

"It worked, Lieutenant. We are in a hurry. It worked quite well. Recall that I told you this isn't in any of your military manuals."

Luke maneuvered over to the courier. Despite being tied up, oozing blood on the front of his shirt, and scared half to death, he was ready to help. "How far are we, Bill?"

"Half-day without your cannon." Luke was surprised at how close they were. He knew the lieutenant heard the courier's comment about the cannon.

"Does Biggs know you?"

"He's seen me once or twice."

"Would anyone in the hacienda know you?" Luke pressed.

"No. Mr. Biggs doesn't let us get to know each other much."

"Is there any secret password?"

"No," Bill answered.

Luke looked over at Three Toes. "If you're lying, I'm going to give you to my Comanche chief friend here."

The courier gave a frightened glance at Three Toes. "No, there's no password."

"Lieutenant, leave eight men and the cannon here. We've got to move out right quick." Luke scanned the troop. "Lieutenant, we can't send the courier ahead given his condition. I need one of your bigger men to volunteer to take the courier's place. Dress him in my spare shirt and take the courier's hat and horse. He'll wear no military equipment."

Belknap understood Luke's plan, and one of his men volunteered and dressed up as the courier.

Luke and Belknap rode off out of earshot. "Lieutenant, if this goes according to plan, Biggs will send Brown out with an escort to Austin. We can intercept him easily, and you'll have fulfilled part of your mission. Once we have Brown in our hands, we can bring the rest of your troop forward and see if we can draw Biggs out. Frankly, I'd hate to see his family get hurt. We've been very lucky so far, but luck is a flimsy ally."

Belknap nodded. "Captain, I don't understand the Comanche. I've encountered him twice before. The first time, he was headed to his people at Camp Cooper. The second time, he successfully attacked me and my men but spared a couple of us. Why?"

"The Comanche have long memories, Lieutenant. They remember favors and slights. He must have respected you enough to spare your life. So long as you respect him, your scalp is safe." Luke suppressed a grin. "Understand?"

"I think so."

"Lieutenant, someday when you're off fighting Indians somewhere, this will make sense. Remember that they are human and are protecting their way of life. I for one think there's a way to live peacefully with them, though we must also be willing to defend ourselves. Ultimately, the frontier will push them out of their territory. It's survival of the fittest. It's brutal, Lieutenant, but it's the way it is." He was tempted to share his own story of being pushed out of Ireland by the British. More advanced civilizations seemed to supplant lesser ones. It was the way of the real world. Attempts to prevent this phenomenon invariably failed.

They followed roughly a quarter-mile behind the soldier dressed as the courier. Every now and then he'd look back toward the prisoner to be certain he was headed in the right direction. Luke was concerned that Biggs would have some sort of lookout system to warn of impending trouble. Three Toes stayed closer at hand but still ahead of Luke and the soldiers.

They'd ridden for a couple of hours when the disguised soldier was approached by two heavily armed men on horseback. They spoke animatedly. One of the men remained on lookout while the other rode on next to the disguised man they thought was a courier.

One of the armed men relieved the disguised courier of the envelope and sent him on his way. Apparently, he wouldn't be allowed to see where the hacienda was. As the soldier began to ride away, one of the armed men fell back, waited for his partner to disappear with the envelope, raised his rifle, and began to take aim.

Three Toes had quietly ridden to a position behind some trees. The armed man just got his shot off as he took an arrow through his throat and slid in a heap from the saddle. But the damage had been done; the soldier fell mortally wounded. The chief rode over to where Biggs' man lay. Once again, he was tempted to take a scalp, but held back. He motioned Luke and the soldiers on. The track to the hacienda wouldn't be hard to follow.

Luke now knew that they were close to Twin Creeks. He turned to the courier. "I promised you your life. Don't make me regret it. You are free to go."

Horatio Thorpe figured he might yet make use of Thaddeus Brown. He had an impressive array of connections for selling his illicitly acquired goods and was a good judge of merchandise value.

He impatiently awaited the completion of the transaction with Biggs. The entire deed had cost Thorpe more than two thousand dollars, and Brown hadn't been delivered yet. Too much could still go wrong. At least, with Truax gone, it would be nearly impossible to trace anything back to Thorpe.

Roy Biggs spotted his man on the horizon riding in at a fast pace. He was anxious to get paid as well as to rid himself of Thaddeus Brown. On the other hand, he wondered why he was riding alone.

He realized that, in their anxiousness to please him, his men had fallen prey to stupidity and inadvertently revealed the location of his hacienda. He lifted the Sharps rifle into position. Punishment was swift.

Luke and the soldiers caught the report of a large bore rifle in the distance. "Someone's fired a big rifle." They'd no sooner heard the shot than Three Toes appeared. He rode over to Luke.

"Ghost-Who-Rides, the soldier has been killed," he whispered.

Luke turned grimly to Belknap. "Terribly sorry, Lieutenant, your man has apparently been killed."

Belknap's initial reaction was to want to charge at the hacienda that couldn't be very far away.

"Hold your fire, Lieutenant. We're going to wait here and see what develops." It was a sternly delivered command.

Belknap's face turned a deep crimson with seething anger. This wasn't the sort of fighting he'd been taught.

"Send one of your men back to fetch the rest of your troop and the cannon." Luke was purposely ignoring Belknap's emotional reaction.

Cautiously, they followed the trail made by Biggs' man. It wended its way through what passed for forest in that part of Texas. Soon enough, they came upon an open expanse and Biggs' hacienda came into view. This was Twin Creeks. At the forest edge, Three Toes halted. "Turn back, Ghost-Who-Rides." At his feet was Biggs' armed thug. There was no envelope to be seen, but there was a large wound in the man. If he'd been shot from the hacienda, Biggs' reputation as a marksman was intact.

Luke noted that the area around Biggs' hacienda had been cleared for a considerable line of sight. There was no way they could approach without being seen.

FIFTEEN

The Hacienda

Perhaps an hour passed. They watched Thaddeus Brown being escorted from the hacienda. Brown was guarded by two of Biggs' men. They rode in a northeasterly direction toward Austin. It didn't take long for them to cover the ground from the hacienda and into the wooded hills. Luke was surprised that they weren't heavily armed. Something didn't quite smell right to him.

"Lieutenant, when your men get back here with the cannon, set up camp a couple of miles back in the hills. I'd be surprised if Biggs hasn't been told that troops are nearby. He likely doesn't know how close we are. Just keep a low profile and don't do anything that will attract attention."

"What if Biggs leaves the hacienda?"

Luke had to think a moment on that one. "If you think you can take him, go for it, but I don't think we'll be long capturing our friend Mr. Brown."

Soon enough, Luke and Three Toes were hot on the trail of Brown and the escorts. It was already late afternoon, and they fully expected their prey to stop for the night.

Luke was surprised that the trio rode another two hours before they made camp. It was near a creek with plenty of low-lying tree cover. From the look of it, they weren't even setting up any sentries. They ate and drank a bit and told a few jokes. This was far too easy.

Darkness seemed to come on quickly. "Three Toes, let's move in close and wait for them to sleep."

Luke heard the cocking of the hammer of a rifle behind him. "You that damned Ranger everyone's been talking about?" Luke froze. "You turn real slow-like and drop your guns."

In the dim light, Luke couldn't make out who it might be. "I think Mr. Biggs is gonna be right happy to see you, Mr. Texas Ranger."

Apparently, Biggs had learned the trick of adding a trailer escort, a man that followed well behind a traveling group so as to pick up anyone tracking them. Luke had fallen into the trap. Question was, where was Three Toes? Luke dropped his weapons per the man's order.

"You be a big sonofabitch. Don't go making any sudden moves." The man looked beyond at the men around the campfire. "Hey, Jim, lookee what I got!"

Three Toes nocked an arrow, aimed, and let it fly. The wound was mortal but not quickly enough to keep his target from getting off a shot. The bullet grazed Luke's shoulder, but the noise startled the men around the campfire.

Luke picked up his Walker Colt. He had to be careful not to shoot Thaddeus Brown. One of the men had a thick beard. Brown had no beard. The bearded man started shooting in the dark at nothing in particular. Luke took careful aim at the man, squeezed the trigger, and dropped him.

Brown and the second escort stopped shooting and raised their hands in surrender. "Don't shoot. We give up!"

Luke moved in. His shoulder wound was painful and bleeding, but it wasn't slowing him down. "Mr. Brown, it's a pleasure to meet again."

While Three Toes held Brown and the other man at bay with his bow and arrow, Luke manacled the two men and tied them to a tree for the night.

The chief prepared a poultice for Luke's shoulder. It stopped the bleeding and alleviated the pain enough to enjoy the meal Brown and his escorts had prepared. "You still have strong medicine, Ghost-Who-Rides." Truth be told, Luke's good fortune and strong medicine had been having Three Toes nearby. "Your woman will not be happy with your shirt, my friend."

Luke realized they had literally dodged a bullet. If the man hadn't been thrown off by Three Toes' arrow, the outcome might not have gone so well. "We'd better be more careful. We best not underestimate this man Biggs."

"Hey, Captain?" Thaddeus Brown called out from the edge of the darkness, "where you taking us?"

"If it were up to me, Mr. Brown, you'd be meeting your Maker. As it is, we're taking you back to jail."

"Just you and the redskin?"

"Three Toes? He's a Comanche chief, Mr. Brown. You'd better treat him with respect." Luke looked at the man with knitted brows. "And, as to your fate, you're going to be escorted by a troop of soldiers. Likely as not, they'll hand you over to a U.S. marshal in San Antonio."

Brown smiled sardonically. "They'll never get me there."

Lieutenant Belknap stared out into the brisk morning air with a degree of wonderment. A stagecoach, an old Concord model with leather springs, had departed the hacienda. There were six horses pulling with three outriders as armed guards. There was a driver and a man with a long gun.

Belknap couldn't know that Biggs was sending his wife off for shopping in San Antonio. The lieutenant needed to make a decision. Somebody important was quite possibly in that stagecoach. The rest of his troop had arrived with the cannon, and he clearly had a numbers and firepower advantage.

"Sergeant, form up the men."

The military art of mounted soldiers, or what was called cavalry, had not been perfected in the U.S. Army. The standard strategy was to dismount and form battle lines. Only what were called dragoons remained mounted. In this case, these were mounted infantry and would be up against a very mobile enemy. Dismounting was going to place them at a distinct disadvantage. The sergeant shook his head but followed orders.

Moments later, the stagecoach came barreling along the road from the hacienda. The outriders saw the ambush and strove to turn the stagecoach away from the danger.

"Fire!" A volley of gunfire riddled the air. Nobody fell.

The outriders returned fire, hitting a couple of soldiers.

"Fire at will!" The soldiers fired as the stagecoach hurried to get out of rifle range. One of the guards was shot from his saddle, and another soldier fell.

The stagecoach disappeared in a cloud of dust just as Luke and Three Toes arrived on the scene. Luke looked around and got uncharacteristically angry. He directed his ire at Belknap. "Why the hell aren't your men mounted and pursuing?" Luke shook his head in dismay. The stagecoach already had a considerable head start.

Three Toes rode over to Luke. "The wagon was empty."

"What do you mean?" Luke cooled for the moment.

"It rides light. It carries no load."

Luke was amazed at Three Toes' powers of observation. "A decoy?" He turned back to the officer. "My apologies, Lieutenant. It appears you not chasing the stagecoach may work to our advantage."

Belknap was relieved that Three Toes had kept them all from falling for Biggs' ruse. "You were correct, Captain, about me not following the standard military strategy."

"Back in County Kildare, we learned these sorts of tricks,

Lieutenant. We were vastly outnumbered by the Redcoats and had no choice but to resort to trickery. It was a matter of self-preservation. Now, we'll wait to see what Roy Biggs' next move might be." He glanced around. The sergeant was getting the troop back in order. "How many of these men did you say have been in a battle, Lieutenant?"

"Perhaps four or five, Captain. We've got three men wounded, but they say they're ready to keep fighting."

Luke appreciated the men's fighting spirit. "Well, they're going to learn a lot before some spit-and-polish know-it-all unteaches them. What they're learning here will serve them all well." Luke gazed thoughtfully in the direction of the hacienda. "Lieutenant, I think it's time to start flushing out Roy Biggs, to force him to show his hand. We'll conduct what you military folk might call a pincer movement. Have your sergeant go with Three Toes and six men around to the north of the hacienda. Keep a small group here to man the cannon. You and I will take six men and circle around to the south of the hacienda. Hopefully, we'll be able to respond to whatever Biggs has in mind. If we can, we need to capture whatever emerges."

The shooting of the decoy stagecoach had been heard back in the hacienda. Biggs smiled with satisfaction. His hunch had been correct. He thought there might be a threat near the hacienda and sent out the decoy. If all went according to plan, the attackers would pursue the stagecoach into an ambush. He looked forward to their return.

Meanwhile, he readied a second stagecoach with his wife and children onboard. While confusion reigned in the surrounding hills, they'd sneak out the back way.

He laughed confidently at how easily the soldiers had been fooled. Pity he never asked himself why it was so easy. His ego had begun to get in the way of his judgment.

He kissed his wife and children good-bye and sent them on their way. There was always a risk, but he felt he'd done his best to limit it.

He wished Maria wasn't so insistent about shopping in San Antonio.

The stagecoach emerged from the back entrance of the hacienda and headed northward toward Three Toes' position. The six-horse team had a driver and one guard with no outriders.

As the stagecoach lumbered beyond the edge of the cleared area, Biggs' final view was of some Indian shooting an arrow into the driver. The guard was shot from his seat by a couple of soldiers. In seemingly no time, his wife and children were in mortal danger.

Biggs' wife struggled to fend off the soldiers and protect her children. She looked back pleadingly at the hacienda. Squirming to no avail, she and her children fast became captives. "Please, please… help!"

Biggs flushed with rage as he called for his men to mount up. He'd been caught in a spider web he'd woven himself. As he prepared to charge out and rescue his wife, one of his men pointed to the southwestern horizon. Luke and more soldiers had circled from the south and were headed to rendezvous with the stage.

The soldiers with the cannon watched with excited fascination as events unfolded before them. The corporal decided to unlimber the cannon. Biggs reflexively ducked as a cannonball whistled over his head, followed by the booming report that echoed around Twin Creeks.

Luke pulled up near Three Toes' position. He sent Belknap on to have the cannon cease firing. It was time to parlay. "Sergeant, tie the woman up spread-eagled to the stagecoach wheel in full view of the hacienda." The two young children clung tightly to their mother's legs.

Biggs watched helplessly from a parapet. Another cannonball blasted into the hacienda wall, spraying stone chips and dust.

"Three Toes, take out your knife and threaten the woman."

Luke tied a white kerchief to the muzzle of his rifle and rode toward the hacienda. He saw the business end of Biggs' Sharps rifle poked out through a slot in the parapet. Luke already knew of Biggs' skill at long-range ambush, so he slowed Big Horse to a cautious walk. "Biggs! Biggs! Do you hear me?"

"Come any closer, you sonofabitch, and I'll blow your head clean off your body."

"Do you know who that Indian is?" Luke yelled.

"Should I give a damn?"

"He's a Penateka Comanche chief name of Three Toes. Do you know what Comanche do to women and children?"

Biggs fired a shot purposely aimed at narrowly missing Luke. "You wouldn't dare!"

Luke raised one hand toward Three Toes. His knife cut through the length of the bodice of Biggs' wife's dress, leaving her chest exposed. "You ready to surrender?"

Biggs aimed over Luke's head. He squeezed the trigger, and a .50 caliber slug blasted through his wife's chest. An evil smile crossed his face as he shouted, "You can have my damned wife!" He turned the muzzle toward Luke, who spurred Big Horse out of harm's way in the nick of time as another slug pierced the air too close for comfort.

Luke made a zig-zag ride back to the stage. "Clear out, get out of range!" As he sped by, he took in the image of Biggs' wife slumped from the wheel with blood pouring from a gaping wound. The children were crying inconsolably. Luke thought to grab them, but another bullet from Biggs' Sharps rifle whizzed by. Realizing he was being shot at by a cold-blooded maniacal killer who had just killed his own wife and disowned his children, Luke took off in retreat after the others.

Seeing the action at the hacienda, Belknap again unlimbered the cannon at the parapet. The crew fired as quickly as they could load. The top ten feet or so of the parapet were quickly reduced to rubble. A cheer went up from the cannoneers.

Biggs appeared on a second parapet. His aim was true, and a cannoneer's laughter was silenced.

They took aim at the second parapet. Before they could fire, a second soldier fell. Belknap dismounted and lit the fuse. A huge chunk of the parapet was reduced to rubble. A bullet ricocheted off the cannon barrel and through Belknap's left arm. He crumpled in pain.

The weapons Luke and the men with him had were useless at the distance where they found themselves. They'd have to get closer. They had to divert Biggs' attention. Luke signaled Belknap to pull back while they reconsidered their situation.

Biggs was hunkered down with a half-dozen of his men. They'd wait until nightfall to make their next move. He should have been lamenting what he'd done to his wife and worrying about his children, but his stone-cold heart could only see his next diabolically contrived move.

The tunnel was dark and dank. The air was thick. Biggs had only used it once before, to test it out. He and his men had to hunker down, but every hundred yards or so was a place they could stand upright and rest. They were standing in one of those places when they heard the warning buzz of a rattlesnake. It struck one of Biggs' men. Biggs nodded at one of his men who promptly unholstered his pistol and shot the snake. Then he aimed his weapon at the bitten man, but Biggs responded, "No, no." The wounded man was momentarily relieved. Biggs pointed to the shored-up tunnel ceiling. He made a cutting motion across his own neck. His man promptly slit the throat of the victim. There'd be no baggage, no dead weight to slow them down.

They finally emerged from the tunnel well beyond the tree line. They had been traveling west from the hacienda. Biggs looked out to his right and saw the distant campfire of the soldiers. It appeared Belknap thought Biggs had likely escaped and was long gone by now, so permitted his soldiers to light small cooking fires.

Biggs tested the wind. It wasn't strong, but it was moving west to east. Importantly, it was dry. They hadn't seen a raindrop in weeks. They snuck to within a couple of hundred yards of Belknap's bivouac.

They began gathering dried brush and piling it just out of view of the camp. When Biggs figured they'd piled enough, he set it afire. The wind took the flames and swept them rapidly toward Luke and the soldiers. It began to spread, eventually engulfing the stagecoach with his wife's lifeless body still tied to the wheel. The children had been rescued by the soldiers while Biggs was being diverted by the cannon, but their screams as they watched the stage burn in a huge conflagration enveloping their mother were pitiable to hear.

Three Toes was first to smell the smoke, and he sounded the alarm. "Run, run! Fire!" They leapt to their horses and raced from the flames into Biggs' ambush. His gunfire drove them toward Belknap and the cannon. Luke rode hard into the lieutenant's camp. "You have grapeshot?"

"Yes," Belknap offered groggily, just then seeing the fire and hearing the gunshots.

"Load the damned cannon, man!"

Belknap spun the cannon toward Biggs' general direction. Biggs' men were on foot, firing as quickly as they could. Half a dozen soldiers were already dead or wounded.

The bandits were perhaps a mere hundred feet away when Belknap lit the fuse. With an earth-shattering roar, the space in front of the cannon was rent with the whining sound of grapeshot. Biggs and all his men fell in a jumble of screams before the fusillade. The scene fell silent but for the moans of the wounded.

Luke dismounted and drew both his Walker Colts. In the light of the full moon, he began the task of finding Biggs.

After a half hour of searching, Luke came upon a Sharps rifle. There was no Roy Biggs with it. Everything else around was dead or dying, but no Biggs. The grapeshot had a devastating effect.

Luke sat where he'd been standing. He was exceedingly tired. Three Toes joined him. "It has been a long day, Ghost-Who-Rides."

Roy Biggs left arm was virtually useless, and he had wounds in both legs. He had managed to drag himself away from the scene of carnage. He'd underestimated the Texas Ranger, but resolved not to let that happen again. He'd paid a heavy price. Far too heavy.

He made it to the burned-out tree line, found a stick for a crutch, and managed to stand. He had people to the north in Uvalde if he could make it without bleeding to death. He took pieces of sod and strapped them to his leg wounds to apply pressure and stem the bleeding. With one functioning arm, it was especially difficult. He thought about resting, but couldn't risk falling asleep and being found by that damnable Texas Ranger. He realized he'd lost the Sharps rifle, but the thing was too heavy to carry, much less shoot, in his condition.

Luke awakened and began to survey the battlefield, and battlefield it was. Two small but mighty opposing armies had fought and men had died in what would become known in Nueces Strip lore as the Battle of Twin Creeks. If there was a distinctive difference in the opposing sides, one was acting out of loyalty to country and higher purposes while the other was motivated by a wholly evil agenda.

Luke's shoulder wound, the one he'd received during the skirmish capturing Thaddeus Brown, still throbbed. The lieutenant had lost seven soldiers killed and eight wounded. Like Belknap, those wounded would recover to fight again; however, the lieutenant had to make a tough choice as concerned the dead soldiers. He didn't feature riding several days with bodies draped over saddles. He decided to bury the men there near the hacienda that they'd given their lives trying to capture.

After they tended the wounded, buried the dead, and prepared to move out, Luke stared over at the hacienda. "Lieutenant, let's take a few moments and go see what's inside that hacienda or whatever we're to call it."

They moved out cautiously in a column of twos, pulling their trusty cannon behind. They thought they might have to blast their way in. Upon arriving at the entrance, they found its massive door standing open. It was suspicious to say the least. Biggs wasn't one to be so careless. One of Belknap's soldiers walked toward it.

"Stop!" Luke shouted out in the nick of time. A spring-loaded spiked arm swung out, narrowly missing the man.

"Lieutenant, now that we know where this place is, perhaps we should let some folks come out here and dismantle it piece by piece. There's no good purpose served in putting your men in further danger."

Belknap was relieved. Biggs' spiked booby-trap had been too close for comfort, and it was likely there'd be more such deadly devices strategically placed inside the hacienda. They had Thaddeus Brown in custody and could turn him in at San Antonio with their heads held high. No point in further risk.

Belknap rode over to Three Toes. He remained silent for a moment, staring intently into the chief's eyes. "Chief...I am sorry for not respecting you. You have been a big help in accomplishing this mission. Thank you."

Luke nearly fell off Big Horse at Belknap's display of humility. "Dang, Lieutenant, we're gonna make a general out of you yet."

It had been easy to understand Belknap's hostility toward Comanche and Indians in general, given what was talked about throughout the military and what Belknap himself had witnessed of their barbaric behavior. He'd begun to understand. He could never forget what he'd seen, but he could strive to put it behind him toward establishing peaceful, respectful relations with the tribes.

The sergeant smiled approvingly. It had been a hard lesson, but the lieutenant had gotten a huge practical education.

Three Toes had had enough of the white man's fighting for now. "I head back to my people, Ghost-Who-Rides."

"Thank you, my friend. May your travels go well." Luke watched as the chief rode off to the north toward his peoples' Pedernales encampment.

"Lieutenant, you've got your prisoner, though we seem to have lost Mr. Biggs for now." He gave Belknap a friendly salute. "Winter is coming upon us, Lieutenant. I'd be inclined to hunt down Biggs, but it'd be like trying to find a needle in a haystack and time is not our friend. I must see to healing my own wounds, tend to my pregnant wife, and look after my cattle back in Nuecestown." Luke's conflict between ranching and Rangering came through loud and clear.

He surveyed Belknap's men. A few had been killed and several were nursing wounds. "For your part, you need to get back to Fort Mason with your wounded men. You can be proud of how they responded in battle." Luke said it loudly enough for the troopers to hear.

"Thanks, Captain Dunn. I hope we get to work together again." Belknap appreciated the learning experience Luke had afforded him. "Safe travels."

SIXTEEN

Perez's Revenge?

"*Buenas dias*." Carlos Perez permitted himself a smile. They had brought in two dozen head of prime cattle. That was a big haul. His *Caballeros* were in great spirits.

Dónde encontraste el ganado? Perez didn't recognize the brand, so was curious as to where the cattle were from. It was still early in this restart of his hider business. Hides were still bringing top dollar, but ranchers were fighting back against the thieving hiders more aggressively.

The *Caballeros Negros* smiled with satisfaction. "*Rancho Dunn al oeste de Corpus Christi.*"

Perez scowled. It didn't bode well to rustle cattle from a ranch owned by a member of the Dunn family. It might unnecessarily add greater incentive to that damnable Texas Ranger. He hated to steal their joy, but wouldn't tolerate carelessness. They should have known about the reputation of the Dunns. "*Aléjate de esa region.*" He made it crystal clear that they were to stay out of the region between Corpus Christi and San Diego.

As it was, Perez felt as though he had to keep looking over his shoulder, as he had no idea when Captain Dunn might show up. He knew the Rangers were undermanned, so rightly concluded that Dunn was diverted to other missions. Still, it wouldn't be long before Captain Dunn would be turning his attention back to Perez's operation. "*Malditos rinches!*" He cursed the Rangers.

Rinches was a special pejorative term the Mexicans had created for the Texas Rangers. There was no love lost between Rangers and Mexicans. Mexican songs were filled with themes of the intercultural conflict between Texans and Mexicans. The resentment felt by many Mexicans was most easily focused on the Texas Rangers. In turn, the Texans held little respect for Mexicans in general, viewing them as cruel by nature, cowardly and treacherous by inclination, and holding a mindset of thievery, especially of livestock. Men like Perez tended to validate that image. In reality, the ill feelings between Texans and Mexicans was mutual, as Texans were viewed by many Mexicans as cruel and disrespectful. Worse still, the Mexicans viewed the Nueces Strip as having been stolen from them.

Each day, Perez was feeling more confident of the loyalty of this new gang of *Caballeros Negros*. He even ventured to postulate that a third confrontation with the Texas Ranger might turn out successfully. Killing the Ranger would open the opportunity to chase down that Laredo whore. She haunted his dreams, or more rightly, his nightmares. Every time he relieved himself, he was reminded of the damage she had wrought to his manhood.

Luke pulled Big Horse up at the entrance to Heaven's Gate. He looked out over the ranch. Several longhorns were grazing lazily in the comfortable late-fall temperatures. He expected a couple of them would be calving soon. That, in the way of cowboy thinking, got him thinking about Elisa. Her time was drawing ever closer.

He spurred the big gray to a canter and quickly found himself tying Big Horse to the hitching post in front of the cabin. He'd walked the big horse the last few feet so she wouldn't hear him coming. He knocked on the door.

Elisa dropped her sewing and waddled over to peek out the window. In barely a heartbeat, she'd swung the cabin door open and pulled Luke to her. "You're home! Praise God, you're home! I've missed you, Lucas." Her voice was muffled in the folds of his coat.

Luke had thought of this moment from the time they'd left Biggs' hacienda. He never imagined missing anyone so much. He breathed in her sweet fragrance and nestled his chin in her golden-red hair. "And I've missed you, my sweet Lisa."

She eased off his coat, then stood back aghast. "What happened?" The dried blood around the hole in his shirt made it just a bit obvious.

"Nothing serious, Lisa. We recaptured that Brown fellow. It got a little heated."

In the emotion of the moment, Elisa's tears went from joy to fearfulness. "You might have been killed, Lucas Dunn."

What could Luke say. "But I wasn't. I'm here with you."

She offered up a sigh of resignation. "Get cleaned up and I'll fix something." She put her hand over the beaded amulet Three Toes had gifted her with. She smiled to herself and turned to the cooking fire. With the cooling weather, she decided to whip up some stick-to-the-ribs beef stew for her man.

Luke stepped onto the gallery and eased on over to the cistern to wash off the trail dust. As he finished up, he took a gander at the gathering clouds off on the horizon. Some sort of storm was brewing. He led Big Horse over to the stable, unsaddled him, and lovingly curried him. He was glad he'd built the stallion a separate stall, as he could tell that the big gray appreciated it. That's how it was between a man and his horse on the frontier. They spent a lot of time together.

Big Horse seemed a bit unsettled. Luke looked around. Sure enough, a rattler had found its way into the stable to warm up. Luke drew one of his Colts and disposed of the pest. Big Horse settled down right quickly thereafter.

As he headed for the cabin, Luke found himself just a tad worried by the dark clouds. He walked through the door. "Lisa, there's a storm brewing. I closed up the stable, but we should keep an eye on the dang weather." Given the changeability of weather on the Nueces Strip, the storm could disappear or pass them by. There was no way of knowing.

"You shooting varmints, Lucas?"

He was typically nonchalant. "Rattler was unsettling the livestock in the stable." He pulled up a chair and took a long sip of the coffee she'd brewed. Luke had come to crave Elisa's stew and wouldn't be disappointed. "What do you think, come spring, of looking for a bigger spread?" he asked her.

Elisa smiled. Seemed there was yet hope that Luke might chose ranching over Rangering.

They talked about the possibilities of a bigger spread as they ate. It would mean hiring some *vaqueros* to help with the additional cattle they'd have to manage. Luke's cousins owned a couple of large ranches farther west of Corpus Christi, and he committed to seeking their advice.

Luke stretched back in his chair after savoring the bowl of stew and clasped his hands behind his head. He watched admiringly as Elisa flitted about the cabin doing chores, and it struck him that she worked very hard. He tried to imagine her with a couple of little ones playing at her feet.

She walked over to the window and peeked outside. "Lucas… Lucas, come see."

Luke joined her at the window, wrapping his arms around her as he shared her view. It was snowing. It didn't look as though it would settle much on the ground, but the sight was as beautiful as it was unusual.

She placed his hand on her belly. "Feel that, Mr. Texas Ranger?"

He could feel a kick, then another. It brought home the reality of the gifts that would soon be gracing their lives.

It was going to be tough for Luke to have to go face Carlos Perez or Roy Biggs or whatever other assignment he'd be given. It would depend far too much on the political goings-on in Austin. In any case, he'd delay as long as he could. He definitely didn't want to be off chasing down lawbreakers when Elisa's time came.

As Perez sat out front of his little hacienda, one of his men eased on over. "*Patrón, he oído que la put peliroja está en Nuecestown.*"

The news struck him like a lightning bolt. His face turned red. The red-haired whore was in Nuecestown!

"*Y ella tuvo un bebé.*"

She'd had a baby! "*Maldita sea, si hubiera sido tan largo?*" He lamented the realization that much time had passed since he'd crossed paths with her. He looked round his hider ranch. His face began to return to normal color. He'd been operating a sort of semi-legitimate business for a couple of months and had even begun having success selling hides.

"*Es hora!*" He announced that the time had come.

Over the next couple of days, the *Caballeros Negros* brought together the supplies and weapons they would need. There were a dozen men in camp, but Perez decided to leave half of them and only take the ones he judged to be most loyal and capable.

It would take about a week to travel to Nuecestown. In that time, Perez would send a scout ahead to gather information on where the whore was staying and what lawmen were around. He'd acquired a new Sharps .50 caliber rifle, but he wasn't sure it would be useful given his terrible accuracy at long-range shooting. He cursed the loss of his eye that took away his sense of depth perception. Ultimately, he'd have to rely on his pistols and plan to engage his enemies at close range. The image of torturing Luke and Scarlett still dwelt deep in recesses of Perez's evil soul.

There was a feeling of relief coupled with excitement as the *Caballeros Negros* began their journey. By now, Carlos Perez had fully healed physically, and riding was far less uncomfortable. He no longer needed the extra padding on his saddle. For their part, the *Caballeros Negros* were mostly unaware of their patron's physical infirmity. To hear Perez talk, you'd never think he had any physical challenges at all save for his lost eye. If they were aware of his impotence, they knew better than to discuss it openly. Perez would as soon slice a throat for a slight.

The road to Nuecestown was clear. There had been a few snow flurries, but they'd melted before they hit the ground. He barely needed a coat. Whelan rode into town, intent on spending some time with Scarlett. Things had quieted down a bit in Corpus Christi, and Colonel Kinney had allowed Whelan to hire a deputy sheriff.

He rode up to Bernice's boarding house, dismounted, and knocked on the door. As he waited, he looked over at the jail. It was in need of some upkeep. He figured to stick around a few days and see to that.

"Why, Sheriff Whelan, fancy seeing you." Bernice was all smiles as she invited him inside. "Hang on a moment, and I'll check on Scarlett and Margaret." She put a bit of emphasis on the child's name.

"Just a minute, Bernice. How's Scarlett getting on?"

Bernice paused, then turned to face Whelan. "You'll have to ask her yourself. I will say that she's learned to sew and knit. She's right good." She pointed to a chair. "Grab a seat, Sheriff. I'll be right back."

Scarlett soon appeared in the doorway to the parlor. She held Margaret on her hip. The little girl seemed to have grown a bit in the month since George had left Nuecestown to think on how to woo Scarlett, if at all. Margaret was no longer a shriveled-looking, slightly prematurely born baby.

"Hello, George. Good to see you."

He stood. He wanted to touch Scarlett, to wrap his arms around her. He moved forward, and she extended her hand. She wasn't ready for anything so intimate as a hug.

"I've missed you, Scarlett."

"You've had a funny way of showing it, George." Her words were full of frustration for the way men seemed to think.

What could he say? He met her eyes. "I had to think things out. I'm sorry it seemed to take so long."

Scarlett smiled knowingly.

They sat opposite each other in the parlor, he on a chair and she on a settee. They looked at each other for a couple of moments. He prayed she could feel that he sincerely wanted to make things right between them. No…more than right. He wanted to settle down with her. He was in unfamiliar territory. His experiences with women had run along the lines of dominance and objectification. Relationship hadn't been part of his consciousness.

For Scarlett's part, she'd been used so often by men, it was surprising that she wasn't more jaded. She wanted to feel love, but a love that was reciprocated, a love she could trust.

"I…I want to show you that I love you, Scarlett. It's more than about making things right. We can't undo what's done. I've been looking at the Good Book of late, and it says that forgiveness is a first step." He leaned forward. "Will you forgive me, Scarlett Rose?"

She was taken aback. This wasn't what she expected from Whelan. She reached across the space between them and took his clasped hands. "George…George, I do forgive you." A sense of relief swept between them. She looked deeply into his eyes. Yes, he was sincere. "George, come look at her pretty little face, her green eyes."

A couple of tears almost welled up in the corner of Whelan's own eyes as he stood and came around to better take in the sleeping form of little baby Margaret. As if on cue, she opened her eyes. She blinked, smiled, took a breath, and cried out. George stepped back in surprise.

"Easy, George. She's only hungry." Scarlett began to loosen her bodice. "You sit back down while I feed our child."

He sat fully amazed as he watched Margaret suckle at Scarlett's breast.

Scarlett smiled. "Welcome to my world, George."

"She's beautiful." He smiled as tenderly as a rough man could. "And you're beautiful."

"Are you staying in town for a while?"

"Yes. The sheriff's office needs some repair, and I hired a deputy back in Corpus. I'm afraid you're stuck with me being around for a few days." He realized that didn't sound all that interesting. There wasn't a lot to do in Nuecestown. "If it warms up a bit, maybe we could go have us a picnic."

"I'd like that, George. That would be right nice."

Bernice knocked at the parlor door. "Say, you two, Agatha and I are going to invite some folks for a Christmas dinner. It's only a couple of days away. You'd be most welcome to join us."

Scarlett and Whelan exchanged glances. She nodded.

"Why, thank you, Bernice. We'd love to come." It struck Whelan that it would likely be appropriate to give Scarlett a Christmas gift… maybe little Margaret, too.

The *Caballeros Negros* had traveled to within a couple of miles of Nuecestown. They'd passed through San Diego a couple of nights before and had striven to not bring attention to themselves. Perez's intention was to be far more stealthy in his approach this time. He was committed to controlling his emotions, having begun to realize that hate was his enemy.

They made camp up on the south bank of the Nueces River near a thick grove of trees. It afforded natural shelter from prying eyes. He cautioned his men to keep noise to a minimum and light no campfires.

One of his *Caballeros Negros* sauntered over to where Perez was preparing to settle in for the night. "*Jefe, va a ser la Navided mañana. Luchamos?*"

It hadn't occurred to Perez that it was Christmas Eve. The diabolical realization that his prey would never expect an attack at such a time floated through his mind. He hadn't given a thought until now.

"*Si luchamos mañana.*" Yes, they'd fight on Christmas. This could work out perfectly. He leaned back against his saddle and gazed up at the starry night.

"*Jefe, muchas personas se reunirán en lac pensión par la cena de Navided.*"

The news that the townspeople would gather in one place for a Christmas meal was the most valuable information his man could have brought him. "*Cuando?*"

"*Mediodía, Jefe.*"

At midday, the light would be excellent for what he had in mind. With everyone in town occupied, Perez was confident that he'd likely be able to ride into Nuecestown unnoticed. His plan would be to surround the boarding house and put one of his men at each of the windows. He'd enter and wreak his vengeance. With any luck, he'd get the *rinche* and the whore.

Luke had returned from a trip to Nuecestown for a few supplies. He'd spent the earlier part of the day, beginning at the crack of dawn, checking their herd of cattle. After he'd unloaded the goods from the wagon and unhitched and stabled the mules, he felt it was time to relax just a little.

He entered the cabin and saw Elisa uncharacteristically sitting down. He sensed she wasn't feeling well. "Bernice and Agatha have invited us to Christmas dinner, Lisa. Are you up to going?"

Elisa had been having just a touch of morning sickness the past couple of days. "Let's decide in the morning. If I'm up to it, we'll go." She smiled gamely.

"If you don't feel well enough, I can ride in and deliver Christmas wishes," Luke said.

It was broad daylight when Perez and his *Caballeros Negros* rode into town. No one was on the streets. He vaguely recalled the layout of the town, as he'd noted on his rather fast ride through it many months earlier. Riding at a gallop while being shot at can tend to blur the memory. But it was a small town and familiar enough to him.

They tied their horses across from the boarding house. Perez directed his men to stand at the windows on either side of what he understood to be the dining room. At his signal, they'd smash the windows and point their guns at the folks inside. He'd crash through the front door and confront them. It took but a few moments, and he saw that his men were in position.

Bernice's and Agatha's guests had just settled down to the meal. The local priest had offered a Christmas blessing. As he finished his prayer, his peripheral vision caught sight of something at a window.

All of a sudden, there was the crashing of window glass and the muzzles of four rifles were aimed into the room. Whelan instinctively stood and drew a pistol, but a single shot from one of the *Caballeros Negros* at a window felled him. Scarlett screamed and collapsed at his side.

Perez crashed through the dining room door. "*Levanta tus manos!*" He scanned the room, not seeing Scarlett at first. There were eight or nine people in the room, and they all quickly complied with his command.

She recognized that voice, that evil voice. She stayed low and picked up Whelan's Colt. She saw that he was bleeding badly, very badly.

"*Quien esta alli?*" He saw that someone was hiding below one of the tables. He grabbed Agatha and put a gun to her head. "*Sal, o la mataré!*" He ordered Scarlett to come out or he'd kill Agatha.

Scarlett realized that, with Agatha in the way, she had no clear shot at Perez. She stood and placed the Colt on the table.

Perez smiled broadly. "*Ven aca!*" He pushed Agatha away and ordered Scarlett to come to him. Someone in the back of the room pulled a gun. A shot rang out from a window, and there was the thud of a body hitting the floor. "*Ahora!*"

Scarlett took as long a time as she could to make her way to Perez. He cast his one eye with all the sinister evil he could muster.

Whelan was coming around enough to begin to search for his gun. He had enough remaining consciousness to be wary of the men at the windows.

Perez stepped toward his red-haired Laredo whore. He couldn't suppress a wide toothless grin. He stuffed his gun in his waistband. With both his hands, he tore her bodice in two, exposing her breasts to everyone. He reached out and lasciviously fondled her. His hand slid down to her hips and pulled her dress down, further exposing her.

Scarlett's fear at what he might do transcended any embarrassment.

With Elisa feeling poorly, Luke saddled Big Horse and headed out to Nuecestown. He was within a mile when he heard the first shots. He instantly spurred the big gray to a gallop, only slowing when he drew within sight of the town. He saw the horses hitched in front of Doc's place and then noticed the armed men at the windows to the boarding house. Dismounting, he tied Big Horse to a nearby live oak, drawing his rifle from its scabbard. He'd like to get as close as he could before doing any shooting.

He stayed as low as possible in the surrounding prairie grass. He estimated that he could shoot two of the men on the side of the house near him before anyone could react. He heard a Mexican voice from inside and recognized it as Perez's. He could hear him threatening the guests.

Perez forced Scarlett onto her knees and unbuttoned his pants. He sneered at the dinner guests. He sought to humiliate Scarlett right there before all these people. There was an audible gasp from the guests as he dropped his pants and revealed the scarred remainder of his manhood.

"*Besame!*" He commanded her to kiss it. His smile turned sour and his mouth dropped in surprise with the sound from outside of two shots ringing out. Two of his men had disappeared from the windows.

The men on the other side of the house ran around to see what had happened, only to run into a hail of .44 caliber bullets from one of Luke's Walker Colts. His aim was unerring, and they both collapsed to the ground. He then turned his attention to Perez. "*Carlos Perez, sal con las manos levantadas.*" As he gave Perez the command to come out with his hands raised, he moved toward the front door. He stood to the side in case Perez decided to fight it out. He pulled the second Colt from its holster.

Perez heard the order to surrender delivered in that hated Irish-Spanish accent. He pulled up his trousers and managed to button them sufficiently to free his hands. With gun in one hand and holding the barely clothed Scarlett in front of him with the other, he emerged from the boarding house. He saw Luke out of the corner of his remaining eye. He twisted to try to get a shot. Scarlett was hampering his aim, so he pushed her aside.

Another shot rang out, and Perez froze. He looked down at his chest to see blood gushing from a gaping wound. His gun dropped as he fell in a bleeding heap on the boarding house steps. The bullet had gone clean through the hider, barely missing Luke as it whizzed on to oblivion.

Luke was surely grateful that the bullet that hit Perez missed him. He peered inside to see Whelan lying on the floor with smoke wafting skyward from his own Colt revolver. Luke could tell from the doorway that the sheriff was in bad shape.

"Scarlett...Scarlett." Whelan could barely speak as he motioned her to his side. He coughed up blood. "My God, it hurts..."

Someone threw a blanket over Scarlett's half-clothed body as she knelt over him. She wiped the blood from his chin.

Whelan's face had already become ashen, as he'd lost a lot of blood. His breathing was labored. "Scarlett...love you...Scarlett."

She held him close as he took his final breath. "I love you, too, George. I love you, too." She felt certain he'd heard her. She kissed him tenderly.

Luke strode in. Everyone was huddling in fear. "It's okay, everything's safe, folks." He walked over and gently lifted Scarlett. "He's gone, Scarlett. I'm sorry, but he's gone."

Bernice escorted Scarlett from the dining room. There was an unearthly silence, and then someone began spontaneously singing. *"Amazing grace! how sweet the sound, that saved a wretch like me..."*

Luke walked from the dining room, stepping over the corpse of Carlos Perez as it lay in the foyer. He didn't even bother to look at the scoundrel. He shook involuntarily as he experienced a range of emotions. Luke reached the front step of the boarding house and sat. He wondered at what the world had become. Evil seemed to lurk at every turn. Could he...should he...continue the fight for justice on the Nueces Strip? Heaven's Gate seemed like a protected oasis from all that was evil.

Luke knew that wickedness would always be around. There was simply no escaping it. Even the most God-fearing people were not insulated from its effect. Would the world get better? Could it get better? Could truth and faith and justice prevail?

He'd miss George Whelan. The man had taught him early on the ins and outs of being a lawman, and they had developed a deep mutual respect, if not friendship.

It came to him as he sat deep in thought that Perez's body smelled badly. It needed a quick burial, if for no other reason than to get rid of the man's stench.

Most everyone from the boarding house was still in some state of emotional recovery. It would not be a Christmas soon forgotten.

Scarlett was beside herself with grief. George had raped her and imprisoned her, but she'd actually come to forgive him and had even begun to truly care for him. She'd made so many bad choices in men, and George in his contrition had become a contrast. At least he'd been reliable and on the right side of the law. She'd see to burying Whelan and then deal with whether to stay in Nuecestown. She had a sense of relief that Carlos Perez was finally out of her life. She no longer needed to look over her shoulder in fear of the man.

"Scarlett?" It was Doc. "I'm sorry, but I need to take George's body over to my place to get him ready. Just wanted you to know." He meant ready for a funeral.

Meanwhile, Luke took care of burying Perez, while Dan buried the remaining *Caballeros Negros*. Having done his duty, Luke decided it was time to head back to Heaven's Gate. He had a lot to share with Elisa, though it would once again feed her fears over his safety. In a day or so, he'd go into Corpus Christi and let Colonel Kinney know he'd need a new sheriff.

After wishing everyone well and ensuring that all the loose ends of taking care of bodies were tied up, he mounted Big Horse and gave him his head for home.

SEVENTEEN

Connections

Roy Biggs sighed as he rode northwest toward Uvalde. He sought to get as far away from the Nueces Strip as he could while his wounds healed and he could gather his wits. He detested being vulnerable. Uvalde was regarded by some as the northernmost limits of the Strip, or what some folks called the Wild Horse Desert. He was also traipsing across the Comancheria and had to stay alert for Comanche and Kiowa war parties, but he was plenty savvy so far as avoiding such encounters.

He'd walked for two days after sneaking from Twin Creeks. As chance would have it, he came upon a small hider ranch. Most of the hiders were away, literally rustling up business. There wasn't much cattle ranching quite yet in this part of Texas, so the hiders had to range far out into the hills to work their thievery. There were only two adults guarding the three hovels that served as housing. They turned out to be women and looked to be Mexican. They were unarmed and feeding some chickens when Biggs came upon them. He was surely a sight to behold with his near-useless left arm and bandages wrapped around his legs. He didn't appear to be much of a threat.

"*Buenas dias, señoras. Me venderán un caballo?*" In as friendly a way possible, Biggs let the women know that he wanted to buy a horse.

Surprised, one of them ran to grab a rifle leaning against a nearby fence post.

Biggs sighed. He pulled the Colt from his holster and shot her just as she reached the rifle. He looked at the other woman. "*Repito. Me venderás un caballo?*"

She vigorously nodded her head yes as she raised her hands. "*Señor, toma uno del corral.*" She pointed toward the corral.

Biggs prodded her along in front of him to the corral. He didn't want her grabbing some other hidden weapon. He picked a buckskin stallion of fair size and looking to be in good health. "*Poner una silla de montar en este.*"

She complied, haltering and saddling the steed for him. Biggs climbed painfully into the saddle. Once seated reasonably in comfort, he tossed her two silver coins. "*Gracias y adiós.*"

He turned the horse and rode off. He looked back to see her tending to the woman he'd killed. He shook his head resignedly, thinking how foolish she'd been. It had been a cheap notch in his gun, a wasted bullet even to his perverse mind.

Thoughts of that damnable Texas Ranger dragged on his head. The loss of his wife and children didn't weigh nearly so heavily. Dunn was one tough, savvy hombre and as worthy an opponent as he'd ever met. It was time for some extreme actions. He decided to find his old friend Cutter John up in Uvalde.

"What?" Horatio Thorpe was beside himself. "Biggs failed?!"

Samuel had been fearful of Thorpe's reaction from the moment he first learned that Thaddeus Brown was once again in U.S. Marshal custody and on his way to Washington, D.C. He silently awaited instructions as he let Thorpe vent his anger.

"I want my damned money back!" Of course, Thorpe knew that was impossible. These were the sorts of risks assumed in nefarious operations of this kind. Even Biggs wasn't perfect. On the upside, the general and the major were permanently silenced. What might be his next step? Were there any loose ends that needed to be cleaned up? It occurred to Thorpe that he still had connections in the nation's capital. Perhaps he could yet eliminate the Thaddeus Brown problem.

"Samuel, invite Mr. Culthwaite to meet with me at the Bullock Hotel at six o'clock." Berne Culthwaite would drop just about everything to meet with Thorpe, and he knew it. Thorpe needed to solve a Texas Ranger problem, but Thaddeus Brown would come first.

"Yes, sir, Master Thorpe." Samuel left immediately. Thorpe wasn't in a mood to tolerate delays. He didn't envy Roy Biggs if Thorpe decided to exact his own brand of justice. Samuel had seen stronger men made to suffer. Then again, Biggs just might be a match for Thorpe's brand of *quid pro quo*.

Luke rode easy-like back to Heaven's Gate. The ride was long enough to give him time to mull over the events of the past few weeks. At the least, Carlos Perez hadn't been able to dodge his fate. Luke expected that he'd eventually have to find Perez's hider ranch and close it down. That Roy Biggs fellow still haunted him. He knew that Biggs would yet be nasty to deal with. He also wondered about what might become of Scarlett. By the time he reached Elisa's outstretched arms, he was physically and mentally tight as a drum. He desperately needed time with her.

"What happened?" Elisa had an uncanny ability to read her man's face. She knew it was serious and that, likely or not, Luke had been at some risk.

"George Whelan got shot and killed."

Tears welled up in Elisa's eyes as she thought of the impact on Scarlett and on baby Margaret growing up with no father. She could see there was more, like how had Whelan been killed?

Luke read her expression. He knew he'd have to tell the whole sordid tale. "It was Carlos Perez and his cutthroats. They surrounded Bernice's boarding house while everyone was seated at dinner. I just happened to ride up as the attack began. George was mortally wounded early on. By God's grace, I shot and killed the four men in Perez's gang. Whelan killed Perez with his dying breath as the bandit was attempting to rape Scarlett in front of everyone." He let her fill in the gaps that likely swirled about in her mind as risks to her man. "Scarlett was heartbroken at George's death. I think they were going to try to make a go of it. The poor woman has had such bad luck with men."

"Were you shot at?" Elisa's eyebrows furrowed a bit.

Luke had been avoiding getting into that issue. "Closest I came was the bullet that George fired at Perez. It went clean through the man and missed me by inches. Even Perez's gang never got off any shots at me." Luke smiled, satisfied at having gotten that all off his chest. "Shame Three Toes wasn't there with his arrows."

At the thought of Three Toes, Elisa touched the beaded amulet Three Toes had given her. She snapped out of her brief, thoughtful trance, and offered Luke a winsome smile. "Lucas Dunn, what am I going to do with you?" She stood before him with her hands on her hips. Her belly seemed ready to burst under her over-sized dress. "What do I do…?"

He deftly slipped her dress up and over her head. "Love me?" He laughed, swept her off her feet, and deposited her gently on the bed. "Merry Christmas."

She buried herself in his well-muscled but tenderly enveloping arms. He stroked her delicately, his fingers like a breeze wafting across her skin. His touch set her heart fluttering, and the lives within her began to kick up a storm as they sensed her arousal.

Berne Culthwaite kicked back in an easy chair on the veranda of the Bullock Hotel. He much preferred his hacienda overlooking the sparkling blue waters of Galveston Bay and enjoying a cooling breeze wafting in off the Gulf of Mexico. Today, he had to settle for a much warmer breeze in Austin. Gentle gusts pushed the cigar smoke lazily back in his face. He enjoyed the aroma of the fine Cuban tobacco. In Galveston, he could look out on the bay and make out his ships. They all sailed low in the water, packed as they were with merchandise for eastern cities and even Europe. At last count, he had better than two dozen ships plying the trade routes. Today, he'd have to settle for watching a few carriages plodding along the streets of Austin.

"Angelina, where's that drink?" He looked back over his shoulder.

Soon enough, she slinked through the door, purposefully kissed the edge of the glass, gave the drink to Culthwaite, and then seductively slipped over to the railing. With the sun behind her from the southeast, her diaphanous negligee revealed a silhouette that any man would kill for. Her golden curls fell in gentle waves across her shoulders.

Culthwaite was about to enjoy some mid-morning delight when a knock interrupted. Culthwaite was annoyed. "Excuse me?"

"Begging your pardon, Mr. Culthwaite. I have a note from Mr. Thorpe." The man bowed solicitously and nodded admiringly at Angelina. He handed the note to Culthwaite, glanced again at the woman, and beat a hasty retreat.

Culthwaite ignored the man's leering, read the note, and shrugged. "Damn," he uttered under his breath. He'd have to bail Thorpe out of a situation again.

"Is there a problem, my love?" Angelina slinked over and rubbed her legs against Culthwaite.

He pulled her down to him and kissed her passionately.

He went through the motions of sex, but his mind was already wrapping around whatever thorny problem Horatio Thorpe would bring to him.

Three Toes walked his pony into the encampment near Camp Cooper. He was immediately struck by the absence of warriors. Where had they gone? There were no more than a dozen teepees.

Moon Woman emerged and was the first to greet the Penateka chief. As she moved toward Three Toes, his other two wives followed. They were both pregnant. Moon Woman uncharacteristically embraced the chief. She was clearly relieved at his return.

"Where are the warriors?"

Moon Woman was about to speak when the Indian agent coincidentally arrived. She bowed to Three Toes and headed back to the teepee.

"Three Toes, welcome back. Where have you been?" The agent had already firmly established an us-versus-them environment with the Comanche. He was wanted as an accessory to murder in the Indian Territory, so he didn't exactly have a reputation as an upstanding citizen. That being said, he was a lawyer and even had been elected to the Texas state legislature. He'd only been agent to the Comanche on the Clear Fork of the Brazos since September 1855, but his relationship with the tribe deteriorated rapidly. Nearby Camp Cooper was not his favorite place. The agent also resented losing the extra cash he'd earned when Thaddeus Brown had been plying his trade. He knew that it had only recently been made legal per Texas law to set aside state lands for Indians. The Comanche, like other tribes, didn't think farming was to be a seriously undertaken part of the Comanche culture. They tried to farm, but extreme weather inclusive of drought worked against them.

"Three Toes has traveled far. Where are my people?"

The agent knew that the 2nd U.S. Cavalry had been unable to keep the Comanche from ranging far and wide in their traditional habits of raiding settlements. It was easy for the Comanche to follow their old trails south to Mexico and southwest Texas. Men like Brown made matters worse by trading in whiskey. "They have left. I doubt they'll be back." He strove to be respectful, though his hatred of Indians came through in his body language and facial expressions.

"Where are the bluecoats?"

"Back at Camp Cooper."

"Not chasing Chief Sanaco?"

The agent shook his head. "Are you staying, Chief?"

Three Toes looked around. An encampment of more than four hundred warriors had dwindled to a handful of mostly women, children, and old men. He stared hard at the agent. "You go now. I must talk with my wives."

The agent, sensing a frustration growing in Three Toes, bid farewell and headed back to the agency. He knew better than to rile a Comanche war chief with a reputation like this one. Discretion was certainly the better part of valor.

Three Toes entered his teepee and sat near Moon Woman. He accepted his pipe from her and smoked it thoughtfully. "We must leave this place." He looked at his two pregnant wives. Travel would not be easy and the uncertainty of the Texas winter on the trail in the northern reaches of the hill country could be dangerous. He hoped they could catch up to Sanaco's band. Before leaving, he'd have to make his peace with Chief Ketumse and perhaps the aging Buffalo Hump.

Horace Rucker examined the paperwork. He'd now be known as Horace Rucker, Colonel, USA (Retired). His work to help Texas by participating in the capture of General Truax and Thaddeus Brown salvaged his name sufficiently to avoid dishonorable discharge. Kind words from Rip Ford had even saved him the embarrassment of a court martial. Perhaps most important, his sons would still have a clear track into West Point.

He would be forever grateful to Luke for having talked some sense into him and given him a chance to show his true value. He'd taken some time to sort out his life. Rucker knew and was mostly relieved that he wasn't going to spend the rest of his life sitting around, taking in the Austin social scene (he'd pretty much given up on Washington, D.C.), and being respectfully referred to as "the Colonel."

Given his past association with General Truax's criminal enterprise, he wasn't a candidate for elected office, even though politics remained one of the most sordid of callings. Likewise, and despite his recent heroics, he hadn't the *bona fides* to become a lawman. Besides, he wasn't getting any younger. Farming or ranching weren't his forte either. He loved horses, but didn't see making a living breeding them. He needed to come up with something that would be meaningful, something that would make an honorable contribution. He'd learned a lot in his military career and had been fortunate to survive battles mostly unscathed. What was to be his future?

Rucker began to write a note to Rip Ford. He recalled how Ford had gotten the nickname "Rip," which stood for "rest in peace." It had been a byproduct of all the letters Ford had been ordered to write to the loved ones of soldiers killed in battle while he'd served as an adjutant under General Zachary Taylor in the Mexican-American War. Rucker figured Ford must be a God-fearing man to have endured such a depressing task. Then it struck him; Ford must not have seen it as depressing. He likely had a strength of faith that saw him through all the letters.

It was as though a light had begun to turn on within Horace Rucker's very being. He determined to take a hard look at his faith toward finding some answers. He'd rarely gone to church since childhood, much less read the Bible. It seemed to be time to find out where men like Luke Dunn and Rip Ford found their strength of resolve to remain positive in adversity, do good in a harsh world, and trust in a God that couldn't be seen.

★

Uvalde had been evolving in fits and starts over the past couple of years. In 1855, it got discovered, and the population began doubling every year. By 1857, it stood at nearly three hundred fifty folks. Little wonder that Roy Biggs headed there to hide or that his friend Cutter John plied his profession among the quaint and practical Folk Victorian style buildings of the town. It had experienced a momentary economic lull with the Army ordering the closing of Fort Inge, but settlers came nevertheless. Fort Inge had represented a veritable treasure trove of merchandising opportunities for the fledgling community.

No surprise when Biggs entered the local watering hole, sidled up to the bar and, with a quick scan of the room, he quickly found Cutter John sitting at a table playing cards. He noted that Cutter still didn't drink, at least as evidenced by the glass of water near his cards. The man always kept his wits about him. It was rumored that his skill with a knife was such that he could fully skin animal or human in mere seconds. It was legendary, even though there was no clear evidence that he practiced the craft on humans…except maybe an occasional Comanche or Apache and even a Mexican or two…that many whites didn't consider civilized humans.

Cutter glanced up from his card hand. His eyes acknowledged Biggs, but he dared not lose his concentration on the game. He pushed a couple of coins into the pot and called the hand. With just a hint of self-gratified flare, he laid down a straight, ten high, in multiple suits. As he was about to rake in the pot, the player opposite him called him out.

"Excuse me, but I think I have you beat." He proceeded to lay out a full house.

Cutter didn't cotton to being challenged, plus he was convinced that he'd seen the man slip two cards from his sleeve. "Not so fast," he whispered through clenched teeth as his knife appeared. There was a silvery glint, and the man's hand was suddenly pinned to the table. Cutter's eyes drilled into the man's own eyes. "Now look what ya did, you cheatin' sonofabitch, you got blood on the cards."

The man grimaced with pain, letting out a low growl.

Cutter saw the man's other hand move toward a small pistol in his vest pocket. "No, no, you don't want to do that." A second knife materialized in Cutter's free hand.

Biggs was leisurely sipping his drink and thoroughly enjoying the entertainment. A quiet had settled over the clientele as they too watched with anticipation tinged with trepidation. Folks in Uvalde knew the card cheater, and no one had called him out before.

The cheater pulled his hand away from the pistol and displayed it palm open to Cutter.

Cutter pulled the knife from the man's hand. "I gotta believe you've seen a deer get skinned, mister. You ever seen a human skinned?"

Abject fear replaced the uncertainty that had come over the man. There was even a touch of panic in his demeanor.

"Now, I suggest that you leave Uvalde, my friend." Cutter nodded toward the door. "Now!"

The card cheater left as fast as his feet could move him. He wrapped a bandana tightly around his hand as he ran out.

Biggs sauntered over to the table. "Cutter John, how the hell you doin', my friend?" Since the card players had all scattered, Biggs took a seat opposite Cutter.

"A few dollars richer at the moment, Roy. A few dollars richer." He allowed himself a smile and took a swig of water. "Hell of a way to make a dollar, though."

"Well, you haven't lost your touch. That was impressive."

Cutter looked judgmentally at Biggs' whiskey. "See you still tip the booze, Roy. What brings you to Uvalde? Thought you'd pretty much settled down." He gave Biggs a visual once over. "Damn, but you sure look like hell."

Biggs absorbed Cutter's observation. "Lost my wife in a shootout." He failed to mention it was his bullet that killed her. He likely did look pretty bad as exacerbated by a couple of days growth of beard. "Lost the kids, too. Don't know where they are." He didn't offer up that he'd left them behind. He stared thoughtfully at his whiskey. "I have a problem that could use your artistic talents."

Cutter eased back in his chair. He casually cleaned the cheater's blood from his knife. "What sort of trouble did you get into this time?"

"It's about a Texas Ranger."

"Not that Dunn fella?" He stared back at Biggs, who'd blinked at Cutter having guessed about whom he was talking. He thought how evil the man had come to appear. There was a darkness about his old friend Roy Biggs. He figured Biggs was wondering how he knew about Luke Dunn.

"You've heard of him?"

"I've heard he's a one-man wrecking crew. That man is one tough piece of work, Roy." He smiled. "I suppose it's the Irish in him. I hear tell that a bunch of Dunns have come to the Nueces Strip from Ireland. They have strong family loyalties and are understood to be great Indian fighters. Nobody messes with them."

"You saying you wouldn't want to take on one little Texas Ranger?"

"I understand your little Ranger is six-foot-three, an accomplished tracker, and a hell of a marksman. Word travels fast out here, Roy, and I heard the other day that Dunn destroyed Carlos Perez's hider gang almost single-handed. Even the Comanche respect him."

Biggs fixed a you-can't-be-serious look at him.

"Look, Roy, normally I'd leap at a chance to team up with you, but I've got to really think this one out."

"Appreciate the consideration, Cutter. I expect I'll be around Uvalde for a spell. Got some healing to do." His grim countenance turned to a smile. "Remind me not to cheat if we play cards."

Cutter grabbed the two Jacks that the cheater had used, turned the deck face up, and spread them on the table. "Lookee there, Roy, I'll be damned if there aren't six Jacks in this deck." He laughed heartily.

Three Toes had the remaining Penateka Comanche families

packed up and ready for travel. They had broken camp before sunrise and were miles to the west, tracing the Brazos River. In another day or thereabouts, they'd turn southward, following the mesas and tablelands of the Llano Estacado. He'd left behind Chief Ketumse, who'd departed with three Comanche to check out the possibilities in the Indian Territory.

Three Toes rode out front with two of his warriors. The weather was quite cool, reflective both of the coming onset of winter and the higher elevation. Food and water were plentiful along the route. They felt confident that the Indian agent and the soldiers from Camp Cooper would not follow them. They were wary of the volatile nature of Texas weather. The Comanche were outfitted in their cold-weather gear featuring ornately beaded buckskin shirts and, if needed, fur capes.

In the course of Three Toes' travels back to Camp Cooper, he had acquired an upgrade to his arsenal of weapons. He was now the proud owner of a Walker Colt revolver. He found it at a campsite where the previous owner had been killed, apparently by bandits of some sort who had overlooked the opportunity to add to their own arsenal. The chief had fired it a couple of times to practice, but was intent on saving the dozen rounds he'd acquired with the firearm. He still much preferred the bow and arrow, but he quickly understood the advantage the Colt gave to his enemies.

He wasn't certain what he might do once he found a wintering place he'd feel comfortable with. His plan was to reach the headwaters of the Nueces River. In the inner reaches of his memory, it was isolated and featured plentiful game. He might be able to buy some time for his people before the frontier swept over them. As to the Comanche concept of land, the nearly nineteen thousand acres the government had set aside on the Brazos near Camp Cooper meant nothing to the Comanche. It was more a way of demarcating the place that the white man was to steer clear of. Fact was that settlers had already begun to encroach on reservation lands.

Once his people were settled in, Three Toes would venture out to hopefully find a place where they could be free to live in their ways without encountering the white man and his bluecoats. He'd need to go off alone for a period to meditate and get guidance from the Great Spirit. He wasn't certain that his vision quest had been fulfilled. It seemed like there was a sort of hole in his soul that gnawed at him. It was an incompleteness of spirit, no doubt exacerbated by the circumstances of the current plight of his people.

They finally made their turn southwestward along the Llano Estacado. In a few days they'd reach the headwaters of the Colorado River. It would be a good place to camp for the winter. Along their route, he noticed signs of the encroachment of white settlers.

The trappers and frontiersmen had become history, as mostly white settlers were now seeking places to establish themselves, to make their lives. White man's towns, their hubs of trade, were springing up and facilitating the process of settlement. Farms, ranches, and towns were beginning to dot the countryside. Three Toes knew the Indians would eventually have to accept this invasion of their lives or die opposing it.

He looked up at the distant horizon. Dark storm clouds were gathering. The growing coldness in the air was a harbinger of snow. He knew that a sudden snow storm in the hills they were traveling through could have a devastating effect. As if on cue, a couple of snowflakes floated to the ground in front of him. Three Toes led his people to a great limestone rock outcropping. They'd make camp in this place to ride out the storm.

"Berne, glad you could make it." Thorpe lifted his prodigious frame enough to extend his hand to receive Culthwaite's handshake.

"I've rarely been one to turn down a free dinner, Horatio, especially from someone of your culinary tastes." Culthwaite sat in the chair opposite Thorpe. He glanced at the partially smoked cigar on the dish alongside Thorpe's place setting.

"Care for a cigar?" Thorpe offered.

"Perhaps after dinner." Culthwaite had no idea as yet what trouble Thorpe needed to be extricated from or otherwise helped with.

"I seem to recall your partiality for steak, Berne, so I've taken the liberty of ordering for you."

Culthwaite knew from experience that generosity and thoughtfulness were not at the forefront of Thorpe's nature, so he figured that whatever problem he had must be hugely significant.

They ate mostly in silence, making occasional small talk about the weather, cotton and beef prices, and the political goings-on in Austin.

Dinner finished, Thorpe ordered coffee and offered a cigar to Culthwaite. He clipped the end of a Cuban of his own and lit it. He took a few pulls and puffed smoke into the air. He waited while Culthwaite lit his cigar.

There they sat, two of the most powerful men in Texas. By design, there was no one within earshot. Thorpe had paid off the staff to keep the surrounding tables free to provide a privacy zone of sorts. Finally, Thorpe leaned forward and opened the topic of soon-to-be-mutual concern in a low, serious voice. "I need something taken care of, quietly and discreetly."

Culthwaite had an urge to roll his eyes. Quiet and discreet. Of course, that had always been the nature of their relationship. He wanted to shake Thorpe and have him get to the point. What was the something he needed fixed? "You've always been able to count on me, Horatio." He sat back casually, determined not to play Thorpe's intense theatrics game.

"I need a witness eliminated." He let those words hang in the air, then added, "and a Texas Ranger killed." It came out uglier than the mere words. From the disgustingly overweight figure of Thorpe fairly bursting from his white three-piece suit, it was almost like he'd vomited up his dinner. Thorpe punctuated his statement with a belch.

Culthwaite hadn't seen quite this sort of demeanor from Thorpe before. The plantation magnate tended to be more collected. This was emotional, even tinged with fear. "Horatio, I sense that one of these is protecting your business dealings, but the other…well…I sense revenge. That's far more complicated."

Thorpe ignored Culthwaite's assessment. "The witness is on a train heading east to bear witness against me for my business with the Indian agencies. He's escorted by two U.S. marshals. They're taking him to Washington, D.C."

"That's no problem, Horatio. Usual fee plus extra consideration, as I'll have to contract the job." He was rather matter of fact. This was normal business between them. Thorpe would have a problem and Culthwaite would fix it. It was how he'd earned his nickname: the fixer. "What about this other matter? A Texas Ranger, you say."

"The Ranger…yes…the sonofabitch tore my operations apart on the Nueces Strip and shut down half my business in Texas. He's based out of Nuecestown, down near Corpus Christi."

Culthwaite gave him an "oh crap" look.

"What is it, Berne? Is there some sort of problem?"

"You're talking about that Dunn fellow. You know I don't take on revenge jobs, Horatio."

"I'll pay triple."

It was clear that Thorpe was desperate to get rid of the Ranger. "Horatio, I've heard about this man. He's a one-man Texas Ranger company cleaning the Nueces Strip of lawbreakers. There are a lot of folks that would like to see him retired…permanently."

"He's not perfect. In fact, his so-called perfection is likely his weakness."

Culthwaite looked back with curious anticipation.

"He's married, owns a ranch, and his wife is pregnant."

Culthwaite was figuring whether to take this job on at all. Thorpe would have to pay far more than triple the usual fee. "I'll take it on, Horatio, but it's going to cost you ten thousand dollars in gold with half paid in advance."

Thorpe's eyes grew wide. He pushed back in the seat he was stuffed into. "Ten…!"

"Not a penny less. And you pay, whether I get him or not." At that, Culthwaite wasn't really comfortable with the deal. This was to be a high-risk endeavor.

Thorpe was between a rock and a hard place. Roy Biggs had already failed him. He was running out of alternatives. He looked at Culthwaite resignedly. "Okay, Berne, we've got a deal. Let's cement our agreement over at the Red Rose." The Red Rose was one of Thorpe's network of brothels. This one was a relatively high-end expression of the profession that catered to a wealthy Austin clientele.

Thorpe's mind lingered on the Red Rose for a moment. It reminded him of that Laredo whore he'd missed out on. What was her name? Oh, yes, Scarlett Rose, he recalled. And to Berne, "If, in the course of your work, you run into a red-haired woman named Scarlett, I'll pay a bonus if you help me add her to my stable of whores." His smile grew positively wicked over the mere thought of it. What General Truax and his fool colonel had failed to accomplish, perhaps Berne Culthwaite could get done. He uncinched his belt a notch. He really was going to have to be fitted for some new suits.

His dark reaction as concerned the whore certainly wasn't lost on Culthwaite.

"Berne," Thorpe added, "I've got to take care of some business back at one of my plantations. If you need me, Samuel will know where to find me."

EIGHTEEN

Battle of Evil Minds

Notoriety has a price. Luke Dunn was beginning to realize that he'd created a sort of monster by virtue of his successes at bringing justice to the Nueces Strip. Seemed that every desperado was now aiming to put a notch in his gun, to build his own reputation by killing a famous Texas Ranger.

With an eventful Christmas behind them, Luke and Elisa were focused on awaiting the impending birth event. Making sure their cattle were all right despite the colder weather seemed more of an afterthought in terms of priorities of the mind. Luke made his daily rounds of Heaven's Gate, but found himself trying to spend more time close by their cabin. They hoped there'd be enough warning that Doc or Bernice would be able to come help. It pretty much went without saying that they prayed for Doc to be sober.

With the increased awareness of his own vulnerability, Luke was concerned that there were enough lawmen in the Corpus Christi area. "I wonder whether Colonel Kinney has found himself another sheriff?"

"It was thoughtful of him to attend George's funeral." Elisa was feeling just a bit uncomfortable. She felt as though her belly might explode, and the kicking had become unmerciful. Like Luke, she was striving to keep her mind off the lives she was carrying. "I can't say as I was impressed with that deputy sheriff he dragged along with him."

"He asked me if I could help in Corpus Christi until he found a full-time sheriff."

"And you said…?" Elisa was naturally worried that Luke would over-extend himself.

"I told him I'd do what I could, but had higher priority responsibilities here with you."

Elisa smiled. She felt a little more secure. She put her hand over the amulet Three Toes had given her. Between that and her Bible, she felt pretty much up to weathering just about any challenge.

The momentary quiet of the cabin was broken by a noise from outside. They heard a horse approaching. Luke grabbed his Colt rifle and cautiously peered out the window. "Lisa, it's Scarlett come to visit."

He hustled out to greet Scarlett, who was carrying little Margaret in a papoose sort of sack. He held her horse while she dismounted and ushered herself into the cabin.

"Welcome, Scarlett. How's the baby?" Elisa greeted her with a broad smile.

Scarlett warmed her hands at the fireplace. "She's doing well, Elisa. How are you feeling?"

Luke was standing back just a bit awkwardly as the ladies went through their greetings. He wondered what had brought Scarlett out to Heaven's Gate. Was it just a friendly visit or was something important on her mind?

"Seems to be getting colder this season." Elisa took Margaret in her arms. "She's so pretty, Scarlett. She has your eyes…and hair."

Luke couldn't take it any longer. "So, what brings you all the way out to Heaven's Gate, Scarlett?"

Elisa gave him one of those "don't be in such a hurry" looks.

Scarlett continued before the fireplace. "That weather just chills you right to the bone, doesn't it?" She acted as though deep in thought for another moment. "I'm thinking of moving to Corpus Christi. I'd love to move to Austin, but something deep inside me is fearful that some sort of danger lurks there. I suppose it's what they call a woman's intuition."

From Luke's perspective, at last they were getting somewhere. "Can we help?"

"I was thinking of setting up a seamstress shop. Bernice and Agatha have been teaching me and feel that I'm ready to be on my own. Do you know anyone in Corpus that might be helpful? I have some money saved."

Luke thought back to the long ride across the Nueces Strip with Scarlett as she escaped Laredo and chased her murderous lover. It was quite a history. She'd been through a lot since then, and her terrible luck with her choices of men seemed to be a curse no one should have to endure. Perhaps she'd find a man worthy of her in Corpus Christi, though it wouldn't be so easy with her being a single mother. But for a few more weeks of George's relentlessly courting her, she might have been a widow.

"I'd be pleased to introduce you to Colonel Kinney, Scarlett," Luke said. "He'd likely as not be helpful toward finding you a place." Luke pondered a moment longer. "Oh, and I also have a cousin in Corpus that's a blacksmith and farrier. I'm certain he and his family would be pleased to give you some connection to the community."

"That's so generous, Luke Dunn. Elisa is so fortunate to have you as her man."

"I think it's the other was around, Scarlett. I'm the lucky one." He looked over at Elisa. She'd turned just a tad pale, grimacing as one of the twins kicked hard.

"Whew, they're kickin' up a storm, Lucas. I'm thinking they're anxious to see the world." The combination of rambunctiousness in her womb and a touch of morning sickness were working on Elisa mentally and physically. "I pray this won't go on much longer. I'm

220

still a couple of weeks away if Doc is right."

Luke wanted to help, but was nevertheless helpless.

Scarlett smiled sweetly. Having experienced childbirth, she could fully appreciate Elisa's condition. "I'll help in any way I can, Elisa."

Cutter John was up unusually early. It had snowed during the night, and Uvalde had become a winter wonderland for those inclined to appreciate those sorts of things. "Damn," he thought. It meant any trails out of town would be deadly slippery. Thankfully, there'd been no blizzard, and the snow would likely melt by nightfall. He wasn't anxious to face Roy Biggs with any decision as to helping him give Luke Dunn his come-uppance. He generally didn't fear much of anything, but knew that a bit of fear in any endeavor kept you careful. As he figured it, you never wanted to be too complacent.

As fate would have it, Cutter's morning idyll was shattered by Biggs' voice. "Cutter. Mornin', my friend. Looks like we got a touch of snow last night."

Cutter ignored Biggs' stating of the obvious. In his mind, he saw the snow as delaying any escape from facing Biggs' pressure to help in his quest. He resigned himself to having to face the question. "Let's get some coffee, Roy. I've been thinking about your Texas Ranger problem." Cutter threw on his coat and gingerly ventured out onto the snow-covered road in front of the boarding house.

Biggs took a step onto the slippery wooden step, slipped, and half-fell backward against the door jam. "Damn." He winced in pain, as his leg wounds were still raw. Turned out his left arm had also been briefly dislocated at the shoulder and popped back in back at Twin Creeks. He'd done enough damage that it had become painful and useless for several days. With his leg wounds healing and the arm feeling better, he was getting the itch for action.

Cutter suppressed a laugh. It wouldn't do to make fun of Roy Biggs, even as a friend. Evil respected evil.

They finally slipped and slid their way to the hotel down the street. Soon enough, they were ordering breakfast and sipping hot coffee.

Cutter stared thoughtfully into the coffee mug. "You know, Roy, approaching this Texas Ranger business as revenge is a fool's game. Revenge is emotional. It robs you of your wits."

Given Biggs' history of killing, you'd have thought he'd understand. He was a cool operator except in those flash-anger incidents where he felt an inner passionate impulse to kill. "It drives me, Cutter."

"Look at what you have, Roy. You've got your life, still plenty of money, and likely as not a lot of years ahead if you don't put yourself in front of the muzzle of a certain Texas Ranger's gun."

"I sure could use your help in this, Cutter." Biggs' turned his squinty, snake-like eyes to stare intently at Cutter. He didn't even look down at his breakfast as he stuffed some steak and egg into his gaping mouth. "The man caused me to lose my family and my home."

"What about the soldiers? You gonna chase after them, too? And wasn't there some Comanche you mentioned?" Cutter paused to let that sink in. "You gonna get them after you get...or if you get the Ranger?"

Biggs was frustrated. He'd expected support from his old friend. Instead, he was getting arguments against his quest. "You think on it a bit more, Cutter."

"Damn, Roy, killing that Ranger won't make your pain go away." Even a diabolical murderer like Cutter John was smart enough to know this. "Move on. Rebuild. Then, if you're still of a mind, go after the sonofabitch. You've gotta have your head right, Roy."

Biggs stared stoically across the table. He knew Cutter was right.

"Now, Roy, if you're lookin' for some real action, let's go kill us some Comanche."

Biggs gave him a look as though he was nuts.

"Seriously. I hear there's an Indian agent up toward Camp Cooper on the Brazos River that hates redskins so much, he's putting a bounty on them."

"Cutter, you can't be in your right mind. You think I'm crazy for wanting to kill a Texas Ranger? Comanche would as soon scalp and castrate you alive and breathing as look at you."

"Just sayin', Roy. I've heard the tribes have weakened considerable since the days of Buffalo Hump's big raid back in '40. There's some chief name of Three Toes that's camped a few days ride north of here. It's a small encampment on the Pedernales River of mostly women and children."

"You are serious." Biggs pondered Cutter's suggestion. "If we go up and grab some Indian scalps and I still want to go after that Ranger, will you help me out?"

"Likely, Roy. No promises."

Biggs thought about asking Cutter if he was scared, but decided that would be far too provocative. No one could ever say Cutter John was fearful of anything. Careful for sure, but not fearful. Yep, no point in riling up a man that was so handy with a knife.

The alley was dark as alleys went. It held a stench of urine, vomit, and booze. To make matters worse, if such could be imagined, there was a body long moldering at the end of the passageway. Culthwaite wasn't exactly excited about passing through, but it was the only way to get where he had to go without being seen. He held his breath as best he could, covering his face with a bandana for the final few steps. He saw that his boots had some sort of alley slime on them, and he hoped he'd find a place to rinse them off.

He turned left up a wider alley. Blessedly, it was cleaner, not antiseptically clean, but better than what he'd just emerged from. At the end, he came to a dark, well-aged door. He knocked four times, then heard a latch release. Slowly, the door opened a few inches.

"Whatcha want?" It was a gnarly voice. The muzzle of a pistol snuck out just enough so Culthwaite knew it was there.

"*Está Jabalí aquí?*" He offered his best attempt at Spanish. *Jabalí* was the nickname for Kern Roberts. Translated, *jabalí* meant "wild boar," about as tough and nasty a critter as could be found in Texas.

"*Jabalí's* not…"

Culthwaite flashed a silver coin in front of the pistol muzzle.

The door opened wide enough for Culthwaite to enter.

"Berne? Berne Culthwaite?" The voice emanated from the opposite side of the darkened room. It was in stark contrast to the bright sun pouring down on Austin that day.

"Kern, what the hell are you doing in this dark, God-forsaken place?"

"Easier on my eyes, compadre. Had a bit of a gunpowder accident the other day and was told to rest my eyesight for a few days." He gave an ironic sort of smile. "So, why are you traipsing through Austin's back-alley slime?"

"Low profile, Kern."

"Humph. Another big client, eh?"

"Big is as good a description as any." Culthwaite thought on Thorpe's girth. It brought a smile to his face. "One of them plantation owners. You know the ones. They sprinkle money around Austin and act like they own the place." He shook his head. "Maybe they do. Anyway, he's back tending to his slaves and cotton while I see to cleaning up his mess."

"So what do you need?"

"Two U.S. marshals are escorting a prisoner to Washington, D.C. He's a witness that could expose my patron."

"Have they left Austin?"

"Heading out on tomorrow's train."

"I know a few marshals. If these are men I know, it'll be an easy job."

"It's worth five hundred dollars to my patron. You just need to dispose of the witness."

"Happy to oblige, Berne. But, say, how come you're not handling this personally?"

"Got a bigger critter to hunt. I'm lookin' to kill a Texas Ranger."

"You're not goin' after that Ranger that's been tearing up the Nueces Strip, are you?"

Culthwaite nodded.

"Damn, Berne. You've got a death wish."

Culthwaite nodded. "It's gonna be tough. But, if you'd be kind enough to dispose of this Thaddeus Brown fella, I'd be much obliged."

"Ha, I've heard of Brown. What a snake! Heard he'd been stealing from Army inventory and Indian agencies all over Texas. Not sure whether to be jealous or envious…or both. Kind of look forward to this one, my friend." He rubbed his hands with a certain gleefulness. "You got the money?"

"You know the deal. Half now, half when the work is done. Hey, and there's a bonus. My client wants me to bring back a certain prostitute. She's a redhead that he's obsessed over. When I've had my way, I just might give you a turn." Culthwaite handed him a small bag, turned, and exited. He looked ahead. He didn't relish navigating the alley slime again so, against his better judgment, he turned away from the alley. He pulled his hat low over his face. He didn't see a certain passerby note his emergence onto the street.

Culthwaite headed back to his hotel. He still needed to clean his boots.

Moments later, Rip Ford was knocking on Kern Roberts' door. As it opened a crack, Ford kicked it in. "What's up, *Jabali*?" The man who'd cracked the door open lay sprawled out on the stone floor.

Roberts blinked as a shaft of light unexpectedly shot in through the open door. "Huh?"

"What sort of no good is Culthwaite up to?" Ford found the stench in the room quite unpleasant and determined not to stay any longer than needed.

Roberts wasn't about to mention the Thaddeus Brown job or intimate at the side action with the whore. "He's talking about going after some Ranger in Corpus Christi."

"You watch yourself, you hear?" Ford pointed a threatening finger at *Jabalí*, then turned and left. He'd have to send Luke a warning.

NINETEEN

New Life

Three Toes walked slowly around the encampment in the early morning mist. With only six teepees, the camp was small. He saw that as an advantage, since its size, along with the protection of the huge rock outcropping, meant they were not so vulnerable. From a distance, it would take a practiced eye to find them. He wrapped his blanket more tightly around his shoulders as a chill wind began to herald the beginnings of another early winter day.

With two of his wives pregnant, more duties were thrust upon Moon Woman, his first wife. The men had conducted their first hunt at the new encampment and had brought back three deer. Moon Woman was hard at work preparing the meat and had already mounted the hide on a stretching frame to begin the tanning process. She was diligently scraping off fat, flesh, and fur toward eventually making buckskin clothing. Soon enough, she'd be smoking the skin to make it soft and supple.

Three Toes' pregnant wives busied themselves with repairing moccasins and ensuring that his chiefly robes were in good order.

The chief looked out to the mostly wooded area surrounding the encampment. He still had twenty of his original herd of more than a hundred horses. He'd see to adding to his herd come spring and warmer weather. He squinted to better see into the trees for signs of anything amiss.

Bear Slayer approached the chief as he was contemplating the tribe's situation. "What are your thoughts, my Chief?"

"I don't like this place, Bear Slayer. It speaks bad medicine to me, and I don't like what I hear. We must move again soon."

Bear Slayer nodded. He held Three Toes in highest regard. "We are small in number, my Chief. Enemies might find us an easy target."

"You are wise, Bear Slayer. That is my concern as well. We have only three experienced warriors among us." Three Toes saw this warrior standing before him as the future of the Penateka Comanche. Bear Slayer might eventually become a chief, but it would be of a decidedly different nature of tribe, as they would learn to live among the white man. He knew they had perhaps two or three more years of true freedom before they'd have no choice but to return to the white man's reservation. For now, they'd be constantly on guard while trying to enjoy hunting and fishing and the various traditions of their lives as practiced for many centuries.

Three Toes sniffed the air. Something wasn't right, but he couldn't quite figure it out. He peered again into the trees. Nothing moved; nothing stood out.

Bear Slayer watched. He sensed it, too, but he'd take the lead of his chief. He stroked his left forearm. It was heavily scarred and ached just a bit in cold weather. The scarring had been earned in the bear fight that gave him his warrior name. He'd slain the black bear with only his knife as weapon. It may have been a badge of honor, but that didn't stop it from aching.

"Let's go back to our village." The two turned and walked briskly back to the cluster of teepees. "We must post a sentry from now on, Bear Slayer. I will take first duty."

Horatio Thorpe picked up his newspaper at breakfast. He was in a bit of a hurry, as he had an appointment with his tailor before he headed back to his plantation.

He scooped an out-sized forkful of eggs while simultaneously filling his mouth with an out-sized bite of heavily buttered biscuit. Below the fold of the newspaper, a headline blared out at him. The fork fell with a clang onto his plate. It was enough to draw attention from other diners.

Thorpe glanced around apologetically. "Federal Witness Killed in Custody of Marshals" blared out from the page. Thorpe enjoyed a broad smile. His "fixer" was already delivering as promised. Now, he'd await news of the fate of that damnable Texas Ranger and perhaps even enjoy the company of the red-haired whore from Laredo.

With the welcome news, he became even more ravenous and ordered a second breakfast. He didn't notice the judgmental looks from diners around the room as they observed this rotund man further engorging himself.

"I have to head to Corpus, Lisa. I told Colonel Kinney I'd help when I could. I'll return tomorrow."

"Promise?"

"Promise." He swept her to him and then put on the heavy buckskin coat Elisa had made for him. The Colt revolvers seemed to know where to go as they slid into holster and waistband.

Elisa gave her husband the once-over. She was at once proud and fearful. His six-foot-three, well-muscled frame struck fear in the very inner core of any lawbreaker. Yet, this same larger-than-life physique could be incredibly gentle, even tender. She loved it when he regaled her with stories from his growing up in County Kildare in Ireland, about his large and loving family, and his loving, but rebellious spirit.

NUECES REPRISE

He had an instinctive dislike of injustice, especially by tyrannical government. It had led to his having to leave his birthplace and begin anew in Texas. "I love you, Lucas Dunn." She gave him one last kiss before he strode out the door to saddle Big Horse and hit the trail to Corpus Christi.

Alternating between walking the big gray and cantering astride the stallion, Luke arrived at Colonel Kinney's house in the early afternoon. He hitched Big Horse and walked purposefully to the door.

To Luke's surprise, the door opened before he could knock, and Colonel Kinney stood before him, welcoming him inside. The merchant turned politician and speculator was fresh from an ill-fated attempt to establish a colony in Nicaragua. It seemed he was unable to take advantage of the U.S. policy of manifest destiny, as he lost to a more powerful, better-connected foe. "Welcome, Captain Dunn. I happened to see you riding toward the house, and figured I'd greet you myself. I'm truly glad to see you." He ushered Luke to his library.

"You'd asked me to check in from time to time, Colonel."

"Far as I know, there's been nothing that the deputy sheriff hasn't been able to handle. He's not the best, but he's trying his best and slowly learning the ropes."

"Have you found a good candidate for sheriff, Colonel?"

"Recall when we first met?" the colonel asked.

"You mean just before the cock fights?"

"Yes. There was a man I'd hired to blend in with the crowd and keep an eye on everyone." Kinney offered Luke a cigar, which he politely refused. "Well, I'm considering this fellow for the job. I'm trying to lure him away from Houston. It's a matter of money, of course, but I think he'll join us down here."

"Sounds promising. I thought I'd check on your deputy and head back home tomorrow. Anything special I need to be aware of?"

"Oh, this arrived for you last night. A messenger rode pretty hard from Austin to bring it here. If you hadn't shown up today, I'd have sent it on to Nuecestown." He handed a sealed envelope to Luke.

"And here's a bit of what I promised you for keeping an eye on things around here." Another envelope found its way into Luke's hands.

"Thank you, Colonel." Luke pocketed the second envelope, but felt a certain immediacy attached to the first. After all, it had been specially delivered by courier. He tore it open. Inside was a hand-scrawled message in a script he readily recognized.

Colonel Kinney anxiously anticipated whatever news Luke had received. "What's it about, Captain?"

"It's from Rip Ford." Luke read the note, then reread it. He handed it to Kinney.

"Whew, Berne Culthwaite's looking for you?"

"You know the man?"

"They call him the fixer. He fixes problems for high-placed folks; ties up loose ends, so to speak."

"Wonder why he'd be interested in me?"

The colonel marveled at Luke's occasional naiveté. "I suspect it has something to do with those folks that were cheating the Indian agencies and Army forts. They still haven't found the head of that snake. I expect he's a very powerful person."

Luke thought on how vulnerable he was in Nuecestown, especially with Elisa drawing closer to her delivery date. He had a family to protect. "This Culthwaite fella, how does he work?"

"I hear he's plenty cautious. They've never been able to pin anything on him. Here, look at this." He thrust the newspaper at Luke. He'd drawn a circle around the story of Thaddeus Brown meeting his end and the two U.S. marshals not knowing how it could have happened. "This is typical Culthwaite work. If possible, he contracts his work, lest he dirty his own hands. He doesn't like confrontations. I've heard he's right handy with a .50 caliber Sharps. No surprise what well-placed money can do, Luke. Oh, and this Culthwaite fellow owns a successful shipping company. Has about two dozen ships."

Luke shook his head thoughtfully. "Thanks, Colonel. I'd best be on my way." He knew he had some serious thinking to do as to how to best protect his family while meeting his lawman duties. The justice business seemed to grow tougher all the time.

He hadn't made any long trail rides in quite a while. Given the cooler winter weather, Berne Culthwaite didn't especially appreciate the contrast of his warm house in Austin and the wind cutting through him riding astride the back of a horse.

He had found his old Sharps .50 caliber rifle. It was a great weapon for bushwhacking unsuspecting victims and suited his style. He slid it into the scabbard attached to his saddle. The Sharps was indeed essential to his strategy. Confrontation was something to be avoided. He would avoid close-in gunplay at all costs.

Just in case, he slipped a Walker Colt into his holster. He wasn't exactly heavily armed, but he had weapons that he was fairly comfortable with. He felt obliged to take this job on personally. Besides, the money was quite handsome compensation.

He outfitted two horses, one for riding and the other for packing his equipment. The pack horse held the creature comforts he'd otherwise miss while on the trail. Culthwaite was not one for roughing it. He shuddered at the thought of the trail ahead. Given his inclination to sleep late, he calculated it would take him about ten days. With the winter on hand, he remained concerned with the changeability of the Texas weather. He'd given passing thought to hiring a manservant for the brief gig. However, he recognized that such a situation could impact the stealth factor essential to his mission.

He mounted up and headed south. A half-day into his journey, he began to have regrets. It was too damned quiet, for one thing. The chill Texas breeze was wearing him down already. He regretted not hiring the manservant, as he could have disposed of him later. At least, he'd have had someone to talk with. In about four days, he'd be riding into San Antonio. He determined to take a couple of days off to shake out the trail dust and warm his bones.

Luke left Corpus Christi early. He wasn't sure what to expect of this contract killer. It could be days before he showed up. Not much he could do.

Alerting the folks in Nuecestown would serve as a sort of early warning of trouble. Dan had returned from Corpus Christi, having taken Elisa's advice to learn a trade. He'd worked at learning to be a farrier, and figured to ply his new skills at the Nuecestown livery stable. Luke expected that Dan was still fairly handy with a gun. He'd sure been an asset a few months back, when Carlos Perez rode at breakneck speed through the town's defenses. With all manner of shooting going on, Dan had remained cool.

With Elisa closer to her due date, Luke prayed for no confluence with Culthwaite's arrival.

Soon enough, Luke rode up to their cabin. He dismounted and walked Big Horse over to the corral, currying and feeding the big stallion before heading to the warmth of the cabin.

He opened the door and strode in. He held out a couple of tiny blankets he'd bought in Corpus Christi for the twins.

Elisa was lying back on the bed. "Lucas, thank God you're back… it's time…they're early, Lucas."

Luke noticed the damp pool on the floor near the fireplace.

"I've watched Doc. Warm up some water, Lucas. Hurry."

Obviously, there was no time to fetch help from town. This would literally be a labor of love between the two of them. Luke threw off his heavy coat and rolled up his sleeves. He pushed Elisa's skirt up and slipped an oil cloth sheet under her.

Elisa moaned. "Oh, Lucas…help…it hurts." She took deep breaths and pushed. She remembered what Doc had said about breathing and pushing. She wrapped her hand tightly around Luke's.

Luke managed to stay surprisingly calm. "Push…" He encouraged her. "Oh, my God, Lisa, I see a head." Luke gently caught the first in his huge hands. It was a boy who quickly gasped for air and screamed a greeting to the world. Luke lay the child on the blanket.

No sooner had Luke turned back to her, Elisa let out another low moan and pushed. "Lucas, I feel another…oh, my…" She pushed hard. Once. Twice. A second boy slipped into Luke's waiting hands. Instinct had taken over her young body as she delivered the new lives within her. Amazingly and certainly blessedly, she'd delivered twins in a span of a mere twenty minutes.

Luke was caught in total amazement at what had just transpired. "Lisa, we've got a family!"

Both boys were screaming with new-found air in their lungs as they entered an unfamiliar world. Luke began to tenderly wash them.

"Tie off their cords, Lucas." Despite exhaustion, she worked at cleaning herself up as Luke tended to their sons. "Names? We need to give them names, my love."

Luke really hadn't thought about names. "They sound like Irishmen, Lisa. What do you think?"

Elisa had sunk back exhausted into the bedding. Luke wrapped the twins in the new blankets and placed them on either side of her. "I think they're hungry already."

Luke could contain himself no longer; tears of joy ran down his cheeks. He sat on the bedside, watching the marvel of his wife feeding the twin boys. "How about Peter and John? They're good strong biblical names, Lisa."

"Peter and John. I like those names, Lucas. I like…" As she nursed, tiredness overcame her and words trailed off.

He watched as she fell asleep with their sons at her breasts. He was now a father as well as husband. Once again, he began thinking about being a lawman versus a rancher. It would now be tougher to be both. They'd be growing their ranch holdings soon enough; it would be a lot more to care for. He'd likely need to hire some *vaqueros*, too. Was it selfish to place himself at risk chasing desperadoes across the Nueces Strip?

It was a reprise of an earlier theme for Elisa and him. What price was justice?

He got up and peered thoughtfully out the window. A tumbleweed bumped along with the breeze across the open space in front of their cabin. Where was it headed? It certainly had no particular direction, dependent as it was on the wind. It was surely going to get to wherever it was headed. If tumbleweeds could think, they'd likely be frustrated at not being able to determine their direction. Luke appreciated that, while he had decisions to make, he wasn't dependent upon the randomness of the wind.

Cold reality struck him. Regardless of his decision, his success had bred notoriety. Whether Texas Ranger or not, thugs like Culthwaite would come after him. For some it might be business, for others revenge and, for still others, the ability to boast at having killed a famous lawman. The reason didn't matter. He couldn't hide, and he had to protect his family from harm. He decided he needed to hire men who were more than *vaqueros*.

He turned from the window and heard a horse approaching. He pivoted and glanced back outside. He threw on his coat and eased the door open so as not to awaken Elisa, Peter, and John. He said their names under his breath. It felt good. He stepped onto the gallery.

"Horace…Horace Rucker. I'm glad to see you, my friend."

Rucker dismounted and tied his horse to the hitching post. He extended his hand to Luke, but Luke walked past the proffered hand and hugged the newly retired colonel. As his chest was compressed in Luke's vice-like grasp, he managed, "Good to see you, too, Luke. What's new?"

As he stepped away, Luke noted that Rucker was lightly armed and held a Bible in his hand. "Elisa…we just had twin boys, Horace. It was only a bit ago." He smiled broadly, and took in the man before him. "I see you're changing professions. You a man of the cloth now?"

"Congratulations, Luke. That's great news." He smiled. "I remember my first."

"You can see them when they wake up."

"In answer to your question, Luke, I was never that great at soldiering."

"What brings you down this way?"

"I needed to get away from certain folks in Austin. Thought I'd establish myself in Corpus Christi, then bring my wife down here."

"Great news. We could use more preaching around these parts." Luke grew suddenly serious. "But it's hard to escape, Horace. I've been warned that someone has been dispatched from Austin to kill me. It's apparently linked to that business you were involved with."

Rucker shook his head with deep concern. "Sounds as though we're going to need more than prayer, Luke. Maybe I should hole up in Nuecestown for a spell. In fact, that's what I'll do. Shucks, those folks could use a bit of religion."

"Much obliged, Horace."

"Oh, and I can still shoot, Captain Dunn. I'm not what they call a pacifist." Truth be told, Rucker had become aware that there were folks on the Nueces Strip that didn't cotton to religion. In fact, a number of priests and preachers had met their Maker at the hands of men who were fearful of religion, for whatever reason. It didn't have to make sense. Just a few days previous, Rucker had met two priests on the road from Corpus Christi to Laredo, and they were armed to the teeth.

"Having another armed citizen around just might come in handy, Horace." Luke had a passing vision of a preacher in a gunfight. "Colonel Kinney still hasn't hired a new sheriff. I expect you heard about George Whelan?"

"Yeah, good lawman. Heard he'd just become a father with that woman…what's her name…Scarlett Rose. Pity. I expect I'll always regret not getting to apologize for chasing after him on General Truax's orders. Pity indeed."

Peter and John began to cry. It would always be in unison. "Mr. Rucker, you're about to meet our family. Just give me a few moments."

Luke ushered Rucker inside. "Elisa, Horace Rucker is here."

"Hang on, Luke. Good to see you, Horace. Please sit." Elisa went off to a sheltered corner of the cabin to nurse the boys.

"Say, I don't want to be any trouble."

Elisa talked over her shoulder. "You set yourself back down, Horace Rucker. You are our guest for dinner. You'll have plenty of time to get back to Nuecestown." It was almost as though delivering twins had merely been a pause in her routine, as she displayed the strength typical of so many women on the frontier.

Dinner invitation settled, Luke and Rucker busied themselves in talk about Texas and the issues facing the state. Luke dipped deep into thought. "You been hearing about this slave and free state business? What do you think, Horace?"

"I've heard about some upstart politicians trying to end slavery. I'm not so certain they'll succeed. There are too many folks preaching violence. Shoot, it could even wind up dividing families."

"I've got a cousin with a lot of cotton acreage. I know he has slaves. I'd pay a wage to the couple of *vaqueros* we need. Can't imagine owning people." Luke's gaze wandered off. "We were nearly slaves to the English back in Ireland."

Elisa walked over with a child on each hip. "Mr. Rucker, meet Peter and John."

"Pleased to make your acquaintance, boys."

Elisa placed the boys in a seat Luke had made. "As to those black folks, I've heard they bleed red just like us."

Rucker sat back. "It's interesting here in Texas. Up toward Austin, the German immigrants are mostly opposed to slavery, even for economic advantage. I just hope and pray that it doesn't divide the nation any worse than it has and hope especially that it doesn't divide Texas."

"We'd best stick to our knitting, Horace. You're learnin' to preach and we've got a ranch to run. Hopefully, the slave business will get resolved without us sticking our noses into it." Intuitively, Luke sensed that it would become everyone's problem soon enough.

Elisa stirred the stew that had been brewing. The duties of mother had now been added to her role.

Cutter John realized early on that Roy Biggs was a reluctant companion. Nevertheless, he appreciated the company. If they happened upon any of those disgustingly barbaric Comanche, he'd at least be of some help. A downside was that Biggs kept up pretty near constant chatter. And he couldn't seem to get that Texas Ranger from his mind. Cutter recognized that he'd eventually have to either separate himself from Biggs or join his perverse revenge quest.

They were into the heart of the central Texas hills and woodlands, wending their way around stands of oak and juniper. The trails also accessed more heavily wooded areas of pecan, elm, sycamore, walnut, and hackberry in the major drainages. They found a reasonably shallow passage across the Pedernales River and waded northward through the frigid waters. Cypress, buttonbush, and ash grew thick on the terraced shore beside the river.

Cutter noted the dark threatening clouds swelling up to the northwest. He decided it was time to find shelter for what was fixing to be a blizzard of sorts. "Roy, we need to travel quietly from here on. I sense that our prey is close at hand." He looked back at Biggs trailing behind with their pack horse. "Let's take cover over there under that rock outcropping. I'm thinking there's going to be a pretty fair snow storm, and pushing on could get just a tad riskier than I care for."

They rode their horses up under the rock shelf and dismounted. They'd be afforded shelter on three sides. Importantly, it faced south such that the wind wasn't in their faces. Cutter began to set a fire.

"What are we going to eat?"

Cutter put a finger to his lips to silence Biggs as a stupidly curious deer got within fifty feet or so. The swiftness with which Cutter threw the knife and felled the doe caught Biggs by total surprise.

"Damn, Cutter."

Again, Cutter placed finger to lips. In a matter of but a few minutes, he had the doe skinned and choice cuts ready to cook. He whispered, "This might do for a couple of days."

Within the hour, the temperature dropped precipitously, wind picked up to a banshee-like howl, and snow began to fly horizontally past their shelter.

Not ten miles away to the north, Three Toes had his people ready to withstand the coming blizzard. From the warmth of his teepee, he listened to the roar of the wind and heard the snow pelting its walls. Moon Woman kept the fire stoked, and she and Three Toes' other wives kept their minds off the storm by busying themselves with chores.

Three Toes thought on Bear Slayer's concerns. The end of the Comanche as marauding warriors dominating the landscape was drawing near.

He still had a sense within his inner consciousness that something in this place was not quite right. He vowed to explore the area once the storm abated.

With the morning came the end of the storm. The chief peered from the entrance flap of the teepee. Snow had covered everything in sight. With the sunrise, the warm rays would melt nearly all of the six inches or so of snow that blanketed the encampment. He instinctively grabbed his white robe, stuffed the revolver in his waistband, picked up his bow and arrows, and slipped out of the teepee. Moon Woman and the others were still asleep. He mounted his best pony, a white stallion and, on instinct, headed southward. The whiteness of his trappings and horse were like a camouflage against the backdrop of snow.

Culthwaite watched the storm pass far to the northwest. Here on the road to San Antonio, the sky seemed stretched such that judging distances was a deceptive endeavor. He decided that he'd been lucky so far as the storm was concerned.

He rode into San Antonio, and it didn't take long to find the essentials for a traveler of his ilk: hotel, saloon, and brothel. The hotel clerk was helpful in recommending the saloon, which would lead to a ringing endorsement of a brothel that turned out to be part of Thorpe's string of establishments. Culthwaite was impressed with extent of the man's business reach.

"You new in San Antone?" The bartender tried to strike up a conversation.

"Can't say that I've been here for a while. Place is growing." Culthwaite tried to be friendly. He didn't want to draw too much attention, as his business depended on working in the shadows. Had he known he'd been seen doing business with *Jabalí* up in Austin, he'd have been far more concerned.

"Stayin' long?"

This barkeep was asking too many questions. Culthwaite chose not to answer. In fact, the brothel began to sound unattractive. He decided to get some rest in a comfortable bed and head out early toward Corpus Christi. He thought again about hiring a manservant, but decided it would cause more problems than it was worth. He could struggle with living on the trail for a few days longer.

He was on the road toward Corpus Christi just as the sun peeked over the eastern horizon. He looked forward to riding with the sun's rays before him, warming his chilled face and hands as best they could. Looking into the blinding light was a small price to trade for the warmth. It would be another five days or so before he reached his final destination. He gave thought to stopping in San Patricio, but judged it would be no better than San Antonio. He needed to focus on his mission. The distractions of saloons and brothels could wait. Still, San Patricio could offer a needed break.

Today was no exception for Roy Biggs. He liked to sleep late.

The fact that it was cold and snow was everywhere in sight did not motivate him to change his routine. Besides, Cutter was cooking up a fine venison steak and had coffee brewing. The smoke from the fire twisted straight up, as there was no longer a breeze. The aroma of sizzling venison was finally enough to draw him out of his bedroll.

"You're quite handy, Cutter."

Cutter gave him a condescending glance. "You do what you have to do, Roy." He looked at Biggs and thoughtfully stroked the couple of days of beard growth he now sported. He was beginning to think Biggs might be more liability than help. Here they were, out in the wilderness of the Comancheria, having endured a heavy snow storm that was nearly of blizzard proportions. For all Cutter knew, there could be Comanche lurking most anywhere in this region. The soldiers were not known for venturing out at this time of year except when there was some serious suspicion of Indian threat. He had heard that the Comanche had mostly dispersed from the Brazos River encampment up near Camp Cooper.

He couldn't know that Three Toes had spotted his campfire, and certainly couldn't know how very near the chief actually was.

Three Toes had ventured out a few miles and, upon seeing the distant smoke, had given passing thought to doubling back to get Bear Slayer. However, he feared going back might mean losing whatever possible opportunity lurked in the snow-draped hills ahead. The smoke was too thick to be Comanche or trappers. He suspected that it was from a small group of perhaps two and no more than three in number. He was confident he could handle this himself, especially if he maintained the element of surprise.

The trail featured occasional icy spots that the chief had to be wary of. He had to trust the sure-footedness of his pony. As he drew closer, he dismounted. With the terrain turning even icier at slightly higher elevation, it was best not to take chances. He moved off the trail and stayed low, all the better to blend among the trees.

He heard men talking. The voices weren't especially loud, so they were exercising some modest amount of caution. He decided there were only two, and they were white. Of a sudden, a horse neighed. Apparently, they were in the process of breaking camp. Three Toes' practiced instincts knew they'd be at their most vulnerable.

The snow effectively muffled the chief's approach, not that Cutter and Biggs would have heard him anyway. The white blanket continued to camouflage him visually, as he'd also worn his near-white buckskins. He breathed slowly, lest vapors give him away. His prey were blissfully unaware of approaching danger.

Three Toes thought about the Colt revolver in his waistband, but his gut inclination was to use his trusty bow and arrows. The two men finally came into view. He nocked an arrow and watched for just the right moment.

Cutter lifted the sack onto the pack horse. Both his hands were occupied.

Biggs was partially screened behind the pack horse. "Damn, Cutter, this cold weather stinks. Is this really worth a few bounties?"

Cutter grunted as he let the sack settle on the horse's back. There was a whoosh, and he found himself staring down at an arrowhead protruding from his chest. Before he could react, a second shaft followed, not but two inches beside the first. Cutter was a dead man standing. "Roy, I'm hit!" They would be his final words as he fell beside the pack horse.

Biggs dove onto the nearest saddled bronc and hung on for dear life as it leaped from the shelter. Three Toes simply had no time to nock another arrow as the fast-moving target sped by. By some fortune, Biggs' horse didn't slip and fall on the ice-laden trail.

Three Toes calmly put his arrows away and pulled out his knife. Cutter John was still struggling to breathe as Three Toes added a scalp to his collection. He left Cutter John to bleed out. The chief would never appreciate the irony in scalping a man who had lived by the knife. He mounted his pony and led the remaining saddle horse and the pack horse on a track back to his encampment. In addition to Cutter's scalp and the horses, he had captured equipment that could prove useful back at the Comanche encampment. He especially appreciated the venison and deer hide.

Roy Biggs was scared half to death. The horse galloped for at least half a mile before it slipped on a rock. Biggs heard the foreleg break and found himself tossed over the beast's head. He almost hated to waste a bullet putting the horse out of its misery. He was certain that whatever Indian had killed Cutter must have heard the gun's report. The blast seemed to echo into the hills forever.

Biggs took stock of his situation. He decided to take the saddle blanket and rifle. He grabbed the saddle bag and unloaded anything not absolutely necessary so as to lighten its weight.

He became very aware of his vulnerability, finding himself alone and on foot in some of the toughest country to be found in Texas. To make it worse, he had no food or water. He had no choice but to head south, retracing from whence he and Cutter had come. He gave a fleeting thought to following the Indian who'd attacked them. Instinctively, he knew better. He and Cutter had avoided anything resembling civilization on their travel northward, so there was hope that he might happen onto a ranch or stumble onto a trapper's cabin. He cursed the Indian. He cursed Cutter.

He was cold. He knew he had at least three icy rivers to cross, and shivered at the thought. He second-guessed himself as to why he had agreed to join Cutter on this now ill-fated mission. He should have remained focused on pursuing the Texas Ranger. On the upside, the snow was melting. He had the forethought to keep some kindling in the saddlebag so was able to make a fire the first night. He had nothing to eat, but at least he was warm and could melt snow for drinking water.

As he trudged through the hill country wilderness, he was fortunate to find an easy crossing on the Medina River. He began to feel more confident that he'd get back to Uvalde unscathed. The Sabinal River, on the other hand, posed a far greater challenge.

A frigid rain had begun to fall by the time he reached its banks. If only he could find a way to cross while staying reasonably dry. He had about given up hope when he saw what appeared to be a fairly shallow area to cross. Rocks were just beneath the water surface. At worst, he'd get his boots wet. Once on the other side, he figured he could build a fire and then begin the final push back to Uvalde. He held the saddle bags and rifle up high and stepped gingerly out onto the first rock. Two steps, three.

He was almost across when his foot slipped. He nearly caught himself, but he lost his grip on the rifle and, in going for it, tumbled headfirst into the icy waters. He popped up, gasping for air. As if on cue, a cold wind blasted him, and it was all he could do to struggle, slipping and sliding, to shore. To make matters worse, he'd turned his ankle during the dunking. Crawling up the bank, he took stock of his situation as he was wracked with uncontrollable shivering.

The kindling in the saddlebag was soaked and nothing dry was in sight. His ankle throbbed. He saw a cavity among some rocks and decided to take temporary shelter, using the wet saddle blanket as a sort of shelter from the wind. He brought his legs close to his body and rubbed himself to generate warmth. It wasn't long before the dropping temperature had the effect of making him drowsy. Soon enough, he fell asleep.

Lieutenant Belknap was not especially happy. They'd received word that some settlers had seen Comanche. It wasn't his first choice—nor his patrol's—to be out on horseback in the dead of winter.

They'd ridden out of Fort Mason. He had matured in his thinking about this rough frontier enough to differentiate between Comanche having been seen versus having attacked. He did pray that he wouldn't come upon the aftermath of one of their brutal attacks.

He'd heard that Three Toes had left the Brazos River encampment and was somewhere along the Pedernales River or thereabouts. In any case, he headed toward what was formerly Fort Inge near Uvalde.

They were about three days out from Fort Mason when they reached the Sabinal River. They'd endured the same blizzard-like conditions that Cutter and Biggs had faced. They wended their way along the shoreline looking for a reasonably shallow crossing to minimize the men getting soaked with frigid water in the already freezing air. The scenery was beautiful, but they were too cold to fully enjoy it.

"Lieutenant! Lieutenant!" One of the soldiers near the rear of the column called out.

Belknap brought the column to a halt, turned his horse, and ventured cautiously toward the rear. "What's so important, soldier?"

"Look, sir." He pointed to a large lump half-buried in the snow.

Belknap dismounted and approached the object to examine it more closely, only to discover it wasn't an object at all. "Sergeant, get some men over here." It was a half-frozen man.

"He's still breathing, sir." The sergeant could feel the shallow, struggling breaths.

"Well, build a damned fire. Warm up whoever it is."

Three soldiers wrapped blankets around the frozen man. Soon enough, they had a fire going and began to figure out what had happened. He'd clearly been traveling on foot and slipped in the chilled waters of the river. He'd crawled to the shore, but had no dry kindling or means to make a fire. The man had huddled as best he could for warmth in the concave shelter of some rocks and fallen asleep.

Slowly, the man's color began to return and his breathing improved.

"Sergeant, this man looks vaguely familiar." Belknap stared intently at the man's bearded face.

The sergeant bent close. He wasn't certain the man would be able to hear him. "What's your name, sir?"

Dark eyes blinked and came into focus. The man's mouth opened, but no sound came out. "Co..han…che," finally came out in a barely audible, guttural whisper. He wasn't able to enunciate the "m" sound as his swollen and chapped lips wouldn't come together.

Apparently, the man had run into Comanche but had obviously escaped. "What's your name?"

A bit of panic came into the man's eyes as he realized that he was among soldiers.

"Never mind, Sergeant," the lieutenant said. "I recognize him. Let's get him in condition to ride. "We'll find space on a pack horse."

"Sir?"

"It's Roy Biggs. He's wanted on a federal warrant."

The sergeant's expression grew deadly serious. "Almost hate to suffer the inconvenience, sir." The sergeant recalled Biggs' actions at Twin Creeks. "We could let him freeze to death."

Belknap gave him a hard look. "We're not judge and jury out here, Sergeant. Let's have none of that sort of talk." Belknap was surprised that the usually conscientious sergeant would think such a thing. The officer decided he would have to keep a more watchful eye on the patrol, as the cold apparently worked in mysterious ways on normally sensible minds.

Biggs had soon warmed up sufficiently to be lifted to his feet. A few more minutes before the fire, and he became pretty much ambulatory. The soldiers adjusted the load on one of the two pack horses to make space for Biggs to ride. They covered him with a blanket, and Belknap volunteered one of the soldiers to give him dry clothes. With that, they continued the trek toward Uvalde, given that it was closer than heading back to Fort Mason.

"Mr. Biggs, we'll do the best we can for you. You are now a federal prisoner. While we find it distasteful under the circumstances, we are obligated to protect you." Belknap determined to make the situation perfectly clear. "By the way, Mr. Biggs, your hacienda has been mostly dismantled. There were no casualties from your clever traps."

Belknap couldn't suppress a smile as he watched Biggs' snake-like eyes flit disconcertedly. This devil incarnate had at least gotten some of what he was due. The ironic contradiction of the fires of hell versus the frigid climes of the hill country were not lost on the lieutenant.

Belknap still had to make the effort to search for any marauding Comanche, so decided to temporarily deposit Biggs in the Uvalde jail. His plan was to pick Biggs up on the way back from the patrol and take the prisoner back to Fort Mason.

Luke wrapped his coat tightly against the chill. He appreciated the effort Elisa had made in lining it with sheepskin. Big Horse didn't seem to mind the weather. The steed's coat had thickened with the lowering temperatures to better withstand the winter. So long as he was dry, he could endure the cold. Luke, for his part, was scanning for longhorns that might have gotten lost. They'd put out feed in various spots around the ranch, and the cattle would cluster to eat.

He came upon the tripod he'd made a few months back to pry his longhorn bull from the mud. He smiled a bit; the beast had developed into a pretty fair breeder bull. He'd been well worth saving and had earned the nickname *Lodoso*, or Muddy. The *vaqueros* Luke occasionally hired appreciated the humor in the name. In any case, the Dunn herd was growing, along with their property holdings.

Being out on the pastures of the ranch was actually a relief despite the weather, as Luke hadn't gotten a solid night's sleep in several days. The twins would wail in the middle of the night, and Elisa had to be roused to feed them. They'd been assured by Doc that this would change once they got a bit older. Meanwhile, both Luke and Elisa sometimes felt as though they were only half-awake as they made their way through each day.

True to his promise, Luke had escorted Scarlett to Corpus Christi, and she rented a room near his cousin. Except for the looming warning Luke had received from Rip Ford, life was fairly copacetic.

With a new family and the exhilarating feelings of freedom to be experienced on the wide-open vistas of the ranch, Luke's internal conflict between rancher and lawman had attained new dimensions. The instinct to be at home for his family butted hard against the feelings of obligation to be a protector in the broader context of justice. While loyalty to family was by far most important, there was necessarily a loyalty to the greater community that was vulnerable to and in need of defending against lawbreakers. It was reminiscent of the familial closeness within the Irish clans and sects that had evolved over the centuries. The arrival of Peter and John, combined with Elisa's attentions to their needs, had increased this conflict of loyalties by orders of magnitude.

He scanned the horizon and could see nothing amiss. He turned Big Horse and gave him his head to return home.

Berne Culthwaite headed southeast on the road to Corpus Christi. Soon enough, he'd have the opportunity to add to his reputation as the fixer, as he would seek to solve Horatio Thorpe's problem. He didn't appreciate that the weather had grown colder as he headed south. Intuitively, he expected the opposite. Then, again, this was Texas, and the unexpected could be expected.

TWENTY

Danger Lurks

Three Toes regaled his people several times with the story of his attack on the two men in the forest not far from their encampment. The story got better with every telling. He did regret the one who'd escaped, but he knew the man would have a tough time surviving on foot. The scalp and horses were worthy prizes in any case. And the venison had been a bonus.

He had several discussions with Bear Slayer and White Feather about where to move come spring. It was becoming increasingly difficult to separate themselves from the invasion of settlers from the east. These people didn't seem to be put off by the harsh frontier or the dangers from Comanche, indigenous wildlife, and even themselves. He took note of the frictions among the white man, the black man, and the brown man. They were not so different in that respect as the Comanche in their relations with Kiowa, Apache, Ute, Pawnee, Cherokee, and other tribes. The chief reflected on the irony of the meaning of the Comanche name: enemy. Try as the white man might to get the Comanche to settle peacefully, it ran counter to many years of tribal culture and history.

Three Toes convened a tribal council. Seated around a roaring campfire in his teepee, the largest in the camp, he and the warriors discussed the future. The gathering wasn't nearly so large as it used to be. There were only three warriors, and Three Toes was the only elder. The women weren't welcome in the council and busied themselves elsewhere. It was a humble gathering. There was no place for pride, given the way the Penateka and the other dozen Comanche tribes had been defeated in battles with men and disease and scattered to the four winds. The chief had no idea how many Comanche yet survived. Each time he'd returned to Camp Cooper, there were fewer of his people.

After traditional council opening ceremonies, Bear Slayer opened the discussion. "Are we better to find a remote place away from the white man and with good hunting, or do we go back to the Indian agency?" It was a simple enough question and got directly to the essence of their concerns.

Three Toes took a long pull on his pipe. He nodded to White Feather.

White Feather was the youngest of the three. He'd fought with Buffalo Hump years before and excelled in battle. "Can any of us here tolerate the white man's rules?" It was a mostly rhetorical question. None liked the white man's rigid way of life. The white man required written laws to supposedly protect their freedoms. Freedom was a far easier concept for a Penateka Comanche. "I say we find a new camp."

Three Toes considered that two of his wives were very much pregnant. In another fifteen years, there would be new Comanche warriors. But what of now? In fifteen years, the chief would be an old man…if he lived that long. "We must find the others," he pronounced.

Bear Slayer and White Feather nodded agreement. The greater question now became where might they be found?

"One of us goes north, another south. We look for sign of our people." White Feather looked from Bear Slayer to Three Toes. "Three Toes and Bear Slayer are better trackers; I am a strong fighter. I will stay to protect the camp."

Three Toes agreed that the proposal made sense. They smoked the pipe. The journey to find their people and establish a new encampment would begin with the first day of spring.

Scarlett began to settle into life in Corpus Christi. She'd be forever grateful to Luke and Elisa for helping her out. She used her remaining "fortune" to start a seamstress business. No matter that her gold coins had been obtained under dubious circumstances from her erstwhile romantic fling with the outlaw Dirk Cavendish; she felt no guilt. In fact, the gold seemed like a sort of compensation for what she'd endured over the past few years. It was a new day for her.

She decided to go visit her friends. Wrapping little Margaret up for traveling, she rented a buckboard wagon and headed up the road to visit with Bernice and Agatha in Nuecestown.

The bright, sunny, unseasonably warm day made her journey about as pleasant as could be. She even had some business to conduct at the general store, as she'd made a couple of fashionable-looking dresses to sell to the local ladyfolk.

Scarlett parked the buckboard in front of the boarding house and grabbed up Margaret and her satchel. She was of a mind to spend the night. She paused on the front step. Memories swirled through her mind as she stood where Carlos Perez had been killed by George Whelan's bullet just weeks ago. She took a deep breath and knocked.

Bernice was overjoyed to see the two of them and quickly took the baby into her arms. Agatha impatiently awaited her turn. "You spending the night, Scarlett dear?"

"If y'all will still have me." She smiled. She looked past Bernice at the still black-draped doorway to the dining room where Whelan had breathed his last, professing his love for her with his final labored gasps. She was beyond crying and forced a smile for the two ladies.

Bernice was pleased to see Scarlett looking healthy and even relaxed. Leaving her previous profession was apparently proving to be a blessing. "Of course," she said, grinning as she gazed down at the baby. "You can even use the room you were staying in before."

Agatha took Margaret, allowing Bernice to help Scarlett with her things. "We'll be serving dinner in a couple of hours." Agatha smiled. "And Bernice has a new recipe for her roast." The humor in her intimation wasn't lost on any of them. Bernice knew that her roasts had left a lot to be desired.

Culthwaite felt as though he was drawing close to Corpus Christi. He'd passed through San Patricio the day before. Soon enough, he'd be at Nuecestown. He'd enjoyed traveling south and felt fairly safe despite stories of bandits on the road. He had only been to the Nueces Strip once and was thus not likely to be recognized. The combination of his being incognito and maintaining a low profile would combine to work in his favor so far as finding an opportunity to ambush Luke Dunn. He would have to find a way to casually ask directions to Dunn's ranch without raising any suspicion. He also recalled Thorpe's parting request to find the red-haired whore. There were bonus monies there.

The trip had been uneventful. He chalked it up to the weather. With the colder temperatures, folks tended to stay indoors and were more likely to stay out of trouble. Now, it was warming just a bit.

When he wasn't on the trail, which his rear end was detesting more daily, Culthwaite would find a saloon and listen to folk chatter. He felt it best to minimize his own conversation as he didn't want to slip up and reveal his mission.

Some of the talk did pique his interest. A table full of itinerant drovers told of soldiers finding the infamous Roy Biggs half-frozen to death and locking him in the Uvalde jail. Culthwaite vaguely knew of Thorpe's use of Biggs and found it interesting.

He'd spent a night back in San Patricio where he heard stories of the exploits of Texas Ranger Captain Dunn and how he took the measure of the Mexican desperado Carlos Perez. His feat of single-handedly gunning down Perez's men had impressed many folks. He heard less talk about Bad Bart Strong and Dirk Cavendish. By all accounts, this Texas Ranger's success was a combination of skill, dogged perseverance, and uncanny luck. He hoped the luck part would run out so as to even his own odds.

He was curious about the Comanche chief Luke was said to have allied with. He heard that the chief had a habit of showing up just when the Texas Ranger needed him. He also heard the Comanche admired Dunn enough to have given him a name: Ghost-Who-Rides. That was big medicine. Culthwaite wasn't a man normally to be taken with superstition. On the other hand, a well-placed slug from the Sharps rifle could likely offset any sort of Comanche medicine.

At last, Nuecestown came into view. He considered his situation. Here he was, a stranger riding into town. They likely saw plenty of strangers, thanks to the ferry crossing and being on the road to San Antonio, but not so many came through sporting a Sharps. He decided to pass himself off as a hunter heading west to find buffalo.

He rode up to Bernice's and Agatha's boarding house, dismounted, and knocked.

Bernice opened the door. She was the one who usually answered the door to greet possible guests. "Welcome to Nuecestown, sir. May we help you?"

"Why, yes, ma'am. I'm passing through for some sport hunting." He smiled inwardly, as that technically wasn't a lie. "I'd like to have a room for the night."

"Well, we'd be pleased to have you. You can sign here." She turned a register to Culthwaite. "We take two dollars in advance, and you can put your horses up at the livery up the street for no charge."

"Why, thank you, ma'am. I look forward to a restful time here in Nuecestown." He signed the register as John Smith.

As Culthwaite strode out the door to see to his horses, Bernice looked at the register. "John Smith?" she whispered under her breath. The initials on his leather wallet were "BC." Who was this guest, and what was he hiding? She'd have to alert Luke just in case this was the man he'd warned the town about. "Agatha? Agatha, fetch Dan but don't make a big thing about it."

When Culthwaite returned, she made certain he was settled into a room. She noted that he kept his big Sharps rifle especially close at hand and couldn't help but notice the Colt revolver in his holster. She decided this guest wasn't there to hunt game.

Culthwaite got himself reasonably comfortable in the room Bernice had escorted him to. He decided to wait until later in the day to venture out. He had been told by a talkative drunk in San Patricio that the Texas Ranger lived about five miles east of Nuecestown near the road to Corpus Christi. He was determined to take an exploratory ride.

He decided to partake of dinner at the boarding house. Upon entering the dining room, he couldn't help but notice a very attractive red-haired woman dining with a small child by her side. He soon found himself staring at her and wondering whether this could be the woman Thorpe had mentioned. He nodded in her direction. "Pardon, ma'am, are you from these parts?"

Scarlett was a bit put off by the man's question. After all, who was he to ask such a question of a woman traveling alone? "Why, yes, sir, I've lived here a bit."

Culthwaite decided to be bold. "You ever live in Laredo?"

Scarlett blushed. "No, sir, no, I haven't." Her blush said otherwise.

Culthwaite had his answer. "Sorry, ma'am, I expect I mistook you for someone else." He didn't bother her with more questions. There would be time enough to deal with her after he settled things with the Texas Ranger. He was appreciative that good fortune might be on his side. He finished dinner and headed up to his room.

As he was ready to settle down, he saw the young man from the livery making haste on the road eastward from town. He decided that was just too much of a coincidence with his arrival. Perhaps he'd need to make his move on the Ranger sooner.

Culthwaite grabbed the Sharps, checked that the Colt was loaded, pocketed a handful of .50 caliber cartridges, and headed for the stable. As he passed the sheriff's office where Rucker had taken up temporary quarters, he didn't notice the former Army colonel sitting on the gallery. Rucker thought he recognized Culthwaite from a past association with General Truax at some social event. He recalled the man had a reputation of taking care of problems for important folks on the wrong side of the law. Moreover, Luke had warned Rucker of a potential threat during his visit to the ranch.

As he saddled and mounted, Culthwaite still had only the vaguest suspicion that he might have been discovered. As soon as he disappeared on the road from town, Rucker saddled his horse, armed himself, and picked up Culthwaite's trail. The hunter had now become the hunted.

The features of the land along the Nueces River tended to be characterized as very low rolling terrain. It wasn't flat, but it was easy to find cover by venturing just a little way off the road. Culthwaite soon found a trail off to his right with a ranch entrance archway featuring a sign that said "Heaven's Gate." This was the name of the place Thorpe had mentioned where the Texas Ranger supposedly lived.

He dismounted and began to walk his horse. He noted a motte of live oak on a knoll off to his left. It afforded a bit of shelter from view. He hung his hat on the saddle horn and slipped the Sharps from its scabbard.

Rucker saw Culthwaite stop and take cover at the motte and decided to cautiously hold back. He wanted to be certain of the man's intentions.

About this time, Dan rode by on his way back to Nuecestown. He spotted neither Culthwaite nor Rucker. Just as well, as his job of alerting Luke had been done.

Culthwaite was concerned. His mission was definitely no secret. His prey had obviously been warned, so his situation was compromised. Culthwaite had no idea how vulnerable he actually was. The smart move would be to simply call it off and wait for another day.

He could see the cabin about a half-mile off to the south. Smoke was curling from the chimney, so he knew someone was home. Was the Texas Ranger there? He nestled the barrel of the Sharps in the crotch of one of the live oak limbs. This was a long shot but within the capability of the Sharps and a modest test of his own marksmanship.

Rucker tried to find a place where he could get close enough to Culthwaite without being seen. His own rifle didn't have the range of Culthwaite's Sharps. He'd need to be certain of his shot, and he wasn't a great marksman to begin with. The ground leading up to the live oak motte offered no cover for at least a hundred yards, so he had to crawl his way to a decent position.

Dan's warning had put Luke on high alert. He now knew Culthwaite was in Nuecestown. Of course, he had no idea that the man was already lurking within shooting distance. He and Elisa had talked about defending their home. In fact, he'd dug out a small hideaway under the wooden floorboards. The door was hidden under a buffalo hide that served as a carpet.

"Dan says that this man Culthwaite is in Nuecestown. We can't be certain how long he'll stay there."

Elisa looked as worried as Luke had ever seen her.

"It's time, sweetheart. I've got to find this man. You and the boys must be prepared to hide in the cubbyhole at the least suspicion of trouble." He swept her into his arms and gave her a deep kiss. He sensed her fear but dared not linger as he didn't want it thought of as possibly their final kiss.

Luke checked that the Walker Colts were loaded before placing one in its holster and the second in his waistband. He put on his heavy coat, grabbed the Colt rifle, and opened the door to head to the stable and saddle up Big Horse. He paused at the doorway to scan the horizon. He saw nothing to alarm him.

At the opening of the cabin door, Culthwaite adjusted his aim slightly. He cocked the hammer. In the stillness, the click sounded like it might be heard miles away. He saw a man emerge from the cabin, exhaled, and squeezed the trigger. An explosion echoed across the prairie.

By comparison, the second shot fired was barely audible. Rucker had gotten into position moments before Culthwaite fired. His target slouched onto the branches of the live oak, took a deep breath, tried to rise, and fell to the ground. Rucker dashed for his horse, leaped into the saddle, and charged up the hill. Reaching Culthwaite's position, he noted the unmoving body, grabbed the Sharps from the tree, cut the man's horse loose, and spurred his own horse toward the cabin.

Elisa heard the gunshot and the loud thud as Luke's body slammed into the front of the cabin from the force of the bullet. The slug had hit the barrel of his rifle before slamming with still ferocious velocity into the lower right side of his chest. He lay on the gallery floor with blood oozing from his side. He struggled to catch his breath.

Throwing caution to the wind, Elisa was by his side in a heartbeat. "Lucas!" She pressed her hand hard against the wound to try to stop the bleeding.

Rucker arrived, barely able to bring his galloping horse to a stop, and managed to do so just in time to avoid crashing into the cabin. He jumped from the saddle. "Let's get him inside, Elisa. Quickly!"

They dragged Luke into the cabin, laying him out near the fireplace.

"Keep pressure on the wound. I'm gonna ride back to town and get Doc." Rucker gave a final look at Luke with Elisa over him trying to staunch the bleeding from the gaping wound. He dashed back outside, mounted, and headed toward Nuecestown as fast as his horse's legs could carry them.

Elisa was on her knees, pressing hard on the wound. "Stay with me, Lucas Dunn. Don't you dare leave me." She bowed her head as she pressed hard and blood oozed between her fingers. "Lord, please don't take him. Please, Lord." She felt helpless despite the strength of her faith. Luke's face was turning whiter and his breathing was becoming more shallow. "Breathe, Lucas…breathe, my love."

Berne Culthwaite was in excruciating pain. His own breathing was a struggle. The slug from Rucker's shot had ripped through his lung and embedded itself in his ribcage. It had initially knocked the wind from him, and the wound was bleeding profusely. He shed his coat and strapped his belt around his chest and over the wound to exert pressure and stem the blood flow. The pain was agonizingly intense.

"Damn!" he whispered to himself with a half-groan. "Damn it to hell." He'd been uncharacteristically careless. He flayed himself with regrets at not having checked his surroundings before setting his ambush. He began to get his breath back in shallow gasps despite the stabbing pain and had just noticed that the Sharps was gone. His horse had been cut loose. He looked at the far-off cabin and resolved to finish his work. This wasn't supposed to be happening this way. He'd never been shot nor lost a single drop of precious blood. He asked himself just what kind of people was he dealing with down here on the Nueces Strip? He became even angrier with himself for his stupidity.

Culthwaite began to walk, haltingly at first, staggering toward the cabin, stopping every few steps to catch his breath. He hadn't seen Rucker ride out for help from Nuecestown. He strove to stay singularly focused on his mission as he tried to deal with the sharp pain from the bullet lodged in his rib. He had no idea how much damage the slug had done inside his chest. He couldn't know he was slowly bleeding to death internally. He kept plodding along, with each step more difficult than the one before.

Finally, after what seemed like ages, he reached the gallery across the front of Luke's cabin. He'd begun to grow faint from loss of blood. He lifted one foot, caught the edge of the gallery, and half-stumbled, making enough noise that Elisa heard him. He barely caught himself. He gasped from the pain in his ribs.

Elisa called out. "Horace? Doc?" There was no answer.

Culthwaite held his breath as best he could. His breathing was increasingly labored and it hurt worse as he strove to approach the door.

Instinctively, Elisa slid the Walker Colt from Luke's holster. It brought back memories of the Comanche attack that had killed her father and brother. She'd been cool then; she'd have to be cool now.

From the corner of his eye, Culthwaite saw Luke's Colt rifle lying on the gallery floor with its now misshapen barrel. He cursed the rifle as he checked his revolver to be certain a cartridge was in each chamber. Cocking the hammer, he took another step toward the door, leaned against it, lifted the latch, and pushed it in. He staggered and half-fell into the cabin, and found himself staring down the barrel of a gun.

Elisa instinctively pointed Luke's gun in Culthwaite's general direction, noted it was neither Doc nor Rucker, and squeezed the trigger. In the confines of the cabin, the explosive report from the Walker Colt sounded like a cannon had been fired.

An expression of total surprise swept across Culthwaite's face as the .44 caliber slug tore through his neck. Elisa's second shot to his chest fully took the wind from him and sent him reeling back through the door. He reflexively fired wildly into the air but hit nothing as life rapidly ebbed from his body.

Elisa curled up in a ball, tears flowing profusely. Her Heaven's Gate idyll was being rudely and violently shaken. The acrid odor of gun smoke filled the cabin. Screams emanated from the cubbyhole where Elisa had protectively hidden the twins. She quickly gathered her wits. She couldn't leave Luke's side. "Help me, dear God," she uttered from her heart.

Luke groaned. "Whaaat…help…"

Elisa turned back to her husband and returned to putting pressure on his wound. He was alive. He was pale and chilled, but sweating profusely. She didn't understand that he was in shock, just that he was getting weaker. "You stay with me, Lucas Dunn. You stay with me." Peter and John would have to wait.

At last, she heard Doc and Rucker ride up. It had only been about thirty minutes, but it seemed like a lifetime. It may have been.

Doc dashed inside, pulled Elisa away, and kneeled at Luke's side. He peeled back the Texas Ranger's coat and shirt to get a look at the damage. "Damn!"

Elisa had never heard Doc curse. "What? Is he okay?" She wanted to ask whether he'd live.

"The bullet went clean through, but it tore him up pretty bad. Didn't get any vital organs far as I can see." Doc fished thread from his bag. He'd be doing a bit of suturing. "Get him some water. He's gonna die of thirst instead of blood loss." He looked back at Luke. "Get that preacher back in here to hold him down. This is going to hurt like hell. You can help, too, Elisa. Get me that hot poker from the fireplace." Doc would be doing some cauterizing, too.

Rucker had been on the gallery ensuring that Culthwaite was now truly dead. He grabbed the man's Sharps and bashed it in half against the hitching post. He heard Elisa's call and headed into the cabin. "Elisa Dunn, you are one terrific marks…woman. You finished that monster for sure." He positioned himself to hold Luke's arms.

Just then, there was once again the plaintive cry of a hungry baby, quickly joined by a second wailing. Doc looked at her and nodded for her to tend her children. "Go ahead, Elisa. We've got this. He's going to make it." Doc said a little prayer under his breath. With the loss of blood and so much torn tissue, he knew it would be touch and go. Rucker was already praying as he held Luke down.

Elisa looked at Doc, suddenly becoming aware that he was sober. No smell of alcohol.

An hour later, Doc was bandaging Luke's wound. It'd been a true test of his doctoring ability. So much was at stake; more than this family, it was about winning another battle on the Texas frontier.

Luke was finally resting on the bed, utterly exhausted. Sleep had overtaken him.

"Doc, Horace, I can't thank you enough. You've saved my Lucas." Elisa spoke with her jaw set and a child in each arm. She was beyond crying.

Rucker stood, taking in the scene. "I'd heard that you could shoot a gun with pretty fair accuracy, Elisa Dunn, but that was amazing. I thought I'd finished the man. Thank God you can shoot." He reinforced his earlier observation.

"Thank God, indeed, Preacher. It's by God's grace that this Texas Ranger, my husband, is alive."

Rucker extended Luke's rifle toward her. "I can't say much for this Colt rifle of his. That slug took a bite from the barrel before it hit him. Likely saved his life. Keep this to remind you of God's handiwork."

Elisa lay the twins on the bed close to Luke. Then, stroking the beaded amulet that Three Toes had given her, she took the rifle from him. It struck Elisa that Rucker was apparently trying to help Doc with his drinking problem. Normally after such a stressful circumstance, Doc would have just about totally drained a bottle of whiskey. Not this day.

"We're going to head back to Nuecestown, Elisa. We'll let folks know about Luke and how things worked out here." Doc gathered his instruments into his bag. "I'll check on y'all tomorrow. For now, let that man of yours sleep. He'll need some serious rest. Oh, I'd half-bet that Bernice will send some food out as her way of helping. She's a sweetheart. And praise the Lord she sent out the alert with Dan about this man arriving in Nuecestown." Doc gave Elisa a brief hug and followed Rucker out the door.

Together, Doc and Rucker lifted Culthwaite's body, draping it behind Rucker's saddle. They'd send Dan out to find Culthwaite's horse the next day; meanwhile, this would do to get the man's body back for burial in the Nuecestown Cemetery.

As Doc turned to mount his horse, he noticed a rumpled and bloodied envelope that had apparently fallen from the dead man's pocket. "Hang on, Preacher. What's this?" He bent down and scooped it up. Inside were several bank notes and a slip of paper with some sort of instructions. It was signed with the initials "HT." He shared the note with Rucker. "Looks like this fella was a hired gun," he said, stating the obvious.

"We should be sure to let Luke know about this when he's strong enough. Meanwhile, I'm not sure who I could trust in Austin. Maybe Rip Ford." Rucker stuffed the note in his pocket and straightened out the bank notes. "Doc, why don't you keep the paper money? Call it payment for services. The dead man sure won't be needing it."

Doc smiled broadly as he turned his horse toward the road. "Kind thought, Preacher. I've got what I need. Why not take the money toward starting that church you've talked about?"

The two slowly rode off toward Nuecestown. It'd be dark when they arrived, but regaling the folks in town with the story of the attack on Luke's family would keep them up late.

TWENTY-ONE

Massacre?

The jail cell was dark, dank, and musty. Now and then a rat would slither through, so there was likely a nest under the building with enough warmth to mess with their hibernation. Some might say it was a kinship thing. At least, the cell was warm, the rats happy, and the prisoner was being fed.

The Uvalde sheriff was a slip of a man who was such a wisp of humanity that a stiff breeze might blow him over. His revolver was likely just about as heavy as he was, but word had it that nobody dared underestimate him. A few had tried and a few had died. Sheriff Rollo Warren let just enough gambling and illicit whoring go on to keep it from getting out of hand. It didn't take a mental giant to understand that he was in control of the town.

Biggs' experience with being nearly frozen to death hadn't especially suited him. He was unshaven and unkempt, to say the least. He'd been sitting on the bunk for nearly a day, occasionally standing and walking a small circle around its interior. He was on one of these walks when he realized that the floor boards were loose. He slipped down onto his hands and knees. He found an edge and lifted. A board came up quite easily, as did the one next to it. He carefully replaced them. He'd have to wait for the sheriff to leave for the night.

"I expect you've discovered the loose floor boards, Mr. Biggs." Warren smiled wryly from his seat behind the desk. He was leaning back in the chair with his feet propped up and his hat nestled in over his eyes while chewing on a major chaw of tobacco. Now and then he'd fire a wad of spittle into the spittoon below the gun rack. He never missed. In between spats, he'd work in a sentence. "Trust me, you don't want to know what's under those boards." He fired another shot into the spittoon.

Biggs could sense the sheriff's smile from the sound of his voice. He had to wonder what was under the floorboards. Was the sheriff bluffing? He didn't have long to wait for an answer. He heard a rat scurry beneath the floor. There was a thud as something hit the floorboard hard enough to lift it an inch or so. An abbreviated squeal was followed by sudden silence. Whatever was down there wasn't hungry any more.

Another wad of spit hit the spittoon. "Yep. It's our pet rattler. We call him Buzz 'cause of his rattle. He likes our warm jail and the plentiful food supply." Warren shot another load into the spittoon. "Oh, and I expect he won't show you any professional courtesy, Mr. Biggs."

Biggs sat back down on the edge of the bed.

"Don't you be worrying none, Mr. Biggs." Warren sat up, leaned forward, and smiled at Biggs through teeth deeply yellowed by years of chewing tobacco. "Them soldiers will be back for you in a day or so. I'm gonna go get some grub. I'll bring somethin' back for you." He threw on his coat, headed for the door, and took a final shot at the spittoon as he threw a piece of wood into the iron stove on his way out.

As Sheriff Warren exited, Biggs once again took stock of his situation. It had taken him a couple of days to fully thaw out. His muscles were still a tad stiff from his river experience, and the horse ride hadn't helped. He certainly didn't figure that his fate would hang with some far-off federal jury. In any case, awaiting his fate while sitting in a dilapidated jail in what he considered a flea-bit backwoods town wasn't to his liking. With Cutter John gone, he didn't have any friends that he knew of, especially in Uvalde. His prospects seemed bleak at best.

"I'm tellin' you, Bert. He's sittin' up the street a ways in our very own Uvalde jail. He's got money an' he's mean as a cornered polecat."

"You really think he'd join up with us?"

"I heard he's facin' the noose. If we were to spring him, he'd be pretty much beholden." Cal thoughtfully turned the glass in his hand before putting it to his lips, savoring the smoothness of the whiskey, and setting it back on the table as though punctuating his sentence. "Damn right, he'd join us."

"What you figure to do? That damned sheriff is tough. We gotta avoid stirrin' him up. We gonna pull Sam and Ty in on this?"

"Yeah, sure." He sloughed off the suggestion as he focused on a way to spring Roy Biggs. "Need what they call a diversion."

"We could set fire to that abandoned house," Bert suggested.

"Hmmm. That could work." Cal poured another whiskey. "We'll need horses, too."

Bert was quiet, his mind working.

"You mean to go after them Comanche…the ones that raided your ranch?" Cal asked.

"Damn right." A snarly frown came to Bert's entire face. "They stole our horses an' nearly killed my wife. She'll never be the same woman." He paused thoughtfully. "And there's a bounty."

Cal knew better than to press Bert further on what the Comanche had done to his wife. The savages pretty much did the same thing to nearly all the white women they attacked, no matter whether they killed them or took them prisoner.

"I think that's about enough, Sergeant." Lieutenant Belknap and his patrol had dutifully searched the hills and found no sign of Comanche. "Let's head back to Uvalde and get our prisoner."

"If I may, sir?"

Belknap nodded.

"We could just leave him to rot in that cell. The men are tired and anxious to get back to Fort Mason."

Belknap recognized the condition his men were in. It was cold, a damp cold that was none too comfortable for man or beast. He sensed the unsettling attitude among his soldiers. Roy Biggs had certainly made for a significant inconvenience. Besides, had the Texas Rangers been reauthorized in Austin, the man would be their charge. "Damned politicians," he whispered under his breath.

"Yes, sir? Did you say something?"

"Sergeant, let the men know that we'll rest in Uvalde before heading back to Fort Mason. I'll even buy drinks and dinner."

The sergeant was pleased to see Belknap loosen up a bit and care about the mental state of his troops. Of course, the promise of a respite was roundly cheered.

They turned their mounts southwestward toward Uvalde.

Two days had passed, and Luke had barely stirred. Elisa was overjoyed to see him breathing regular and his color returning. The bedrest, enforced by the seriousness of his wound, was working. She had been lying next to him for the past hour, watching him sleep. All her men were asleep.

"Lisa?" He raised his head.

She sat bolt upright at the sound of his voice. It was indeed music to her ears. "Lucas...I'm right here, Lucas."

"What happened?"

"You were shot, love. You were shot pretty bad, but Doc fixed you up."

He laid his head back. "Dang, but it hurts." He turned his head toward her and moved his hand to touch her arm. "I love you, Lisa Dunn."

"I know, Lucas. I know." She looked deeply into his blue Irish eyes and gently stroked his cheek with its three-days' growth of stubble.

"Are you all right?"

"I am now. Bernice, bless her heart, brought some meals out here. Doc stopped by a couple of times to check on you. Oh, and Mr. Rucker has started his church." She paused thoughtfully. "I think Mr. Rucker has gotten Doc to stop drinking."

Luke offered a tired smile. "What happened to the man that was hunting me? Are we safe?"

"He's dead and gone, Lucas." She didn't think he was quite ready to hear how she had to finish Culthwaite off. Besides, she was conflicted in the sense that evil men were taking Luke's crusade against injustice to their home here at Heaven's Gate. His success was putting them all in danger, and she wasn't sure yet how to deal with it. Likely as not, the desperadoes would come after Luke, even if he quit the Rangers. It would haunt them constantly. So there was hardly any point in troubling her man with this dilemma, at least not yet.

He fell back to sleep.

Elisa got up to feed the twins. She took in the cabin. Sure, she'd cleaned up the blood on the floor near the fireplace, but it wasn't enough. She thoughtfully beheld her six-foot-three hunk of manhood lying helplessly in their bed. When he was well enough, they'd have to talk about a larger home. This cabin held many memories, both good and bad. She'd grown up here. There were joys, not the least having been the birth of their twin boys. But she'd seen enough death here as well. There were four graves under the live oak as eternal reminders. She missed her mother and father especially.

A quiet night in Uvalde had suddenly turned ugly. The abandoned house near the livery was ablaze, with flames shooting high into the dark sky. Townsfolk had gathered to form a bucket line, but their hearts weren't into saving the ramshackle old building.

Sheriff Warren stood back and simply observed. He intuitively felt in his skinny bones that something wasn't quite right. Seeing there was little he could do about the fire other than spit on it, he began to mosey back toward the jail.

As he walked toward the jail, five men raced by at a full gallop. To the sheriff's way of thinking, they didn't seem inclined to help with putting out the last embers of the fire. It was more like they were riding to or away from something. Warren didn't like the next feeling that came on. He instinctively ran toward the jail, leaped onto the front step and threw open the door. "Damn!" The cells were all empty.

Biggs had left a note on the desk. "Your rattler is lonely." He wasn't pleased at the outlaw's sick sense of humor. The wrong snake had escaped. He didn't feature having to deal with Lieutenant Belknap and his troops when they learned that their prize prisoner had flown the coop.

He leaned against his desk. They had a head start, it was a cold night, and he was significantly outnumbered. Last but hardly the least concern, Uvalde wasn't exactly the sort of place where it would be easy to raise any sort of posse.

A familiar whiney voice behind him shattered his internal deliberations.

"Sheriff? Some men stole a couple of our horses."

"I know, Joe. I know." Warren shook his head resignedly. "They're long gone, Joe."

"You gonna chase'm, Sheriff?"

"Go right ahead, Joe. Mount up and ride into the cold." The sarcasm was lost on the simple-minded stable boy.

"Yes, sir. You comin'?"

Warren simply shook his head. "Is the fire out?"

"Yes, sir, it is. Burned itself out. We gonna chase them thieves?"

"Not now, Joe." He couldn't be angry at the young man. "You go help make sure that fire is out."

"Mr. Biggs, what'd you write on that paper you left behind?"

The band of rescuers had ridden about ten miles out of town and holed up for the night at an abandoned cabin one of the men had scouted out ahead of time.

Biggs smiled one of his more diabolical smiles. "Personal between me and the sheriff." It was a clear, definitive statement that dared anyone to ask again. Biggs poured himself a cup of coffee. "I rightly appreciate what y'all have done in springing me from that flea-bag jail." He looked around the room from man to man. "What y'all have in mind?"

For the first time, the men noted the aura of evil that surrounded this man. Maybe they should have let him rot in the jail. Bert stepped forward. He'd become the *de facto* ringleader. "Um…well, we were of a mind to go after some Comanche we'd been hearing about. Bunch of them savages raided my ranch last year. Ruined my wife."

Biggs was well aware of what Comanche did to women, and was equally aware that white men were repelled by women that had been violated by the Indians. It was more than the disfigurement; it was the symbolism associated with the physical violation. The woman was considered unclean thereafter.

"Sorry about that." His gaze riveted in on Bert. "What's it to me?" Another man might have thought better of so insensitive a remark.

Bert was taken aback. His hand instinctively found its way to the handle of the revolver in the holster at his side.

Biggs gave him a "don't you dare" look. "I just got back from chasing after Comanche with Cutter John. Got ambushed. They killed

Cutter. I escaped, but the damned soldiers found me half-frozen from falling in the river."

All the men had heard of Cutter John. They thought of him as invincible. The fact that he'd been killed by Comanche sat heavily upon them.

"Yer not scared of a few Comanche, are you?" Bert asked. It was a reflexive response toward preserving their sense of manhood.

Biggs thought about the deal he'd made with Cutter. "Tell you what, if y'all promise to follow me to take care of some business in Nuecestown, I'll help you hunt a few Comanche."

That's what the men were waiting to hear. "You got a deal, Mr. Biggs. We can start after them savages in the morning."

Biggs shook his head. "The place I was attacked is three, maybe four days ride from here. We need supplies."

"We took care of that, Mr. Biggs. Got a pack horse and supplies around back of the cabin."

Biggs smiled at their abundant confidence that he'd join them in hunting Comanche.

The soldiers passed the still-smoldering ruins of a house as they rode into Uvalde.

"Sergeant, show the men to that hotel up the street and settle them in. I'm going to check on Roy Biggs."

Belknap rode down the street to the jail, dismounted, and knocked on the door.

"Yes?" A low, barely audible voice came from within.

Belknap pushed on through the doorway. He was met with a sweat-and-tobacco aroma that could have killed a buffalo. Warren sat at his desk with tobacco drool all over his shirt. His pistol lay on the desk as though being contemplated. Belknap, holding his kerchief over his nose, glanced at the spittoon. It was a mess. Worse, Warren apparently hadn't visited the privy behind the jail. Last but hardly least, Belknap saw that the jail cells was empty.

"What happened?" He coughed.

Warren looked up through sleep-deprived eyes. "Escaped." He said it as though stating the obvious…which he was.

Belknap pivoted and went outside. He needed some air just to gather his thoughts. He wasn't really a law enforcement officer, yet Biggs did have a federal warrant to be enforced against him. The lieutenant opened the door to help air the place out. The stench was overwhelming.

He stuck his head back inside. "Sheriff, you get yourself and your damned jail cleaned up. I'll be back to deal with you in the morning." He shook his head and headed up the street to rejoin his men. He was of a mind to ignore Biggs altogether and lead his men back to Fort Mason. He rightly calculated that Biggs had a pretty fair head start to wherever he was going. To make matters worse, he had no tracker among his patrol.

As he walked into the saloon, a hush fell over the place. Since the closing of Fort Inge, the townsfolk hadn't seen many soldiers. "Don't stop on my account," he announced. The hush gradually went away and noise returned to the carryings-on they were used to.

"Sir, may I have a word?" The sergeant took Belknap aside.

"What is it, Sergeant?"

"The barkeep says that four dregs of Uvalde society sprung Biggs from the jail, and he'd heard them talking about heading north to kill Comanche for sport. The barkeep thought it might have been a revenge thing."

"Do you think our troopers are up to the chase?"

"Well, sir, they've been riding for days and seen not a bit of action. They might be ready for a fight. I'm thinking these outlaws are likely headed on a path that takes us not far from Fort Mason."

"Wish we had a tracker."

"Sir, I think these men will leave a clear trail. We should have no trouble."

The smoke curled up gracefully from the teepees. The sun had crested the horizon and was casting its warming rays upon their encampment. Three Toes' wives were all busy with their various chores. Bear Slayer and White Feather had just emerged from their teepees.

The chief engaged the two warriors. "I feel called to talk with the Great Spirit. I do not expect to be gone long."

They respected his need to communicate with the Great Spirit. His spiritual medicine was vital to their survival. "Go, my Chief. We will watch over the camp." They assured Three Toes that all was well in hand.

"Be watchful, my brothers." Something in the air that morning felt out of phase with their world. Three Toes wasn't able to identify it, so would commiserate with the Great Spirit in an effort to learn what was amiss. He bade his wives good-bye, assuring them he'd return for dinner. As he headed away, he walked past the small herd of ponies that his small band maintained. He walked over to his favorite, mounted, and headed toward a hilltop perhaps five or six miles away. There he expected to find the solitude he sought.

Horace Rucker had returned to Austin to fetch his wife and son, Stephen, and they soon arrived back in Nuecestown. His eldest boy, Rex, remained at West Point. The powers-that-be had permitted the colonel to retire, and thus had not jeopardized his son's military opportunities.

Colonel Rucker showed his wife and son to a mostly serviceable house in town that had been abandoned by its previous owners. It was a far cry from the grander housing they'd been used to back in Austin. It'd take a bit of renovating, but could be right comfortable.

Mrs. Rucker was actually pleased to have been able to put the pressures of being an Army officer's wife behind her. She didn't aspire for her family to be scions of society.

Soon enough, they began to make friends among the Nuecestown community.

The five men took positions on a bluff overlooking the Comanche encampment. The camp was well hidden, and it was dumb luck that they'd come upon it.

Biggs was carefully surveilling to see how many Comanche were there. "I see only two warriors." He was looking for a particular Comanche but didn't see him. "I thought there'd be more." It seemed almost too easy.

Bert also stared intently. "There are five or six women. Damned heathen polygamists!" He'd done the math. "Hey, at least three squaws are pregnant." He suppressed a snarly, hate-filled laugh. "Do the savages in their bellies have scalps?" The perversion wasn't lost on his companions. Bert's hatred, bred of what the heathen Comanche had done to his wife, brought out evil in its darkest, sickest form.

Even Biggs found Bert's comment offensive. He kept his voice low. They were positioned downwind from the encampment, but couldn't chance being heard. "Shoot the warriors first. The rest will be easy." Biggs enjoyed a smile. If he'd been a snake, his forked tongue would have been darting in and out to sense the excitement in the air. This little Comanche hunt might work out after all. The men would be happy collecting bounty scalps and then be beholden to him to help him go after that damnable Texas Ranger.

"Let's do it."

The explosions of rifle fire in the confines of the ravine made it sound as though the gunfire came from everywhere. Bear Slayer and White Feather never had a chance as bullets riddled their bodies. The women were too horrified to scream and the children ran to their mothers. Biggs and his men stayed in their positions a few moments longer, picking off the couple of small children that straggled.

Biggs surveyed the scene before them, and then showed them the way down the hill to the Comanche camp. The men finished off all the squaws, shooting at close range. The pregnant women were shot in their bellies multiple times. Bert even grabbed a small child by one leg, swung it high, and bashed its brains out on the rocks. The rage of the men seemed unbounded.

For Biggs' part, he just stood back and watched as Bert and his friends unleashed their blood fury. "Okay, men. Let's be quick about this."

They began scalping the men, women, and children. All told, they had a dozen scalps. Once their blood ritual was done, their vengeance sated, they torched the teepees and headed back for their horses.

"Where to, Boss?"

Biggs didn't have to think long. "We'll stop at Fort Mason to collect your bounties, then we're heading to Corpus Christi." His smile would have made Lucifer seem pleasantly harmless.

Three Toes couldn't help but hear the shooting. Since it emanated from the direction of the encampment, he feared the worst. Leaping to his pony, he rode back toward his people.

The terrain was rocky, yet his pony charged forward at nearly a gallop. Folks didn't consider Comanche among the best horsemen on the plains for nothing. Man and beast traveled as one.

By the time he reached the scene, Biggs and the others were long gone. Before him was horror beyond all imaginings. Bear Slayer, White Feather, wives, children…all dead…all scalped. He found Moon Woman. She moaned as he lifted her. She looked into his eyes, and then breathed her last. His other two wives lay on the cold rocks, their bodies mutilated so as to defy imagination. His warriors hadn't even had a chance to defend themselves. The sheer magnitude of the loss was overwhelming.

Three Toes remained outwardly calm despite the rage within that sought to avenge. It didn't matter that Comanche had inflicted as bad if not worse atrocities on white folk. This was personal, very personal.

About five miles to the south, Lieutenant Belknap and his patrol were plodding along, following the sign left by Biggs and his companions. Biggs' gang made no effort whatsoever to cover their tracks. Their trail was not difficult to follow, even for a neophyte like Belknap. It was almost too easy. They'd found two campsites along the way. At one of them, Biggs' crew had carelessly left the embers glowing. Carelessness seemed to be their *modus operandi*. Apparently, they weren't worried in the least about being discovered. Such was the singular nature of their mission.

As they headed down into a rocky draw, the soldiers' attention was drawn by the sounds of the distant shooting. Belknap and the sergeant exchanged glances. The lieutenant didn't hesitate but a moment.

"Quick now, men. Follow me." He spurred his horse and headed toward the sound at a quick trot. He led his men as fast as the rocky terrain would permit.

It took nearly two hours to cover the distance across the rough landscape. By God's grace, they'd managed not to lose any horses or riders. The ice from a recent storm had mostly melted. Toward the end, the patrol slowed; they had no idea what to expect.

Wisps of smoke from dying fires soon came into view. The place was so sheltered that they might have missed it if not for the smoke. Belknap led the way into the small clearing. They were shocked to a man at the sight before them. Bodies lay everywhere. The lieutenant caught some movement on a rise behind the smoldering remains of the largest teepee. "Say, who goes there?" Other than Belknap and the sergeant, none of his soldiers had ever seen, much less met an actual Comanche chief.

Three Toes emerged from behind a small tree. He was dressed in full regalia, as he had been preparing the ground for a mass funeral. He immediately recognized Belknap. "You are late, bluecoat." There was terrible sadness in his eyes. He was already experiencing a deepening guilt at not being there to defend his people. Despite his erect posture and well-muscled frame, he seemed broken.

"I am so sorry, Chief Three Toes." Belknap surveyed the scene again. Being unfamiliar with Comanche culture, especially so far as honoring the dead, Belknap felt helpless. "Can we help?"

Three Toes shook his head. He wanted to tell the lieutenant that the white man had already done enough. Belknap, however, seemed a different breed. He was teachable. The chief thought about his Texas Ranger friend. There might be good white men out there among the others. However, mourning was personal.

"I am grateful for your offer, but I must do this myself." Three Toes would spend the rest of the day wrapping each of the bodies in blankets in preparation for burial. There were plenty of places there along the Pedernales River to bury his people. Each one was honored with prayer, then the bodies were covered with stones. He would burn all the remaining possessions of those who had died and, in a final act, Three Toes would slash his arms in expression of his grief.

Belknap sensed both the sadness and pride in the chief's words. He respected that Three Toes had to do what he must do according to Comanche custom. "We're going to continue chasing the men that did this," he told Three Toes. "Again, we are sorry this happened, Chief." He saluted Three Toes and headed his men out on the trail that the sergeant had already discovered.

The patrol picked up their pace, calculating that they just might catch up to the men by the next day. It didn't take much to figure out that they were headed to Fort Mason to collect their bounties.

Belknap marveled at their sheer brazenness. These massacres needed to stop, whether perpetrated by Indian or white man. The lieutenant was determined to make an example of Roy Biggs.

Samuel knocked softly. This wasn't going to be easy. Horatio Thorpe had arrived just last night from his plantation headquarters not far from Galveston.

Given his near-obesity, he generally eschewed horseback for long rides. He was suffering the ill effects coursing through his hips and legs, despite having had an employee and a couple of slaves to see to his needs on the trail. The rocking cadence of the horse seemed ever-present, and it had not been remotely helped by repeated nights of restless sleep. He cursed not having used one of his carriages.

"Yes, Samuel. Come in. Do you have something for me?"

"Yes, sir...yes, sir, Master." Samuel stepped through the doorway into his master's office and bowed slightly. He noticed immediately that Thorpe was wearing a new suit. It fit far better than the previous suit, the one that made him look like a stuffed sausage. He'd certainly been eating well. Life on his plantation must have been quite profitable. Of course, he dared not mention the fact that his master was quite obviously growing more obese. He reached over and handed him a sealed envelope.

Thorpe nodded dismissively to Samuel, indicating that he could leave. He examined the envelope, turning it slowly in his pudgy hands. It had his name on it in a neat script: "Honorable Horatio Thorpe, Austin, Texas." It had been posted from France. He slowly opened it. The stationary surprised him, as it bore the seal of the French Minister of Trade. Other than trading cotton for finished goods, his only connection with France was having sent his oldest son Gascon to study there.

As Samuel stepped from the office and closed the doors behind him, he heard a thud, the snap of wood, and a gasp for air behind him. He glanced over his shoulder, and then cracked the door open to be sure his master was okay.

Thorpe had at least landed in the chair. He'd partially broken the thing, as the wood on one of the armrests had split. Samuel shook his head at the master's complexion and stroked his own growing goatee. He didn't figure white men could get any whiter.

Horatio Thorpe read the letter again and read it a third time. He was none too happy with the message.

"Samuel!"

"Yes, Master?"

"I want my latest shipment of cotton to France stopped. Please drop everything and be certain that happens immediately."

"It's likely on the ship, Master." Samuel knew it would take several days to carry a message by courier and by that time the ship would have left port.

"It mustn't leave Galveston."

The blessing for Thorpe would be that the telegraph line from Austin to Galveston had recently been completed. It meant he had a real chance to stop the cotton shipment. "Samuel, I hear there's a new-fangled wire system to send messages quickly. See my friend at the Texas and New Orleans Telegraph Company. Now go. Be quick!"

Upon Samuel's departure, Thorpe stood and walked to the window. He pondered at what might have precipitated a letter from so high a level of government, especially one that canceled his trading rights. Could Gascon be up to no good? It seemed enough that the men he'd relied on to get rid of his problems seemed to make them worse. He knew Culthwaite had died trying, and Biggs was out there somewhere. At least, General Truax and that snake-oil trader Thaddeus Brown were no longer a threat to his schemes. But that damned Ranger still lived, and Thorpe found himself still obsessively craving that red-haired harlot he'd had in Laredo.

Luke sat on the gallery, taking in the beautiful rolling landscape of Heaven's Gate. He tired easily during these early days of recuperating. There was still a late winter nip in the air, so Elisa wrapped him in a blanket Scarlett made for them as a thank-you gift. Luke's wound was, in fact, healing faster than expected. It had left an impressive scar on his side, but Doc had done a masterful job repairing the ghastly damage caused by the bullet from Berne Culthwaite's Sharps rifle. A slug meant to stop a buffalo with a single shot generally could be expected to do the same to a human.

Luke's ruined Colt rifle would forever be a piece of memorabilia reminding them of how close he'd come to death's door. Elisa had placed it on the fireplace mantle as a token of her faith in a God who, by never remaining distant from human suffering, was the messenger of hope. Faith and hope were prevailing in the taming of the frontier, and Texas Ranger Captain Luke Dunn would continue to be the instrument in delivering justice and bringing redemption to the Nueces Strip.

Elisa joined Luke on the gallery. Peter and John were sleeping. A tumbleweed tumbled by, carried aimlessly along on the breeze.

Luke gazed lovingly at Elisa as she took a seat beside him. "There goes another of those goldarned tumbleweeds, Lisa. Can't imagine how far those things might tumble or where they'll end up."

"Maybe they're telling you something, Lucas." She looked at him and smiled, then followed the tumbleweed's erratic path with her eyes. "You know your head is telling you to bring justice to the Nueces Strip."

"And my heart, Lisa," he murmured, caressing her cheek with his hand, "my heart is here with you at Heaven's Gate."

It was a dilemma that wouldn't be soon resolved. She took his hand in hers. "I'm proud of what you do, Lucas. I'm grateful that you are a man of principles, a husband that any woman would be grateful for. And to have your love means the world." She glanced at the bandages still covering the wound in his side.

He squeezed her hand gently. "There will be plenty to do come spring, Lisa," he told her. "Guess there'll be no shortage of ranch work." He gave an ironic sort of grin. "And no shortage of lawbreakers." His mind briefly contemplated what might have become of Roy Biggs but, just as quickly, his thoughts turned to Elisa and what might lie ahead for Heaven's Gate.

Roy Biggs was none too happy. He didn't exactly cotton to these men he'd attracted. They were a surly bunch, yet they were drawn to him like so many moths to a candle. He wanted to get the damnable bounty business done at Fort Mason so he could get on with his work. He didn't have any particular feelings for the Comanche they'd massacred, except as a way to get these men's loyalty, however fleeting that might turn out to be.

As the men laughed and carried on, Biggs hung back. He knew that these men would eventually outlive their usefulness to him.

CPSIA information can be obtained
at www.ICGtesting.com
Printed in the USA
LVHW092024200820
663617LV00009BA/969